Praise for La

D A Y S o

"The fearlessness with which Fox frees her women to behave badly heightens both the credibility and the pleasure of her fiction." —*The Boston Globe*

"No contemporary novelist makes me stop as often to mark or admire one of her sentences. . . . Were *Days of Awe* the pilot script for a TV series, elderly actresses would throw elbows to audition for Helene. . . . Poignant." —Jim Higgins, *Milwaukee Journal Sentinel*

"*Days of Awe* is clever, funny, and emotional, the kind of book another writer reads jealously, wishing to have written it. Honest and accurate about female friendship, this is my favorite Lauren Fox book yet."
—Jennifer Close, bestselling author of
Girls in White Dresses and *The Smart One*

"What makes [*Days of Awe*] so special is Isabel's smart, acerbic voice and her way of seeing everything from a sharp angle. . . . Isabel (and Fox) has such an offbeat way of looking at things that you'll eagerly keep reading just to see what she's going to say next. Read it for the magnetic voice and Fox's ever-interesting perspective on work, love, friendship, and parenthood."
—*Kirkus Reviews* (starred review)

"[Fox's] characters are undeniably human. Isabel is messy and imperfect, frustrating yet likable."

—*Entertainment Weekly*

"Beautiful, heartfelt."   —Bookreporter.com

"Raw and darkly humorous . . . Fox's novel is a winner."

—*Publishers Weekly*

"An insightful novel . . . that explores how grief can make every arena of life feel suddenly disorienting. . . . Frank, thought-provoking. . . . Fox once again explores . . . the underside of friendships, marriage, love and loss—and the range of emotions that can plague and liberate the human heart."   —*Shelf Awareness*

"Fox delivers a story about all the things that keep us awake at night: marriage, parenthood, friendship, bereavement, workplace rivalries, aging parents, cultural identity, starting over. And yet with all it encompasses, this book never falters once. The pace is brisk, the suspense high, the heartache intense and the ending so authentic you'll want to turn back to page one and start all over, just so you can experience it again. Kind of like real life."

—*The Globe and Mail* (Toronto)

Lauren Fox

D A Y S *of* A W E

Lauren Fox is the author of the novels *Still Life with Husband* and *Friends Like Us*. She earned her MFA from the University of Minnesota, and her work has appeared in numerous publications including *The New York Times*, *Marie Claire*, *Parenting*, *Psychology Today*, *The Rumpus*, and *Salon*. She lives in Milwaukee with her husband and two daughters.

www.laurenfoxwriter.com

DAYS of AWE

DAYS *of* AWE

·· ——— A NOVEL ——— ··

Lauren Fox

VINTAGE CONTEMPORARIES | VINTAGE BOOKS

A DIVISION OF PENGUIN RANDOM HOUSE LLC

NEW YORK

FIRST VINTAGE CONTEMPORARIES EDITION, JUNE 2016

The Library of Congress has cataloged the Alfred A. Knopf
edition as follows:
Fox, Lauren.
Days of awe : a novel / by Lauren Fox.—First edition.
pages cm
1. Female friendship—Fiction.
2. Mothers and daughters—Fiction.
3. Marital conflict—Fiction.   4. Domestic fiction.   I. Title.
PS3606.O95536D39 2015   813'.D23   2015013533

**Vintage Books Trade Paperback ISBN: 978-0-307-38827-8
eBook ISBN: 978-0-385-35311-3**

Book design by Pei Loi Koay

www.vintagebooks.com

Printed in the United States of America
10   9   8   7   6   5   4   3   2   1

For Molly and Tess

DAYS of AWE

The morning of Josie's funeral was cloudless and knife-sharp, one of those bitter spring days that comes sandwiched between warmer ones and reminds you not to grow accustomed to good things. I was leaning against my car, face to the sun, trying to breathe, when Mark pulled into a spot near mine. I turned and watched as he got out of the car. He wore the scarf Chris and I had gotten him for his last birthday, soft dark blue cashmere, and my heart slammed inside my chest: that beautiful scarf still existed, warm as a blanket, and Josie was gone.

Geese honked overhead. The funeral was in thirty minutes. I shaded my eyes with my hand. The funeral home shared its parking lot with Meehan's Market, a small upscale grocery store, and Mark and I, wearing our funeral finest, didn't look so different from the well-dressed shoppers in their everyday expensive clothes, although we, of course, weren't lugging canvas bags full of fresh bread and oranges and organic baby yogurts and bottles of red wine.

"Stay close to Mommy!" I heard from two different women almost in unison. "Hold Mommy's hand, Olive," one added.

Mark stumbled to me like a zombie, silent and dazed. His skin was pasty in the violent light. His face was unusually clean shaven and dotted with a few tiny, fresh specks of blood. His features seemed just slightly, disconcertingly off-kilter. Watching him, I understood that our pain separates us—that something as monumental as sorrow ought to make us porous, but it petrifies us instead. I understood that, and then, like a goldfish, I forgot it.

"Hi?" I said stupidly, as if we were meeting for coffee, or a blind date.

He mumbled something that sounded like my name and steadied himself on the hood of my car. "This was my fault," he whispered, an agonized croak, and he looked past me, squinting against the glare of the sun bouncing off all the bright cars in the parking lot, the herd of wild minivans.

Josie had died two nights before at 2:00 a.m. on an icy overpass just north of downtown. Her rusty eleven-year-old Toyota skidded off the slick road like a can of soup rolling across a supermarket aisle. It crashed into a guardrail and killed her on impact. There was some alcohol in her blood, we learned, but she hadn't been over the limit. She had, though, been going much too fast for the slippery conditions.

I got the call at 4:00 a.m. Hannah was at a sleepover. The phone woke me, and in a reptile panic I thought, *Hannah.* When Mark, on the other end of the line, said, "Josie's been in an accident," I'm ashamed to admit that I felt a split second of relief. But then I understood what I was being told, and the relief sizzled into horror.

"How could this be your fault?" I said, grasping Mark's shoulders. "It's not!"

A noise came from his throat, a high gasp of breath, a not-quite-human cry: the soft, mad sound of grief. Of course it was his fault. And it was my fault, and possibly Chris's, and most definitely Josie's, and some other people's faults, too: we were all guilty, to varying degrees, the calibrations of which I would scrutinize, often and obsessively, for months to come. And let me tell you, that is one joyless board game. The winner gets a toppling stack of misery and resentment and a free pass to therapy.

"Let's go," Mark said, recovering a bit. He put his arm around me, and we limped into Dalton's Funeral Home together, up the wide wooden steps and into the foyer that was meant to look like a snug, old-fashioned sitting room, with its overstuffed love seats and faded floral wallpaper, as if death had been a more palatable affair seventy years ago, cozy as Mayberry.

Henry Dalton greeted us. He was tall and reedy, with a nimbus of wispy white hair. He spoke quietly to Mark, leaning in close without invading Mark's space. . . . *So sorry for your loss,* I heard him say, . . . *will want to pay their respects.* . . . He managed to seem both rehearsed and completely sincere. *That's quite an undertaking,* I imagined saying to Josie. I could almost feel her elbow sharp against my ribs. After a few minutes, he slipped away and disappeared into a side room.

Mark looked around for him, then turned to me and shrugged. "I think the funeral director is a ghost," he said, and then he cringed. "This is my wife's funeral," he said, scolding himself, reminding himself. His dark gray suit was wrinkled and hung loosely off of his body, as if he were a boy pretending to be grown. "What would she make of this?" He cracked his knuckles. "I feel like I could just ask her! I keep hearing her voice. Like, *Mark, this is a shit avalanche. Let's get out of here and go to a movie.*" Despair sparked in his eyes. "Literally, Iz. I'm hearing her."

My throat tightened. "It's okay," I said. "Me, too. I've been talking to her, too." I swallowed hard. "And I hear her, too," I added, although I didn't.

People began to wander through the front doors, friends, fellow teachers, some of Josie's students and their parents. You could practically smell their collective apprehension, like a perfume. Eau de Dread. I hovered near Mark, suddenly unsure of my place in the hierarchy of mourning.

Josie was my best friend, Hannah's honorary aunt. She was the one who would come over with a bag of chocolate-covered almonds when she thought my voice sounded funny on the phone. She was the one who waited for me in the hospital after Helene had her stroke, and for months she kept me company during the rehab appointments. She had sleepovers with Hannah, cookie-decorating parties, and movie nights, so that Chris and I could be alone—our S.O.S. weekends, Chris called them, when we were first acknowledging how dire things were: Sink or Swim. (And sometimes, I thought, but just to myself: *Same Old Sex.*) I told Josie everything, until I didn't, and she told me everything, except she didn't.

People were arriving now in a steady flow. Josie had few relatives, and they were far-flung: a cousin who lived in London, an uncle in Hawaii she barely knew, the casualties of a family rift a decade before she was born. Her parents had died years ago, a fact which had caused her great pain every day of her life and which right now would have given her solace if she'd been here—that her parents would not have had to suffer the anguish of attending their only daughter's funeral. And that idea muddied my thinking, because if Josie were *here,* she wouldn't have been granted that relief. That's what my brain felt like on the day of my best friend's funeral and for many weeks after: a confounding map of twisted, barely navigable roads that were long and tangled and led nowhere or doubled back without warning and ended up where they had begun.

Mark grew busy and distracted, accepting hugs and handshakes and responding to murmurs of sympathy. I had my first inkling about the comforts of this ritual: the more you were asked to attend to, the less you had to feel. I wandered away and peered out the front window. The sky was such a fine porcelain blue it looked like it might crack.

I had been worried that I wouldn't get through the day without cracking, myself. But numbness seemed to be keeping me together. Relief at feeling nothing shuddered through me. There was probably a long, hard-to-pronounce German word for it: the overwhelming feeling of feeling nothing.

I watched as a small silver car pulled into a parking space, and a trio of teachers emerged from it: Andrea Brauer, Andi Friedman, and Kelly Anderson-Jensen. (Fifth-grade science, sixth-grade math, special ed.) They convened in the teachers' lounge every morning before school and at every lunch hour and at the end of each school day, sitting and sipping their Starbucks half-caff skim lattes or huddled together, tapping away on their phones, or planning their Friday-afternoon drinking sessions at the Leopard Spot, a trendy retro seventies cocktail bar across town where they could enjoy a few well-deserved tequila sunrises away from the prying eyes of local parents. "You're welcome to come," Kelly used to say to us, shaking her head *no* so slightly I'm sure she didn't even notice she was doing it. "I mean, everyone's welcome."

The Andes were ten years younger than Josie and I, smooth haired and hardworking. They assessed us—the dark circles under my eyes, the faint lines on Josie's forehead, the pair of pants one of us might sometimes wear two or three or, let's face it, four days in a row. They took disapproving note of our midcareer shortcuts, those self-preservatory downhill coasts that allowed a person to catch her breath in the midst of the drudgery: a joint sick day from which Josie and I would return with suspiciously pretty fingernails; a multiple-choice test administered when an essay would have been a better measure. They evaluated the sad lunches I stashed in the fridge—peanut butter on Ritz Crackers, one time just a large bag of pretzels and an expired jar of Nutella—detritus of my domestic life huddling pathetically next to their California rolls and their Cobb salads and their tiny portions of pad Thai. We tried, at first, joining them for coffee breaks or tagging along on their Friday-night outings. But their indifference with a thin politeness glaze was too much to bear.

"They reject the decade between us," Josie said over a glass of wine one night in my living room as Hannah pirouetted nearby. "They refuse to admit that they will one day turn forty."

"And then die!" I added, raising my glass, and we laughed, because that was it.

Pleasant, though: Andrea, Andi, and Kelly were perfectly pleasant colleagues, and we moved as separate entities through the school, and so all of that was fine until they clicked into Principal Coffey's office in their slim trousers and their confident low heels and helped destroy Josie's career. So the Andes were to blame for this, too. They were most definitely to blame.

"Mark," Kelly Anderson-Jensen said, the front door blowing shut behind them.

"Mark," Andrea and Andi echoed, "Mark," as if they were setting their sights on a clay pigeon, and he came to greet them. They offered their condolences—which, let it be noted, use the same words as apologies—and hugged Mark, and hugged one another, and first Andrea started crying, and then Kelly, high-pitched little sobs, and before I knew it I was out the door, standing near the building, blinded by fury and trying, once again, to catch my breath. *Josie,* I thought, *you should be here to see this. Josie. You fucking idiot.*

That's when I saw Chris and Hannah and my mother walking across the parking lot. I stepped onto the path in front of the funeral home and called out to them, and Chris and Helene came toward me, Chris supporting my mother with his arm, and Hannah wiped her eyes with her hand and extended her thin arm in a small wave, and there they were, my perfect little family, with their flushed cheeks and their ears and their lips and their bones.

Death smashes a crater into your life, and you're left alone to sort through the rubble. But here's something else I figured out in the long months after Josie died: she would always be my wild, grieving, huge-hearted, selfish, confident, insecure, extravagant, beloved best friend. I would define her. You think, during the worst of it, that it's the other way around, but it's not.

And here's something else I learned: you lose some people that way—fast and blinding. But some people inch away from you slowly, in barely discernible steps.

In the end it almost doesn't matter. They're just as gone.

T w o

Was that birthday party the last time we were all together, Mark and Josie, Chris and I? Surely not. There must have been other gatherings, dinners, brunches, movies. But in the highlights reel of our memories, we don't recall pleasant, uneventful Wednesday afternoons or moderately enjoyable evenings out; we remember occasions—graduations and recitals, holidays and birthdays, and this one was mine. I think sometimes, if the parameters of existence were somehow different, if life were memory, then happiness could prevail, and nothing fine would be lost.

It was my birthday, and we had just finished dinner at Mark and Josie's house. My best friend was a little drunk, which barely warranted notice. It was just how she amplified a celebration, the way any of us might, how she became giddy and charming and magnetic. She had just sliced the cake and dropped an enormous slab on my plate.

"Congratulations, Iz," she said, licking frosting from her finger. "Forty-one is officially the end of the line!"

Chris glanced at me with raised eyebrows. My mild-mannered husband was frequently shocked by the things Josie said; he never quite knew how to respond, so he followed my lead.

"Thank you," I said, smiling. "Happy birthday to me." I took a bite of the cake, banana with chocolate frosting, my favorite and no one else's.

Josie sawed off another piece and passed it to Chris. "Forty-one," she said, "is when you come face-to-face with the void!" She laughed at herself, a low, raspy cackle. "The great yawning chasm of oblivion!" She took a big swig of her wine and grinned at me with purplish lips.

Mark put his arm around his wife. With his free hand he reached for her wineglass and drank the rest of it. "Easy there, cowboy." He looked at me, his face an apology I didn't need.

"Oh, Jose," I said. "I'm not quite ready for my midlife crisis." I thought of Hannah at home with my mother, snuggled up together under a blanket watching *Planet of the Apes,* which for some unfathomable reason they both loved. I thought of the pink-and-orange woven bracelet Hannah had given me that morning and the homemade card: *You're the best Mommy ever!* I'd read that and had to turn away; if she saw me tearing up like an idiot, she'd leave the room. That was the real void, the true earthly terror: being the mother of an almost-ten-year-old girl.

"We're in it together," Josie went on. She was only a few months behind me. "The next box of tampons you buy could be your last!"

"Stop, Jose," Mark said quietly.

Her face reddened, and she glanced at Mark, chastened. "Don't scold me," she murmured. She turned back to Chris and me. "Anyway!" she said, with a merry little kick in her voice to compensate for that blip. "It's not as if it's some kind of a big secret! Doesn't everybody feel that cold lick of mortality on their birthday?" She smiled broadly and held up a paper plate. "More cake?"

"I don't feel that old," I said quickly. I didn't know what I was going to say next. "I don't feel old, but I do think I'm probably no longer eligible to marry a movie star."

"Did you have one in mind?" Chris asked. We were taking the reins. A marriage, the entity of it, was capable of a lot of things, and I was grateful for the ways ours could sometimes move and shift with surprising grace; how together, as a force, we could pick up the slack of social discomfort. Our long connection rescued us. Not always, but sometimes.

"Charlton Heston," I said. I shrugged.

"Of course, he's dead," Josie piped up, "which gives you an advantage."

I took another bite of cake. Josie knew how to establish the perfect ratio of banana to chocolate.

"Mark hasn't gotten any cake," Chris said. It was true. Josie had sliced pieces for me and Chris and herself, but she'd forgotten Mark, or ignored him.

He held out his paper plate, which, like all of ours, had MARK'S BAR MITZVAH! printed on it. Josie and Mark lived in Mark's parents' old house, much of which was pleasantly frozen in 1982. They'd been living there for just over a year, after his parents became snowbirds and headed south, and Mark and Josie hadn't made it their own yet. You never knew what you would stumble on in the attic or at the bottom of a dresser drawer. A rolled-up poster of a cat hanging upside down by its claws. A Jane Fonda aerobics videotape. A few months earlier, Josie told me she'd found a T-shirt in the back of Mark's dad's closet with WORLD'S GREATEST LOVER printed on it in fuzzy block lettering. She tossed it in the garbage before Mark saw it, she told me, saved him from that particular image. How much of our relationships are made up of those little mercies the other person never even knows about?

"Sorry, babe," Josie said, as she passed Mark an extra-large hunk of cake. His hand brushed hers. "Sorry about that."

And then everything was all right again; all was forgiven. We all felt it, the wave of ease that washed over us.

"Oh!" Josie hopped up. "Izzy! I have one more present for you!" She had already given me an orange sweater, a bottle of pink sparkly nail polish, and an enormous slab of dark chocolate.

Chris glanced at me, with an almost-imperceptible twitch of his lips. We both knew what this would be. In addition to teaching, in her spare time Josie was an artist, and every special occasion brought forth a brightly wrapped Josie Abrams original. In college, she'd received an honorable mention in an art department competition. That was enough to keep her going. Twenty years later, she was still at it. You had to admire the commitment, even if the product was sometimes inscrutable. We had seven Josie Abrams sculptures and five paintings on prominent display around our house, because in addition to making gifts for me, Josie was also in the habit of stopping in unannounced.

She dashed upstairs and thumped around above our heads. "Close your eyes, Iz," she called, coming back down the stairs. "This one's not wrapped!" I looked at Chris, then at Mark. Mark shrugged, indulgent, fond. *Don't blame me,* that shrug said. *She's your friend.*

Josie clomped into the dining room and pressed a large, rectangular canvas into my arms. I could still smell the paint on it. "You can open your eyes now," she said. She was like a little kid, vibrating with excitement.

I looked. It was a painting of thirteen women sitting together on one side of a long dinner table, in the style of *The Last Supper* but with middle-aged women instead of apostles. The women were wearing sweaters or high-collared blouses; they wore lipstick and had formal, old-fashioned hairstyles, updos and teased 1950s bouffants. They had vacant, pleasant expressions on their faces, and they were examining clear plastic containers of different sizes. *"The Last Tupperware Party!"* Josie said.

"Oh!" I said, genuinely stunned. I had a fleeting thought about faith and impermanence, about ambition and disappointment. Those dopey-faced women tugged at my heartstrings. "I love it!" I said, and I meant it. I loved the brain that had imagined this painting, the hands that fashioned the women in their pastel tops. I loved Josie, who had baked me my favorite cake for my birthday, and Chris, whose heart was sometimes still a mystery to me, and Mark, who was like a brother. There were invisible tethers that tied us together, and they extended out from us to Hannah, to my mother, to my mother's family, all lost. And beyond: they flowed out beyond us. You didn't get to feel the tug of these ties very often, the fragile net that held us all.

"Happy birthday, Isabel," Josie said. She flung her arms around me, her skinny little body all ribs and hips and solid force. She stood on her tiptoes so her mouth could reach my ear. "I love you," she whispered. "What would I do without you? You're my family."

. . .

Josie and I met at my first staff meeting fifteen years ago. She sauntered in twenty minutes late, took a quick survey of the room, and plopped herself down in the third row, next to me. Bob Coffey, the principal of Rhodes Avenue Middle School, was in the middle of a story. He was in his mid-fifties and fossilizing rapidly. But he was worshipped, an institution in our district. You wouldn't catch anyone saying a word against him. *Mr. Coffey*, parents would whisper reverently, *Mr. Coffey*, like sleepy addicts.

All of his stories, I would soon discover, were about his dog. After taking care of faculty business, he would ramble on about Starbucks the spaniel for a few long minutes, turn the episode into an outdated parable about children and their charming inadequacies, and then adjourn the meeting with a hearty "You are released!" These weekly staff meetings were mandatory. Our school was small, and absences were noted.

"Starbucks woke us up in the middle of the night on Saturday," Mr. Coffey was saying when Josie walked into the room. He turned to her and nodded. "Thank you for joining us, Miss Bryant. As I was saying, Starbucks woke us up in the middle of the night on Saturday, demanding that we take him for a walk. 'Don't give in,' I warned Anita." To everyone's delight, his wife's name really was Anita Coffey. "But Anita gave in, and sure enough, Starbucks needed to empty his bladder. Oh, the chiding I took from her!" He had been walking up and down through the rows of chairs, but now he paused for effect at the front of the room. "Until Sunday night, that is, when Starbucks waltzed into our bedroom at four a.m. and whined to be taken out again. Only this time, he didn't need to, he simply *wanted* to. The same thing happened on Monday night, Tuesday night, and Wednesday night, until finally Mrs. Coffey and I put Starbucks in his crate and broke him of this unpleasant habit."

I leaned forward in my seat. I had been concentrating so hard, trying to grasp the meaning in our principal's strange homily. Only later would I understand that Bob Coffey viewed children as recalcitrant, barely domesticated animals who needed equal amounts of discipline, affection, exercise, and a protein-rich diet. He crossed his arms over his chest and smiled benevolently. "Children require patience, you see, but not overindulgence."

There were nods and murmurs, and Janice Van Dyke, the

seventh-grade math teacher, let loose with an emphatic "So true!"

"If we choose to give them an inch," Mr. Coffey continued, "it is our duty to see that an inch is all they take."

I leaned over to Josie and whispered, "Or they get put in their crates."

Josie looked at me. For a second she seemed puzzled, and then her face opened with delight, her smile huge and toothy and as irresistible as the sun. She nodded to herself. "We need to have dinner," she said quietly. "You and I. Tonight. I need to know you." She reached over and squeezed my arm with startling intimacy, and I felt myself heating up, blushing with pleasure.

That's the way it is with certain people. They set their sights on you. They look at you straight on and they choose you, and they are dazzled by their own brilliant choice. It was the first time anyone had fallen in love with me like that. And I was powerless against it.

· · ·

Lurch forward exactly one year from Josie's death: one tear-lubricated, misery-drenched, grief-addled dung heap of a year. Chris and Hannah and I are meeting Mark at the cemetery for the unveiling of her gravestone.

"I will never get used to this," Chris whispers, hunching over so I'll hear him, his hand on my back, a familiar pressure.

"I know," I say, digging my fingernails into the soft flesh of my palm.

Hannah drags her feet next to mine. She won't look at me. The wind whips up around us. A few drops of rain land, dotting the hard ground of the parking lot, threatening more.

I spot Mark from a few feet away—alone; I wasn't sure if he would be—his hands jammed into his pockets, shoulders hunched. He looks up and starts walking toward us, and relief calms his features. "Hey, guys. Thanks for coming. I know this isn't easy for any of us." He hugs Hannah, then Chris, then, finally, briefly, me. And I feel relief, mixed in with everything else, because I wasn't sure he would; we haven't even spoken in more than three months.

"Of course we're here," Chris murmurs. "God, of course."

Mark pulls away quickly and I examine his face, which, at least, at last, looks like his: today he looks like Mark, my friend, Josie's widower.

That word, he said to me once, drunk, in the midst of it. He raised his bottle of beer. *Who is widower than I? Nobody!*

"Let's go," Mark says, and I can tell he hasn't forgiven me, but we won't talk about that today. Chris and Hannah and I fall into step next to him, picking our way across the pavement and through the dampening path toward the area of the cemetery where Josie is buried: a flat and blanched patch of ground in section E, row 20, as if this were a theater, only the seats are horizontal and the audience particularly unresponsive.

Being only forty-two and in good health, Josie had articulated no specific wishes for her final resting place, so we, her beloved friends and husband, improvised, and this is how she ended up here, at the Eternal Home Cemetery off the highway, may she rest in peace lulled by the honking of trucks zooming down I-94 and the faint but unmistakable smell of fried onions wafting over from Grandpa Zip's Old-Fashioned Diner just across the frontage road. The grass on the western edge of the cemetery is always a lush green because of the year-round humid breath of exhaust. Burying Josie here has made us all wonder: *Will we meet up here in a few years? Us, too? Here? Can we do no better than this?* This death thing, it seems, never gets pretty, but it sure does have staying power.

· · ·

The rain is a steady, spitting drizzle now. We're at the grave site, the brand-new pinkish headstone a shiny heartbreak. Karen Josephine Bryant Abrams. Josie rejected the name Karen in college and never looked back. She would have hated her headstone. Then again, who wouldn't? BELOVED WIFE, it says. CHERISHED FRIEND.

"I prepared a little speech," Mark says, his eyes watery. He looks away and shakes his head. "But now . . . I can't."

Chris moves a step closer to Mark and puts his arm around him, and Mark takes a ragged, heaving breath. "It's okay, man," Chris says. He's a full head taller than Mark, long and lean where Mark is dense and sturdy. Chris's sharp, even features were chiseled by some cold Northern European ancestral winds, a counterpoint to Mark's dark hair and eyes, the craggy hollows of his face, his perennial stubble. Sometimes when I see them next to each other like this, I can't help but think about the strange miracles of DNA.

Chris removes his arm from Mark's shoulders quickly and suddenly, the way men do, and rubs his hands together. "It's okay. I'll say something. Isabel will say something. Maybe even Hannah, if you want to, sweetie."

Here's what I want to do: I want to scream. Chris looks at his feet. He looks up at me, his lips pressed together, and swallows. "She was Izzy's best friend, and Mark's wife, and Hannah . . . well, she was almost like a second mom to Hannah." Hannah, who still won't meet my eye, sobs quietly. "And I miss her for who she was to you all. But, you know, I loved her, too." His breath puffs out into the cold air. "She was always at our house," he says, and I find that I am panting a little bit, trying to contain my fury, trying to hold on to the rhythm of my own breath. As if that solidifies Chris's relationship with her: Josie took up space where he lived!

"She was always around," he continues, oblivious. He takes off his glasses and wipes them on his shirt, then just holds them. His naked eyes are a surprise to me, vulnerable as a fish. "I didn't, um, I didn't have the same kind of relationship with her that you guys did," he says. "Sometimes I'd wake up on a Saturday morning and go downstairs, and she'd still be there, crashed on the sofa from the night before."

An old man carrying a bouquet of pink roses wanders past us, head high, peering left and right, unbothered by the wind and the rain. He looks otherworldly to me, as if he's searching for his own grave. I want to say this to Josie, and for the millionth time, I'm stunned by her absence.

Chris falls silent for a moment, then clears his throat and starts again. "There was always a half-eaten container of something on the coffee table," he says. "Sometimes she would have it for breakfast, no matter how much it had . . ." He waves his empty hand in front of him and smiles a little. "Congealed. She was always so happy in the morning." He glances at me and I can read his mind: *Unlike some people.* "So easy to talk to. We'd have coffee together before Izzy got up."

That's it? I want to say, grief and rage reacting chemically inside me, creating a new and volatile alloy, something bright and flaming. Furium. *That's it? Leftover Chinese food for breakfast? Coffee on a Sunday morning? Tidying up the living room together, maybe? She was more cheerful than my wife!* I want to tear his glasses from his hand and fling them against Josie's headstone. But now Hannah is crying harder, and she pulls up the collar of her red windbreaker and presses her face into her father's solid chest, and I remember how on the night Josie died Chris wrapped his arms around me. We hadn't touched each other in months, it felt like, and he just reached for me in that blank, horrible moment, with everything good that he had. Even if I had wanted to shake his arms off, he wouldn't have let go.

Chris rests his chin on Hannah's head, and they stand there together. The geometry of holding your growing daughter is a changing thing: she fits in your arms a certain way when she's four, another when she's six, unwieldy when she's nine, and hardly at all when she's almost twelve. Some nights when she's sleeping, sprawled out like a starfish on her bed, I crawl in next to her, stealthily, taking up just the smallest sliver of mattress, to feel the ghost of the baby she used to be. Motherhood has reduced me to such a pathetic creature that I don't even care how pathetic I am. I'd like to share that thought with Josie. Having an eleven-year-old daughter is like pining over the college boyfriend who dumped you, I would tell her.

Childless by choice, sweetie! Josie would say.

"It's all right," I say now, to no one. "We all loved her so much." To my surprise, my voice sounds clear and calm. Josie observed one of my classes once, as part of Principal Coffey's peer-review program. *It's a wonder Isabel sings so terribly,* she wrote in her assessment, *with that pretty speaking voice.*

Mark and Hannah are both crying freely now, they're a chorus of sobs, Hannah still pressed hard into Chris's chest; we're just a huddled mass of mourners in the rain, a single entity, despite all the ways we've been blasted apart over the last year. I'm thinking, with a sort of empty resignation, *This is it,* this is how it will be for the rest of my life, lost in this darkness. But then Hannah turns and looks at Mark, and there is a moment, a strange moment between them, and as if by psychic agreement, they both start giggling. It comes over them as quick as a cloudburst. Hannah first: a swipe of her nose with the back of her hand and a chuckle, her recognition of the sad ridiculousness of the occasion offering a glimpse of the kind of adult she will be, savvy and kind. Then Mark, a small part of him opening up to Hannah, a clearing in the bleakness, and then they're both laughing, just shaking with it.

Chris looks at me over Hannah's blond head and raises his eyebrows and smiles. She is one thing we usually agree on, the best thing about us. Lately I find myself thinking about the night she was born, just flipping through the details in my mind. I've told her the story so many times: *It was three a.m. Daddy blew through four red lights. One of the nurses was on the phone when we walked in, ignoring us, chatting. "Lasagna," she said to the person on the other end of the line, and I thought,* Who is she talking to about lasagna at three in the morning? *She held up the "just a minute" finger to us, and Daddy yelled at her. You were upside down, breech, and they were preparing me for a C-section, and then, at the last minute, just for me, you turned. You were born howling, loud as a freight train. But then, when they set you down on my chest, you stopped crying, and we just looked at each other, familiar mammals meeting for the first time.*

I never tell her how Chris circled the parking ramp twice, looking for a good spot. I never tell her how as he walked me slowly down the hospital corridor he said, "Actually, I don't think this is such a good idea, Iz," and then laughed unconvincingly. Some details you keep to yourself; you polish them up in private, smooth, shiny jewels of resentment that you save for when you might need them.

"Okay," Mark says, after he and Hannah have caught their breath and their laughter has subsided and we have all swung safely back to the right side of miserable. "I think we can leave now." It's raining harder. Chris is trying to clean his glasses again. I fumble around for the small stone I've been carrying in my pocket and place it on Josie's gravestone. We were here.

Hannah is quiet in the car, texting. Chris drops her at the library to meet some friends. (*Are you sure, sweetie?* She's sure.) And then he takes me home, driving slowly along the silent streets. He pulls into the driveway and gets out of the car, and before I realize it, we're walking together into the house, word-less routine and muscle memory. In the entryway near the back door he kicks off his shoes, then arranges them neatly on the mat. He shrugs off his jacket, takes mine from me, hangs them up. We're performing the steps of our oldest dance. And even in this strange, sad, suspended state, I know that we are elegant at it.

The house is cold. Someone left the light on in the hallway. Our socked feet pad together past the kitchen, which is still a mess from breakfast, up the stairs, into the bedroom, where the curtains are drawn, where although it's two in the afternoon, it's still twilit and dim: romantic or depressing, depending.

"Well," Chris says, moving toward me. "If there's nothing else . . ."

"Nope," I say, inching closer. "Bye."

After fifteen years together, there is very little about this man that surprises me. His arms around my waist, hands tight against my back: not a surprise. His mouth on my neck, breath heavy and warm: not a surprise. The smell of his skin, like celery and oranges. They say you're attracted to a mate based on his scent, that somewhere, in the simian recesses of your brain, you're sniffing out the smell of genes complementary to yours, the intoxicating whiff of healthy offspring. So there's always that, with Chris. And it, too, is not a surprise. The way he pulls at my clothes as if he doesn't understand the mechanics of buttons and zippers. The speed of his heartbeat, animal desire, heightened now and all this past year, crazier than it has been in all of the fourteen years that came before: well, I guess that's been a surprise.

"Iz," he whispers, the nickname that sounds like an existential proclamation. *"I need you."*

And I laugh out loud. *Who's writing your lines?* Need? Need! I suck in my stomach at the sound of that word. Tiny spider veins crosshatch my thighs, new ones popping up like dropped stitches; I just noticed one this morning. I caught a glimpse of my upper arm in the mirror a few weeks ago and it looked like my mother was in the bathroom waving to me. There are seven wayward pounds that seem to migrate all over my body, like accessories. The signs of disrepair are faint but unmistakable. I flash back to that birthday party, just two years ago, but it seems like a decade: *No movie star will have me now!*

Okay, I'll admit that Chris and I still want each other. But need? Need is for your first lover on your twin bed in your college dorm. And Chris, whose chest hair is going gray; Chris, who has never had any fat on his frame, and so it's his muscles that are softening, loosening a little, his firm stomach growing slightly paunchy, his biceps starting to sag. *Need you?*

But here we are again, all the same, answering death with sex. I peel off his sweater, lift his T-shirt over his head. We've lost so much. I run my hands down his back, across his chest, his body as familiar as my own. I can imagine this with someone different, if I try: the ways passion would, or wouldn't, humiliate you. The ways it would release you.

Chris kisses me, unembarrassed. After a certain amount of time with someone, crisis is an aphrodisiac. It's probably best not to think too hard about the implications of that one. And we are desperate for this, the flotsam of our intimacy. It's true. I can hardly breathe for how much I want him. Need him. "Iz," he says again. "Okay?"

I let him guide me onto our bed, a tangle of soft sheets and heavy blankets. And I don't need to answer, but I do: "Yes."

. . .

I wake up with a start. It must be hours later, still dark, the dead of night. Chris is lying next to me, snoring softly.

"Shit!" I jump out of the bed and scramble for my clothes. "Chris, shit, we were supposed to pick up Hannah hours ago. What the hell? One of us was supposed to get her! Shit!"

Chris glances at the clock and sighs, pulls the covers up to his neck. "It's three o'clock."

"Holy mother of fuck." I fumble with my shirt, pull it on backward, wriggle it around until it's on the right way.

"Izzy, it's three in the afternoon. We've just been . . . dozing for a few minutes." He rolls over and runs a hand through his fine, disheveled hair and peers at me. In our marriage—in every marriage?—no annoyed glance holds only the displeasure of the moment. Each one reflects all the irritated glances he's ever shot at me for all of my transgressions: for lacking discipline, for being brittle and sharp, for overreacting, for swearing all the time, even in front of Hannah, for letting my worst self porcupine out before I retract my quills. Every exasperated look Chris gives me—and there have been plenty—carries the sediment of all the displeasure that has accumulated over the past fifteen years. "Everything is fine," he says. He exhales through his nostrils like a bull.

I shrug. "Well, that's a relief."

He shrugs back at me, an unconscious imitation. "I should be getting back to the apartment," he says, a little embarrassed, and the fact that he is ashamed almost absolves him.

"You don't have to call it 'the apartment,'" I say, suddenly uncomfortably aware that I am standing next to our bed half naked and about to be abandoned by my sort-of-ex-husband whom I probably should not have just slept with. "Just say, 'my apartment. I have to get back to *my apartment*.'" I step into my favorite old pair of sweatpants, which I wear frequently and which Josie used to call a blend of cotton and self-loathing. "You should get back to your apartment," I say, the bitterness in my voice turning the edges hard.

Chris sits up in bed and fumbles for his glasses on the nightstand, then props himself against the headboard with a pillow. "Come on, Iz. Don't. Let's just . . . would you just get back in here for a minute?" He pats the mattress next to him, rubs his hand down the sheet: fifteen years of signals we've been sending each other, fifteen years of fingers and faces, of communication, understood or missed. Our bed. Chris's beautiful face, as alien to me now as it was intimate an hour ago.

"No." I stand over him, glowering, clothed now. "Nope."

Sex with your ex, I imagine Josie saying. *Never a good idea.* I turn toward the door. There's a hallway, then Hannah's room, pink and sweet a few months ago, filled with dolls and pillows and art projects, transitioning now into a sort of burrow, mopey and dark and defiant. (Where did all her stuffed animals go? She used to have a menagerie, a zoo. Where are they? Has there been some kind of teddy-bear Rapture?) There's the bathroom where four pregnancies ended—fourteen, thirteen, six, and one and a half years ago, far away enough that I no longer feel a stab of pain when I think about them, no longer note the anniversaries of what would have been their due dates—December 17, February 4, November 1, April 10—then feel stupid for remembering.

"Izzy, please," Chris says, but I'm already at the top of the stairs, and I'm just heading down, my bare feet cold on the hardwood floor, as I hear him sigh, loud and annoyed. It's the kind of sigh that is meant to be heard, part of the vocabulary of our unraveling marriage.

"I'm trying," he calls after me, and I want to say, *Yes, you are.* He'll get up in a few minutes, put his clothes on, and get in his car and head to his apartment a mile from here, the two-bedroom on the East Side that I helped him pick out, near the lake and full of light, newly decorated with inexpensive but decent furniture and blue rugs and lots of pillows, and far too cozy to be as temporary as we agreed it was.

He'll bring my socks to me before he leaves—he'll have noticed I forgot them. He won't hand them to me. He'll place them in front of me on the table, and he'll stand there for a minute in our messy, darkening kitchen, waiting for me to thank him, to say something, but I won't. I won't say a word.

It's amazing, really, the things two people think they know about each other.

Three

I was the one who introduced Josie and Mark. Mark and I had been friends since kindergarten. We were always seated next to each other, all the way through grade school: Mark Abrams and Isabel Applebaum, two little alphabetized Jews, dark haired and slightly lost in a forest of midwestern consonant clusters, all those strapping, blond Schultzes and Metzgers and Hrubys and Przybylskis—strapping even in kindergarten, if memory serves.

My mother used to tell me things about my classmates, like "Oh, Cindy Eichgrau, her grandparents lived on Locust, right around the corner from us when I was growing up. Once when I was running across their lawn, they yelled at me to go back home and called me a dirty Jew." She would say these things to me casually, while I was decorating valentines for school or making a guest list for my birthday party or eating breakfast. "Allison Metzger . . . Metzger . . . Grandma and Grandpa knew a Metzger family in Frankfurt." Eyebrow raised, head tilted. "Hmm. Probably not the same ones, though. Hope not." The implications were clear. *You never know. . . .*

This is where my psyche took shape, in the clean white kitchen of my parents' house. This is where my heart let loose its first defiant yelp. It's more or less a straight line from Helene

Strauss Applebaum's dark melancholy and gallows humor to my maybe-ex-husband, Christopher Moore: lanky, blue eyed, straightforward to a fault, as likable as Christmas.

But Mark. Mark was my science partner, seatmate on field trips to the nature center and the symphony, and, not coincidentally, Hebrew-school carpool buddy. He was short and quiet and he really, really loved to read, so mostly that's what he did, while I chatted to him. "Mmm-hmm," he would say occasionally, not even looking up from his book, "yup, sounds about right, Iz," and the dynamic served us both well. We were pals through grade school, we lost track of each other in high school, and then we reconnected during our sophomore year in college, in a course on Chaucer. It was a small lecture, an English-major requirement, and for the first few weeks the seats were assigned alphabetically. So there we were again, the two of us. We read *The Canterbury Tales* in translation, but Mark, king of extra credit, can still recite the entire prologue in the original Middle English. All I remember is the strange, sad, musical sound of those almost-comprehensible words, like a dirge, a dream . . . and that the Wife of Bath was a floozy.

We graduated, and there were no jobs, which gave us a certain kind of reckless freedom. My friends and I packed up and moved to cities that seemed appealing—New York? San Francisco? Prague?—as if we were choosing pastries from the bakery case. Then we signed up with temp agencies and, to make ourselves feel better, we applied to law school or graduate programs in Things We Thought We Might Be Sort of Interested In.

I moved to Chicago. I would have gone farther, but Helene doesn't do well when I'm far away. She has a radius of one hundred miles, or a ninety-minute drive, before an anxious tremor creeps into her voice, which I've never been able to ignore. Mark went to Seattle and tried to get a job at a magazine but ended up working temp jobs in law firms and banks. A few years later, demoralized and broke, he and his all-flannel wardrobe moved back to Milwaukee and started a master's program in English literature.

I had come back nine months earlier, at my mother's encouragement, to try to land a teaching job. I moved back in with her and worked as a receptionist at her doctors' office and subbed for the district and then, finally, Rhodes Avenue Middle School hired me. Mark and I picked up where we had left off. We started hanging out, seeing movies, going out for beers after work. I had just met Chris, and I was overflowing with the smug evangelism of the newly coupled. I wanted Mark to be happy like I was happy. I wanted to find him a girlfriend so he could feel what it felt like to be me.

Mark and Josie were both single, which at the time was kind of enough. I figured that two reasonably good-looking, smart professionals in their late twenties were as likely as not to get along. Josie was on my list for Mark, a list that also included my mom's friend's daughter Miranda, who was a couple of years younger and had just moved back from Portland to start med school, and also Lacy, the girl with the pierced tongue and the winking-devil tattoo who swiped my card at the gym. (I had no such corresponding list for Josie, having only just met Chris and still being in the habit of safeguarding available men for myself.)

When, at their wedding, Mark and Josie raised their glasses in a toast to me, Isabel, for having had the brilliant foresight to recognize when two strangers were meant for each other, I just smiled and shrugged, because, really? I hadn't. It was dumb luck.

We met for drinks on a cold night at Heinrich von Raaschke's Gemütliche Bierhaus. It was a loud and rollicking place famous for an elaborate drinking game involving a two-liter glass shoe filled with beer and a dirndl-wearing waitress who would inflict physical punishment for rule infractions. (*Take your turn drinking beer or get a kick in the rear!*) It was my favorite bar at the time, because all my life, whenever Helene drove past it, she would shudder and say something like "Later, after zese beers, ve vill burn down ze synagogue." Frequenting it as an adult made me feel brave and ordinary.

I'm not sure why I elected to come along on Josie and Mark's first date. I had invited Chris, but he couldn't make it, and rather than bow out myself and leave my friends to their own devices, I decided to orchestrate their meeting, to be a conductor of love.

Josie was twenty minutes late. She came bursting through the door as if she had just gotten her cue backstage. Sometimes, with Josie, you half expected the part of the room you were in to darken as a spotlight switched on and encircled her with its glow. She waved at us and walked over to our table. I remember that when she took her hat off, her hair sprang free as if it had been trapped. She draped her magenta coat over the back of a chair and rubbed her hands together to warm them. It was early March but still the bitter, silent depths of a Wisconsin winter, and we all walked around encased in the long, puffy down coats that were fashionable that year, looking like chrysalises, brightly colored and ready to hatch.

"You guys!" Josie announced, before I'd even introduced them. Mark gazed at her, at this dazzling, unruly creature who'd just vaulted through space and come to rest next to him. We had ordered a pitcher of beer, and Josie poured herself a glass and took a fortifying sip. "You guys, I have such a *great story!*" In the years to come, countless get-togethers would begin just this way. *I have such a great story!* She had wandered into the supply room after school, she told us, and caught Mr. Kleefisch, the art teacher, and Señora Doherty, Spanish, in a clinch on the floor near the bottles of neon-blue industrial cleaning solution. Young, newly married Angela Doherty, legs splayed on top of a stack of paper towels, and old, long-married Jim Kleefisch, known both for his creative use of potato prints and for the tufts of gray hair that escaped his shirt at every opening—wrists, chest, back of the neck. Señora Doherty squealed at the sight of Josie. Kleefisch, hairy back to the door, interpreted that squeal as encouragement and groaned, *"Sí, Sí, me gusta, me gusta."*

"Qué escándalo!" Josie said to us, leaning against the cushion of her coat, her eyes bright and delighted. She was radiating with the energy of her tawdry tale.

"They're both *married*!" I said. "And ew, Kleefisch! He's got to be fifty! Oh, my God!" Fifty was decades away and seemed, at the time, like the age at which you would settle in for a short rest before dying.

Josie swallowed another sip, the muscles in her throat working. "Disgusting!" she agreed gleefully.

"Who knew," Mark said under the din, "that a middle school could be such a den of lust." He looked at Josie, and on the word "lust," his cheeks went pink, and she smiled and absorbed the admiration that spilled out of him.

"Oh, you have no idea," she said. "No idea."

A little light clicked on in my brain: this was it. These two, here, this night: they were going to decide to become soul mates.

In my whole life I had not, until Hannah was born and a kind of fear-based maternal instinct kicked in, had any moments of intuition, any bold premonitions of anything at all. I have mostly been an observer of people and situations who later thinks, *Oh, yeah, that makes sense, I get it now.* But at that moment fifteen years ago the night opened up in front of me like a book I had already read. I saw exactly how Mark and Josie would draw closer, fingertips grazing; how they would talk about books and teaching and their families and their dreams; how those details would add up to something specific and amazing (*Really? Me, too! Me, too!*); how Josie and Mark would want to understand each other, and so they would, and that would be love.

I looked at my life at that bright moment and I knew for sure that it would be joyful and that no one I loved would ever leave me. Unlike everyone else, everywhere, in the history of everything.

· · ·

I think now about moments that skittered by but left a trace in my memory. I recalibrate the weight of events, and I wonder: *How did I miss that? How did I not see who she was?*

And so now, of course, I remember this: It was a chilly November afternoon, a Sunday, four months before Josie died. Hannah was sick with a cold and a fever. Josie stopped by, like she did whenever Hannah was sick, with treats for her: a giant bag of M&M's, a little plush stuffed giraffe, a pretty pink notebook. Things had not been great between Josie and me, but I was glad to see her, and Hannah, of course, was delighted.

Hannah was lying on the couch in her pajamas, her forehead sweaty, eyes glassy and tired. "Thanks, J," she said, sniffling. She tucked the giraffe into the crook of her elbow and closed her eyes. She had been dozing on and off and half watching a show about a group of high-school kids who open a smoothie shop. (All of the TV shows Hannah liked that year were about beautiful teenagers in fantastically contrived situations where there happened to be no parental supervision—a group of counselors at a camp for aspiring models, a group of talented surfers at surf school. It didn't take a genius to pick up on the theme.)

Josie bent down and kissed Hannah on the cheek, and then on the forehead. Middle-school teachers don't worry about catching viruses; our immune systems are superpowered. "Feel better, H," she said.

"The customer is always right," one of the gorgeous smoothie-shop girls shrieked to her gorgeous coworker, "except when she's trying to steal my boyfriend!"

Josie and I left Hannah to her laugh track and wandered back into the kitchen. "I miss *Sesame Street*," I said, as we sat down at the table. My voice sounded stilted, even to my own ears, forced and artificial. I was trying hard.

Josie took a white paper sack out of her bag and pulled out two croissants, set each on a napkin, a display of normalcy. "What was that show," she said, "the strange cartoon with the little girl and her parents, and the stories were so, so boring?" She slid a croissant across the table to me. "There was never any conflict. Like the biggest thing to happen in an episode would be the family would go for a drive, or someone would get a letter in the mail." She took a bite of her pastry, chewed slowly.

"Oh, God," I said, rolling my eyes. *"Poca Polpetta."* It was a weird Italian import, inexplicably popular with preschoolers. *Poca polpetta* means "little meatball," and, true to her name, she was a very round-headed little girl. She had preternaturally patient parents and a scampering puppy named Ravioli. When Hannah was little, we used to watch it on the weekends in endless repetition.

"It was so soothing," Josie said.

I pulled off a piece of my croissant. "Once Hannah and I were watching it," I said, "and the image popped into my mind of Poca Polpetta's parents having sex."

"Her cartoon parents," Josie said.

"Yes." Poca Polpetta's mother and father looked just like her: heads like soccer balls, button eyes, pink smiling mouths. "Mama and Papa Polpetta, just screwing their brains out," I said, and Josie snorted. "But how else did Poca come to be?"

The rollicking laughter of a studio audience rumbled in from the living room. "I love you, Isabel," Josie said, "but that is sick, and you should never tell anyone else."

"Okay," I said. "I need a confession from you now. A guarantee that you'll never expose my shame." As soon as I said the word "confession," I cringed.

There was a crumb on Josie's upper lip. Her tongue darted out for it. She reached up and ponytailed her thick hair with her hand, then let it fall back down, loose. "Hmm," she said, and looked at me, and her expression was so serious that I had to look away. "Okay. I had this boyfriend in high school. He, um . . . he dumped me, and then, a week later, he started dating someone else . . . this really pretty sophomore, Dawn Grogan. I was so hurt and just furious. Did I ever tell you about this?" I shook my head. "I went to his house one night and I asked if we could go for a drive and talk."

I sat across from Josie, still and mute. It seemed like she was revealing pieces of something, shards of glass distorting the light.

"We drove for a while," she went on, "but he was being such an ass, acting so smug and . . . *decisive* about our breakup. So before he even knew what I was doing, I drove over to their . . . to Dawn Grogan's house. I pulled into the driveway and turned off the engine, and I opened the car door, and I just marched right up to the front door. I turned around for a second, before I rang the bell, and I saw him. Roger, that is. His name was Roger. I thought he would get out and try to stop me, but he was just sitting there in the car with his mouth hanging open.

"Anyway, Dawn came to the door, and she looked at me like she didn't know who I was, which pissed me off. And so I said, 'Listen, you seem like a nice person, and I just want to tell you that when you and Roger started going out, he was still with me. He was cheating on me. He'll probably deny it, but he was.'

"And by that time, Roger was behind me, jogging up the path to Dawn's door, and he was going, 'No, no, Dawn, it's not true! She's lying!' and I just looked at her and kind of smiled sadly and shrugged, like *See?* And then I said, 'Once a cheater, always a cheater,' like I was some kind of bitter divorcée instead of a seventeen-year-old kid."

She stopped and looked at me, her eyes wide, as if she had surprised herself with the story. "I just really wanted to hurt him. Both of them, actually." She shook her head. "Well, I was in high school," she added quickly, although of course she had already said that.

I stared at her for a moment. I still couldn't make out the outlines of what was true and what wasn't; it was like driving into fog. "Good thing we grow up, huh?" I said, and she nodded. "What happened to Roger and Dawn?" I asked.

"I don't know," Josie said, which seemed strange to me. But before I could pursue it, Hannah shuffled into the kitchen and slumped into a chair. Her hair was tangled and her face was flushed. "I was lonely in there, all by myself. What are you talking about?" she asked, and then before either of us could say anything, she sneezed six times. "I need a Kleenex and a Popsicle, please."

"Poor darling," Josie said, and Hannah sidled over to her and laid her warm head on Josie's shoulder.

I got up from the table and rummaged through the freezer for a minute, and as the cold air swirled around my face, I thought about all the secrets Hannah would collect as she moved further away from Chris and me, as she moved away from us and into the world, and some of those secrets would be benign, but some would be the kind that slam doors inside a person. But for now she was right here, feverish and sweet and in need of tissues and a Popsicle.

Josie and I would never mention her strange story again. Months later, after she was gone, I would put the pieces of it together with everything else I knew, and I would understand that she had told me something half true that day, true in spirit but not in fact—and, in the end, not true enough.

Four

───────

"I saw something interesting on the computer," my mother says to me on the phone on a Saturday morning. I'm sitting at the table, my hands wrapped around a mug of coffee, staring out the window at an epic battle between squirrels and sparrows at the bird feeder.

Hannah has gone over to her friend Delaney's house. Hannah has a slew of friends with names like that, Delaney and Cassidy and Reilly, and even a tiny, owlish girl named O'Malley: names, it seems, that their parents plucked arbitrarily from the Boston phone book. Over the past few months, a new kind of drama has crept into these friendships, whispered stories full of complicated betrayals. From what I can see, from what little she tells me, Hannah is usually brokering peace between warring factions, but who knows; maybe she's right in the thick of it, lobbing grenades, causing her share of grief. You're always going to err on the side of your own child.

I'mgoingtoDelaney'sokay? she announced an hour ago, and before I could say, *I love you, why are you so angry at me lately, you are my life, you own my heart, you are the sole reason I exist, and also close the door behind you,* it slammed shut.

"I said I saw something on the computer," Helene says again.

She's growing accustomed to repeating herself, since so many of her friends have become hard of hearing.

"Did you squish it?"

She ignores me. "So I tried sending it to you on the e-mail, but I don't think it worked. I'm going to read it to you." She puts the phone down for a minute and, after some clattering, picks it back up. "Isabel, it says, 'Your marriage may be over, but your life is not.'"

"Mother, my marriage is not . . ." But I stop, suddenly worn out. It's been two weeks since the dedication at the cemetery, two weeks since Chris and I slept together. Since then we've barely spoken. We're cordial to each other when we drop off and pick up Hannah, polite and embarrassed and chilly as exes.

"It says here: 'You can *recover.*'"

"Good," I say. "I hate my sofa."

Helene sighs, then ignores me again. "I want you to come back to yourself," she says. "Before you tell me to mind my own business, I want to say that I know how hard it's been. So much loss." Her voice catches, and I stare hard at the milky coffee in my cup, let the rising steam dampen my face. "I mean," she continues, "my marriage is over, too! I'll go with you."

I don't remind her, *Your marriage ended thirty years ago;* I don't say, *This is the worst idea you've ever had, and that includes the time we went to Germany and you glared at everyone for an entire week and whispered to me whenever you saw someone with gray hair: Where do you think he was? What do you think she was up to?* Instead, like always with my mother, I stanch the hemorrhaging doubt and agree to the thing she's asking.

· · ·

A woman wearing a HI! MY NAME IS JILLIAN name tag stands up and says, "Hi! My name is Jillian!"

I snort, and then I look around and realize that no one else thinks this is funny. My mother elbows me in the ribs, just for good measure.

"Can we all pull our chairs into a circle?" she asks, squeezing the shoulder of the man sitting next to her. "Can we do that?" I have a feeling that Jillian is fresh out of her social work master's program and that we're her first support group. I imagine that she's newly married and goes home every night with a paper bag full of fresh marjoram and turmeric and dill, and that she and her husband, a young patent attorney, cook elaborate dinners and then eat together at a candlelit table. *Gosh, Tim, they all looked so sad!*

Jillian tucks her blond hair behind her ears and smiles at us so sweetly that I have the urge to raise my hand and say, *I don't know what a circle is.* This is the kind of thing Chris never found funny.

"All right," she says, smoothing her hair again, a nervous tic, as we complete our first group task, and the clank and scrape of chairs subside. "First things first." She looks around with pride: her circle! "Why don't we all say our names and why we're here."

Helene relaxes in her seat, her hands folded on her lap, her left hand gently supporting her right one, a slightly awkward position imperceptible to anyone who doesn't know she's had a stroke. "What are you thinking?" I whisper. My seventy-two-year-old mother is still my emotional barometer. If I know what she's thinking, maybe I'll know what I'm thinking.

"Hush," she says.

The great big bald man two seats from Helene shoots his hand into the air. "I'm Harris!" he shouts, then turns tomato red and lowers his voice. "I'm here because my wife and I decided to end our marriage a few months ago. It was mutual, and we're still great friends." He laughs like he's blowing out a candle. "Nah, I'm just kidding." He looks around the room, assesses his audience, and licks his lips. "What I mean is," he says, even more quietly, "we're not great friends." He shakes his head a little bit. "I actually kind of hate her."

Last night, when I told Hannah that I would be going to the Relationships in Transition support group, she got up from the table, looked me in the eye, and yelled, *"Goddammit,"* which is still one of the worst things she can think of to say. Then she stormed out of the kitchen and didn't talk to me for the rest of the night, her half-finished spaghetti congealing in the bowl until I finally dumped it. I left her alone until bedtime. The house sucked up our sounds and felt huge. Finally, late, I went in to kiss her good night, and she reached up and pulled me toward her, her arms around my neck, her breath warm and a little vinegary. "Mommy," she whispered, half asleep, her eyes closed. "I don't want you to be sad."

"I'm not sad," I said, then immediately, like an idiot, started crying. I swiped my face and hoped Hannah couldn't tell. "You make me happy," I whispered. "Usually!"

She opened her eyes and looked at me, confused for a second, then laughed. The pinkish glow from her ballerina night-light illuminated her face. While the rest of her room has transitioned into a cave, remnants of its previous incarnation remain, like pottery shards from a lost city. "You make me happy *sometimes,"* she said.

"That seems about right."

Now Hannah is over at Chris's apartment, probably belly laughing with him at one of the disgusting reality shows they like to watch, shows about rodent infestations or revolting jobs people have involving sewage.

And here, in the warm basement of the East Side Community Center, Jillian fixes her gaze on the pretty young woman next to my mother who looks like she would rather be yanking out her own toenails than sitting on a metal folding chair, poised to reveal her deepest pain to a roomful of strangers.

The woman's long brown hair is held back from her face by an arrangement of bobby pins. She glances around and realizes that it's her turn, that there's no escape.

"Um?" she says, her palms open in front of her. I have a sudden vision of the kind of girl she was in fifth grade, an occupational hazard of mine. I imagine her hair in a tight braid down her back, clipped by those same bobby pins, her eyes wide and serious. The funny canvas shoes she wears that were popular last year. How hard she tries, the B minuses she gets on her spelling tests and math quizzes. *Good improvement! Super effort!* The small group of sweet, plain girls she hangs out with, steering clear of the clever, beautiful, mean ones. How in that way, she's smarter than she seems.

"I'm Lee Ann?" she continues. "My husband and I met in college, and we've been married for six years." She's wearing a gold band, and when she says the word "husband," she touches it with her thumb. "One night he came home and told me that we'd gotten married too young and that he wasn't in love with me anymore, and that he probably never had been?" Her voice rises and breaks on the last word, but she soldiers on. "Even though he was the one who proposed to me." She sniffles.

My mother is digging around in her purse while Lee Ann is talking, probably searching for a mint. "Mother," I hiss. "Helene!" Helene looks sideways at me and hands Lee Ann a tissue.

"So, last week he moved out," Lee Ann says. "And that's why I'm here."

"That sounds really painful, Lee Ann," Jillian says. "Thank you for sharing." She waits a few seconds, then turns to my mother. She reminds me of a doctor delivering bad news to a patient, dispensing a careful dose of sympathy, then moving on to the next case. "And you?" she says to Helene. "Can you tell us who you are and why you're here?"

"Oh!" Helene says, pretending to be surprised. She shrugs and smiles like the little old lady she is not. "I'm just here to support my daughter."

And then it's my turn, and a river of garbage rolls through my veins, and I just say, "Pass."

"Relationships in transition," as it happens, can mean a number of things. There's the forty-year-old married woman who fell in love with her female yoga teacher; there's the woman who lost sixty-five pounds whose husband no longer wants her. There's the man whose wife died after a long battle with cancer; there's the woman whose husband died after a short battle with cancer. There's Barb, the steely-eyed middle-aged woman whose husband left her to pursue polyamory. "And right before I understood what he was telling me, I blurted, 'Who is this bitch Polly?' It may be my biggest regret that I actually *asked him that!*" There's Neil, the man with the bushy beard who's thinking about leaving his wife and kids and moving to Alaska "for a while" with a twenty-four-year-old woman named Rainy he met in a rock-climbing class at the Y. You can almost feel the air getting sucked out of the room when he tells his story. Barb, in particular, glares at him hard. Last there's Cal, handsome and impeccably dressed and older, maybe in his late fifties, who tells us that he and his wife have been separated for a decade but only recently finalized their divorce. "And I find myself surprised," he says carefully, "by the pain this has unleashed."

At the end of the hour, after the litany of mundane miseries, Jillian shoots laser beams of sincerity out of her blue eyeballs and slays us all. The room, electric before with nervousness and untold stories, is quiet now, hushed and embarrassed as if we'd all just met at a bar and gone home with one another, then woken up the next morning in a fog of regret. Chairs rake backward as everyone gets up.

If Chris were here, he'd be leaking sympathy for the wretched of room B-117. He'd press his arm against mine, barely able to control his kindness. By the end of the night, he'd have exchanged e-mail addresses with Barb; Lee Ann would be nursing a hopeless, mournful crush on him; even bearded Neil would feel understood by Chris, would promise to do better. Then on the drive home, in the private warmth of our car, I would say something sharp and accidental. I would idly wonder if Neil's wife drove him away, or I'd giggle about the way Jillian's makeup stopped at her jawline—and Chris's concern for a roomful of strangers would freeze before my eyes into a block of solid ice.

And Josie? Josie would throw her arm around me and squeeze. *You do not belong here,* she would say, *among the chubby and the damned.*

Helene and I wend our way to the dessert table in the back of the room, her hand on my shoulder like she's the queen. My elegant mother has perfected the art of not looking like she needs help. The table is piled high with sublimated feelings—brownies and cupcakes; biscotti and doughnuts and éclairs; light, jam-filled pastries; fluffy, sugar-dusted shortbreads; *macarons* and macaroons; several varieties of carefully labeled gluten-free chocolate-chip cookies. Not coincidentally, after the broken dam of the last hour, I find that I am jonesing for sugar, almost shaking for it.

Cal, the recently divorced one, stands next to us, pondering the selections intensely. After a minute, he places two small squares of cream-cheese-frosted carrot cake on his plate and smiles at us. His hair is thick and threaded with gray, and there's an appraising, off-kilter sexiness about him, like he's done a thing or two in his life, but he'll just keep those stories to himself. "I believe if I choose carrot cake, I can justify having two pieces," he says, making sure to look first at my mother, then at me.

Helene, her hand still on my shoulder, adds a bit of pressure to her grip. "Definitely true," she says. "You're getting your vegetables."

We introduce ourselves again, and if a person can die of awkwardness, I think I will, my internal organs about to seize up and grind to a halt as sexy, older Cal flirts with my mother. He even goes so far as to brush a crumb off of her sleeve. My mother, and this stud! Well, now I know why she wanted to come here.

I grab three chocolate-chip cookies, a cupcake, and an éclair and pile them on my plate. Carrot cake, my ass. "Mom," I say, trying to pull her attention toward me like the needy nine-year-old I suddenly am. "Mom. *Mom. Mom.* Doesn't this look like the dessert table at my wedding?"

But it's Cal who turns to me and chuckles. "Catherine and I got married at the courthouse," he says. "There was a row of inmates in orange prison jumpsuits sitting on a bench in front of the judge's chambers. We used to say that they were her bridesmaids." He smiles at me, and the weird, small, hibernating rodent of my soul opens one eye and looks around before falling back asleep.

I shove a huge bite of éclair in my mouth and feel the overwhelming need to make a run for it. I'm about to guide my mother to the door when Jillian claps her hands three times, loudly. "Can everybody come on back to the circle for a minute? Just for one more short minute?"

Cal looks at me. "She loves that circle," he whispers. His smile is quick and generous, like he likes to appreciate things.

"Loves it," I say, smiling back and hoping there's no chocolate on my face.

The air in the room has shifted again, or maybe it's my own lungs. As we head back to our chairs, Helene leans into me and whispers, "Is he the kind of person who would hide us in an attic?" which is her litmus test for every non-Jewish boyfriend I've ever had, which is all of them.

My mother and I sit back down, and I hand her a chocolate-chip cookie, which, with her good hand, she accepts.

. . .

Helene was four when she left Germany. In a shoebox in her closet, there's a soft, faded black-and-white photograph of her on the boat, sandwiched between her parents, holding their hands, crying. The railing is behind them and the ocean beyond, gray and menacing in the photograph. I can only imagine how tightly my grandparents must have been gripping Helene's little fingers.

"Oh, Mom," I said when she first showed it to me. In the photo her dark blond hair is in pigtails, her eyes squinting into the sun, her mouth open in despair. "You look so sad. Like you knew what was going on. Like you knew what you had left behind." For a moment I thought I felt that sadness. It moved through me, expanded and lifted me. It was the most I had ever felt.

She took the picture from my hands and shook her head. "Nah. I remember that day. There was a man on the deck who had become friendly with Grandma and Grandpa. Grandpa had a"—she waved her hand, trying to pluck the word out of the air—"a whatchamacallit, a Leica. And this man offered to take our picture. I didn't want him to take my damn picture. I wasn't sad, I was mad."

I was thirteen when we had this conversation. My mind had recently been blown by the revelations of history. I had decided that my mother's flight from Germany made me extremely special and precious. I would lie awake at night sometimes and think, *It's amazing I'm even here! A miracle!* Like I was some kind of unusual, exotic bird. *Me!* I would think, and it was the beautiful bird's rare chirp. *Me, me, me!*

It didn't help that my grandparents fussed and hovered over me, their only grandchild, flapping about, even more so after my parents' divorce, tending to me after school well beyond the age I needed tending, feeding me and telling me to be careful and calling me *schätze,* their treasure.

For a long time, I believed I was destined for something spectacular. I didn't know what, but I thought it would probably involve heroically preventing a genocide or possibly producing some kind of work of art, something of such astounding beauty that, upon viewing, no human being would ever again be capable of cruelty. My ambitions were lofty but extremely vague, which made them even loftier.

How can I explain it now, from the vantage point of forty-three?

My mother and my grandparents sail on a boat from Germany, among the last allowed to leave. The rest of the family, a close-knit bunch of brothers and sisters and aunts and uncles and cousins, think that the little trio is being hasty. They recognize the danger, of course, but they figure that the trouble will resolve itself, as it always has. They stay behind, and then are gone.

Nobody tells me much. I figure it out slowly, and then suddenly it all pops into place. And that's when I see: it's there in my face, my lips the same shape as my grandmother's, my hair coarse and wiry as my grandfather's, sleepy eyelids like my mother's.

I'm living the life they dreamed of, the one they made possible, and so it turns out I'm just the kid I am, trying to memorize the periodic table, watching TV, eating lemon cake, lacing up ice skates, reading *A Separate Peace,* passing my Spanish test. As I get older, my life simultaneously shrinks and grows, shedding delusions as it picks up complications. One day becomes the next. Extraordinary circumstances have given me the gift of an ordinary life.

I had a boyfriend in college named Chad Hansen. He, like all Chads, was from a small town in Wisconsin—his, Waupakakee, was tiny and far north and best known for its native son, Reinhardt Pelican, who, in 1891, invented puffed rice and, subsequently, a sweet puffed rice cereal called Pelican Balls.

Chad wore a baseball cap nearly all the time. He wasn't a jerk, exactly, but he wasn't not a jerk. One morning, sitting crosslegged together on my thin futon on the floor of my bedroom, dust motes sparkling in the sunlight, I tried to explain it to him, this shimmering sense I had of being a child of history, of being destined for something important, and Chad laughed—a loud and genuine *hyuk!*—and he took off his cap and said, "And what, exactly, would that be?" Then he tapped me on the nose and kissed me and told me I was adorable and that he'd never met anyone like me before. We made out on my futon for a long time, and the next day I declared my major in primary education, which was something I'd been thinking about doing anyway.

When I recall that moment with Chad—and I do—I think that it's when I began to grow old and die. Which is, of course, ludicrous.

Everything adds up to where I am now: my mother and grandparents on a ship in the middle of the Atlantic; Chris, mine and then not mine; Hannah (tiny minnow, staying put where the others couldn't). And Josie, setting her sights on me at the faculty meeting, and then, thirteen years later, skidding across the highway on a rainy night. That, too.

Five

Six years ago, Josie and I chaperoned the fifth graders on their Earth Science Weekend. It was an annual event at our school and a coveted volunteer opportunity for teachers, because you could pack most of your required extracurricular hours into one weekend. You could get almost all of them over with at once instead of having to coach eighth-grade soccer every Saturday for a whole season or head up the After-School Mathletes or the Kool Knitting Klub (yes, although no one ever said it out loud: the KKK) for an hour and a half every Wednesday at the end of an already exhausting day. These activities were informally known as Lobster Duty, as many of us felt that they were the equivalent of being dropped into a pot of water and being slowly boiled to death.

There would be some hiking on this trip—Josie and I accepted this unpleasant fact—and much of the weekend would be spent outdoors regardless of the unpredictable April weather, but these were ten-year-olds. The hikes would be easy. Activities would be short and punctuated by breaks. We would not be sleeping in tents but in fully equipped cabins (tents were for the seventh graders and their Outdoor Fitness Weekend in September), and the chaperones would dole out a constant supply of snacks so as to ward off cannibalism if things got dicey. Also, lights-out was at eight thirty, after which our time belonged to us—although in fact, *in actual fact,* as Chris always said—we would be sharing a cabin with two of the Andes, Andrea Brauer, the science teacher, and Kelly Anderson-Jensen, our fellow chaperone.

Andi Friedman had not made the cut. She'd expressed her interest just a few minutes after Josie and I had sent our e-mails, and the selection process was based only on time stamps. When they found out they wouldn't be together on this trip, the Andes had howled at the injustice of it. I saw them in the hallway, hugging and keening. *Oh, no, Andi! Oh, noooooooooooo!* On the bus ride to the Lake Kass Wetlands Preserve, amid the hoots of jazzed-up fifth graders, I imagined Andi alone and angry in her dark apartment, drunkenly creating voodoo dolls of Josie and me out of twigs and cotton balls and old socks.

I was ten weeks pregnant then, and so far only Chris, Josie, and Mark knew. I hadn't even told my mother, although I'd wanted to. Helene would have combusted with joy at the thought of another grandchild, and I wanted to delight her, to add another X in the happiness column of her complicated life. But I had had two miscarriages before Hannah, and so I knew the flip side of that expectant joy for all of us. I carried it with me. I felt a little nauseated most of the time; it was just slight enough to be a comfort. I was beginning to entertain the hope that I might get to be the mother of two children. I imagined—I tried not to, but I couldn't help it—that this one was also a girl, but dark like me, round and playful and quick to laugh, where Hannah was sensitive and serious. I tried not to think about names.

"We can talk about names," Chris had said just a few nights earlier, lying next to me in bed, his hand on my arm. "We can talk about painting the spare room yellow and buying a new crib, or what kind of a big sister Hannah will be. . . . We can talk about anything we want." He moved his hand down to my wrist, circled it with his fingers. "We can be hopeful," he said, and I sucked in my breath with the certain feeling that whatever surprising, encouraging thing he would say next would lift me up. "Because being hopeful won't change anything."

"Oh," I said, deflated. "Right." I marveled at how he could be so expansive and nihilistic at the same time, how his darkly rational mind freed him. And I squeezed my eyes shut and thought the only thought I let myself have about this pregnancy, which was, *Please.*

The bus rolled into the gravel parking lot of the Lake Kass Wetlands Preserve Science Learning and Exploring Center, and our long-suffering driver tapped the horn. A park ranger leaped like a rabbit out of the visitors' center and jogged toward the bus, hoisting herself up the steps as soon as the door opened.

"Hi! My name is Margo! Welcome to NATURE!" she yelled, obviously knowing better than to feed a bunch of fifth graders the line *Welcome to Lake Kass.* The kids screamed and whooped with joy, and you couldn't help but let it seep into you, too. One of the Jakes (there were three of them) struck up a chant: "NaTURE! NaTURE! NaTURE!"

I leaned toward Josie. "Just across the highway is the Nurture Center."

She nodded. "The two camps will duke it out in a series of competitions throughout the weekend."

"Settle down, please," Kelly Anderson-Jensen yelled, waving her hand in the air, and I had the uncomfortable feeling she was talking to Josie and me. "Close your *mouths* and open your *ears.*"

"Yes, friends," Andrea Brauer piped in, the gentler of the two. "Let's show Miss Margo our best Rhodes Avenue manners!"

The Andes were good at this kind of energetic rallying, a skill set available to former high-school cheerleaders. They teased and cajoled and flirted, and then, the second they felt their control slipping, they would turn chilly and withholding. Their classrooms were a charged atmosphere of primal fear coupled with the children's heartbreaking, puppyish desire to please. They always did well on the classroom-management portions of their yearly reviews. Josie had a different kind of rapport with her students. She made them feel as if they would be letting themselves down if they didn't comport themselves with dignity. She was the tween whisperer. My strategy was to speak softly and hope for the best.

"Lake ASS!" Jake hollered, inevitably, and forty-two fifth graders went wild, as they'd been doing all week, because it never got less funny.

"Jake Byers!" Kelly called, her voice high and tinny above the roar. "Jake B, I'm WARNING YOU."

Margo rattled off a loud list of park rules of the *take only pictures, leave only footprints* variety, plus a few more strict mandates about safety: *Never* wander off the path. *Always* stick with your assigned buddy. Just as I was contemplating the syntactic logic of the phrase "assigned buddy," the kids began a massive lurch toward the exit.

"Isabel, come on," Andrea said to me, grabbing my elbow. We were in charge of leading the pack. Kelly would bring up the rear. And Josie would be the sheepdog, herding the stragglers, as well as carrying the small black bag of medical necessities a few of the kids couldn't be more than ten feet from at all times: one asthma inhaler, three EpiPens, and a tube of eczema cream.

I was slow to rouse from my little reverie, stuck in the pregnancy fog I'd been unable to shake for the past few weeks, and Andrea looked at me, her expression a mixture of *What's wrong?*

and *Shape up!* It occurred to me that soon I would be able to spill my secret, wouldn't be able to keep it, in fact, and the thought delighted and terrified me.

"Sorry," I said. Andrea snaked through the aisle and managed to get off the bus before any of the more-squirrelly kids could bust loose and head for the woods. I climbed down the steps and scanned the crowd, beginning the first of the endless head counts we would tick off that weekend. You had to look at these events as prison outings, as chain gangs without the comforting security of the leg irons. I walked more slowly through the mob, patting heads, touching backs, whispering, *Hey, hey, this will be fun, hey, huh.* I was taking a page from Principal Bob Coffey's handbook of child-and-canine obedience, trying to bestow a calm authority.

"Mrs. Moore!" Dylan Nuñez nudged up against me. He tugged on my shirt. They did that, all of them, all the time, yanked and pulled on me, no matter how often I reminded them, *Respect personal space, people!* "Mrs. Moore, look! I found a grasshopper!" He cradled the insect tenderly in his cupped palm and stared at it.

"Wow," I said, leaning down. "That's—" but before I could finish my sentence, he popped it into his mouth.

"Dylan! No! Ew! *Dylan!*" I spun him away from the other children and clamped my mouth shut to keep from screaming.

"Just kidding, Mrs. Moore!" He opened his mouth to reveal a green gummy bear and then began chewing it up with disgusting glee.

"I'm going to sneak up behind you at dinnertime, Dylan," I said, "and I'm going to slip a real grasshopper into your hot-dog bun." He laughed and bumped into me with his shoulder in what I had come to understand was a boy hug, then dodged back into the group.

This was what I loved about being a teacher, back then, when I loved it: that every child was some family's most precious gem, the joy of their hearts, and I could see that, even sometimes when their own parents probably couldn't; I could see that spark of perfection in every kid, in whatever form it took, a devious sense of humor or a disheveled sweetness, and I loved them all for it. They were grubby and loud and chaotic, and occasionally mean-spirited and dim-witted, sometimes feral and once in a while borderline psychotic. But they had beauty in them.

Josie smiled at me over the children's heads—which were, I had noticed on the bus, frankly dirty, along with the rest of them. It was as if their parents had collectively given up on them this week, in preparation for this field trip. They were on the brink of adolescence, these rangy fifth graders, and before the hormone artillery advanced, their bodies were sending out early warning shots. They were greasy haired, gamy little things. As much as I loved them, I also couldn't ignore their collective resemblance to chimps.

I thought about Hannah and felt a sharp pang of longing, almost physical, even though I'd only been away from her for a few hours. She would turn into this species of primate soon enough, but she was six then, still a sweet monkey, just a tall baby who liked to follow me around the house, kissing and petting me. Her body was a satellite to mine. Sometimes at night I would lie in bed and revel in the space between Chris and me, the way my skin touched only my own T-shirt and the sheets. It would be the blink of an eye before Hannah turned into the girl she is now, the one who disdains my affection and cringes from my touch. If I'd known then, I would have ... well, what would I have done? Recorded a caress? Taken notes on a hug? You can't preserve anything; every happy moment is already on its way to becoming nostalgia. That's the problem.

Margo quickly organized the children into a red and a green team for the treasure hunt. We decided to leave their bags on the bus, give them a chance to run around, and then come back later and get them settled in the cabins.

Audrey Franklin and Zoe Meckleheim-Wald rushed over to me as Kelly and Andrea handed out color-coded name tags. Audrey was guiding Zoe, her hands on her friend's bony shoulders, and Zoe, I noticed with alarm, was sobbing.

Mrs. Moore, I! She forgot! Mrs. Moore! Glasses my glasses! Zoe at home forgot! They spoke over each other in a rush to impart this exciting news. Zoe sobbed and wiped her eyes. Audrey smiled at me, expectantly. Audrey was a lightning rod, a heat-seeking drama missile. She was one of those girls who tried to help everybody, especially when they didn't need it.

"What will I do?"

Zoe. It was one of the names on the list I wasn't letting myself make. Also Iris. Phoebe. Louisa. It was so hard to keep this baby an abstraction when every thump of my heart brought her closer.

I bent down close to Zoe, my hands on my knees. "How many fingers am I holding up?" I wasn't holding up any. She tilted her head at me, tears still wet on her flushed cheeks. "How many?" I repeated.

"None!" she said, and started to laugh.

"How well can you see without your glasses?" I asked.

"Mrs. Moore," Audrey said. "She *needs* them!"

"I mostly wear them for watching TV at home." Zoe shrugged.

"I think you'll be okay," I said. "There's no TV here. And it's only two days. Be careful, and don't mistake any of the coyotes for your friends."

"Coyotes?" Audrey clapped her hand over her mouth.

"Audrey, there are no coyotes. Can you be an extra-good friend to Zoe this weekend? Help her if she needs it?"

She nodded and took Zoe's hand, guided her friend away as if she were legally blind. "There's a rock on the path," she said. "And another one! Be careful!"

Josie was standing next to me now, had witnessed my expert land-mine defusing. "Mrs. Moore, I forgot my Xanax," she whispered. "I *neeeed* it."

"Mrs. Abrams, I forgot my vodka."

Josie sighed. "Honestly, I'm exhausted already." She fiddled with her ponytail and looked around. "You know what it's going to be like. The psychological warfare of the girls. The grievous bodily injuries the boys will inflict on one another."

The sun was high in the sky. The spring had been unseasonably warm. Josie and I had assured each other that we were excited about this trip, that we would embrace the intensity of it and enjoy the opportunity to spend time together. And we *had* been excited about it. But that was the thing about teaching—it could be a tightrope. The slightest fumble and you were falling, falling.

"Jose, come on," I said, as we headed toward the lake, which had a wide wooden dock that crossed over and around it, so that you could observe the wildlife almost as if you were walking on the water. "We have to find a marsh wren and a water lily and see if we can spot the beaver dam."

"Sorry, sorry, sorry," she said, falling into step next to me. The kids were darting alongside and in front of us, shrieking and laughing.

When we got to the shore, Margo motioned for us all to gather around. She shushed everyone with a finger to her lips, like magic. "Listen," she whispered. "Look." She pointed, and forty-two ten-year-olds lifted their faces to the sky as a great blue heron glided overhead. We all watched it swoop and soar. Suddenly the sky was a cathedral, the children silent worshippers. The heron landed in a tree, and then four more of them appeared, elegant necks, crooked legs, a prehistoric convention. My breath caught.

"OMG!" Claire Whitley said loudly, and she did a wiggly little dance in place, throwing her shoulders and hips about. Claire was tiny and redheaded and wiry, pale as a cloud, and she liked to rile things up. Her social studies presentations were stand-up comedy routines. She could turn quiet reading time into a hoedown. She was a walking disruption. It was physically impossible not to like her.

The kids around her started laughing. "Shhh," Kelly whispered, laying her hands on Claire's shimmying shoulders. "Hush." And like a miracle, just for a moment, everyone did.

For the next half hour, we wandered around the shore and across the dock, searching for the wildlife on our list. A turtle. A lily pad. A pussy willow. A school of fish.

"It's a fun game," Margo told us, "and being quiet is the only way to win." I was liking Margo more and more.

For many of our students, this weekend was their first experience of nature beyond the brightly colored playground at school, with its giant slide and its one perennially broken swing and its wood-chip-covered ground that was meant to cushion their falls but probably hurt worse than concrete. They were soaking up the day's brilliant sunshine, unfettered and free as the swooping heron. It made them bonkers.

Which is why, when Brady Kieslowski shoved his best friend, Kyle Gilson, into the lake, no one was surprised: not me, not Josie, not Kelly or Andrea or Margo, not even Brady. Not even

Kyle. We heard the scream and the splash, and we went running, our feet making hollow clopping sounds on the dock. *"Stay here!"* we shouted at the other kids. "Stay right here!"

And of course not one of them did. They came tearing after us, a commotion of arms and legs and scrambling feet and fear and delight, and it was only sheer luck that no one else fell in the water.

"Help!" Kyle yelled. "Somebody help me!" He thrashed and sputtered in the four-foot-deep water, coughing and crying, looking tiny and terrified, and even though we all knew the water was shallow, we felt his terror.

Fleet-footed Margo got to him first. Josie was just a second behind her. They squatted at the edge of the dock, and Josie calmly extended her arm to Kyle. In truth he was only a few inches away from the dock in water he could stand in.

"It's okay, buddy," Margo said.

"Take my hand," Josie murmured. A breeze ruffled the wisps of curly brown hair that had escaped her ponytail. She re-arranged herself so that she was balanced on one knee now, braced to pull Kyle up. Her T-shirt blew flat against her stomach.

Brady, who was responsible for the whole scene, hunched next to Josie, his face in his hands, sobbing. I put my arm around him. Some of the kids were screaming and jumping and calling out for Kyle. A few ran back to the shore. Others stood silently, awed or terrified, taking it in. Someone yelled, "Stay calm, dude!" and another cried out, "Oh, my God, he's going to die!" Above the din I could make out laughter. Some kids, predictably, prob-ably from nervousness but maybe it was meanness, just laughed and laughed.

For better or worse we were all our elemental selves for those few moments. I have understood this since the first playground fight I had to break up: how a crisis can reveal the inner workings of our nervous systems before we even know our own hearts.

In just a few seconds, Kyle was out of the water, shaking himself off, refusing comfort, glaring at Brady. His shaggy, dark hair was plastered to his forehead and his cheeks. He gleamed in the sunlight like a seal pup.

"We've got some towels in the visitors' center, hon," Margo said.

"I'm sorry, man," Brady sobbed. "I'm sorry!" But Kyle turned his back to him and let himself be surrounded by the mob of kids eager to celebrate his newfound status as the kid who ALMOST DROWNED AT LAKE KASS.

"I'm really, really sorry!" Brady called after him, high and bereft.

I corralled the children, who were still howling with excitement, back to the shore, and I thought, *This is the end of that friendship.*

But it wasn't. It would take Kyle and Brady all of forty-five minutes to reconcile. They would be pelting pretzels at each other by the end of the day. They would come back together with the purity of ten-year-old boys, until, four years later, Kyle's parents would split up and his mother would move Kyle and his sister to Kenosha, where she would find a job as the manager of an apartment complex.

Josie came up behind me, shepherding her own group. "Jose," I said, "you're an American hero."

She chuckled and held out her hand to me. "I'm still trembling."

"I swear to God," I said, shaking my head.

She leaned into me for a second as we walked. There was a feeling between Josie and me, the goodness and pleasure of our friendship an electric thing humming and buzzing. We had this new story to tell Chris and Mark, and we shared the full and mutual delight of having survived it. I was already picking out phrases to quote to her later. *Oh, my God, he's going to die!*

When more screaming erupted from the horde of kids on the shore, I figured it was residual drama, an aftershock. We weren't even concerned. We wandered back down to the dock. We lollygagged. And the screaming grew louder.

"Ugh, what now?" Josie said.

"I'm gettin' out of this here racket," I said, hooking my thumbs through the belt loops of my jeans. "Thinkin' about gettin' into real estate." We hurried the stragglers along, started jogging toward the confusion. Kelly and Andrea were there already.

"Claire Whitley has been stung by a bee," Kelly announced, her words sharp and fast. "We need the med bag now, Mrs. Abrams. Can you please give me Claire's. Epi. Pen. Right. Now."

The children huddled in little groups, staring and whispering. Claire Whitley was still and scared at the center of it all, tears pouring down her face, which was, impossibly, paler than usual, a blank moon edged in pink. She was holding her wrist. She coughed a few times. Her lips were already starting to look swollen and strange. "I am very allergic," she whispered, which of course we already knew.

And Josie was gone, sprinting toward the bus.

The medical bag was her responsibility, and she had left it on the bus. Later I would think, *It could have happened to anybody. Anybody could have made that mistake,* which both was, and was not, true. It didn't matter. It was Josie's mistake.

I sat on the ground and eased Claire into my lap, and I rocked her while we waited, the longest minutes, endless breaths. Andrea rounded up all the other kids and hurried them over to a spot on the shore about a hundred yards away. Kelly stood nearby, her terrified eyes a mirror to mine. "It's okay, sweetie," I whispered into Claire's fine, red hair, which smelled earthy and sharp and not pleasant, like cheese. I had the feeling that I was whispering to Hannah, the odd sense that I was in my daughter's bedroom in the middle of the night. "It'll be okay."

Claire wheezed. I felt her heart thudding through her narrow back. I thought that she would die in my arms while her mother was oblivious back in Milwaukee, probably enjoying a margarita or watching a movie or sending an e-mail or grilling a steak as her daughter gasped for air.

Lake Kass was placid and clear. There was the sound of birds. My heart pounded with Claire's.

Josie was back four minutes later. The parking lot was two minutes away, down the path and up the hill. We heard her banging on the bus door; we saw her flying back to us, black med bag at her side.

Kelly grabbed the satchel and whipped out the EpiPen, snapped out the syringe, and jammed it into Claire's thigh.

Anaphylactic shock can set in in moments. The slightest delay can affect the patient's outcome. We were subjected to a mandatory student-health tutorial every fall. So we knew.

I held her. She was no bigger than Hannah. *Please.* She slumped over on me, her eyes closed. Kelly crouched next to us; Josie stood, her arms at her sides, fists clenched, breathing hard. Her face was gray and sweaty. I couldn't meet her eyes.

"Claire? Claire, honey?" Kelly touched Claire's cheek, her forehead.

The other children were a brightly colored, frightened flock in the distance: a hassle of children, an irritation of fifth graders, a vexation of tweens. I closed my own eyes for a second to make them disappear.

From far off, an ambulance siren rose and fell, rose and fell: incongruous here, coming closer.

. . .

She drops her littlest sister off at Rhodes Avenue every morning before heading over to the high school two blocks away. Usually she's in a mad rush to say goodbye to Nora and make her 7:55 bell. But every once in a while she pops her head into my classroom and waves to me, her smile bright and familiar. She's not the live wire she was six years ago. Adolescence has rounded her edges and calmed her manic energy. She's almost, but not quite, graceful now—she's still elbowy and kinetic, but I can see that in her, how she'll inhabit her adult body in a few years, balancing a backpack full of books or a bag of groceries, holding someone's hand, a husband's, a child's.

"Mrs. Moore," she says, when she has time to pause. "Have a good day!" And to any of my other former students I would just wave back and say, "You, too!" but with Claire, when I can, when I'm not surrounded by children or trapped in the middle of some minor crisis, I'll hurry over to her and give her a quick hug, just to feel her sharp little shoulders beneath my arms, her breath and her bones, the working machinery of her fragile body.

. . .

Maybe Earth Science Weekend should have concluded then and there, after little, limp Claire was carted off on a stretcher to Kass Memorial Hospital, after Kelly snarled at Josie, "You should have had that bag with you!" and stalked off, and Josie bowed her head, horrified, remorseful, defeated. But we decided to soldier on. After all, there were still mallards to identify, inchworms to count.

But the molecular structure of the field trip had disintegrated beyond repair. Josie was remote, barely functioning. Kelly and Andrea were icy and efficient. The kids were uncharacteristically snarly and combative with one another. We separated so many children so many times that day that enemies had to be seated together by dinner; girls who had made each other cry at lunchtime were paired up in cabins by nightfall. We trudged through the swamp, all of us, weighed down by the psychic burden of one ten-year-old's near-death experience.

Some darkness descended on Josie that weekend, and it never quite lifted.

And I barely noticed that my pregnancy nausea and lethargy had disappeared, until two days after we got home, when I started to bleed.

Six

"Promise me you'll never let Hannah go skydiving," my mother says. "I just read the most awful story in the newspaper." She breathes out, a familiar little *achh* that signifies her disapproval of a world in which anyone thinks skydiving is ever a good idea. "I want you and Hannah Banana to come over for dinner tomorrow night," she says.

"Okay," I say. "Right after her parachuting lesson."

"And you need to wear decent clothes," she says.

"What? Why?" I look down at my sweatshirt, which is decorated with a little archipelago of coffee splotches from this morning.

"Because I'm tired of seeing you in sweatpants. And I'm cooking something nice."

The last time my mother made us dinner, a few weeks ago, it was boiled carrots, boiled potatoes, and a chicken so overbaked that by the time it came out of the oven it had turned into a vaguely chickenish kind of cardboard. "Hey, I have a super idea, though! Let's order from DiPalma's."

"No, no, no," she says. "I want to cook for you."

"I won't even tell Hannah. You can come out of the kitchen wiping sweat off your brow, like you slaved over a hot stove. It will be our little secret."

Helene laughs, and her voice turns girlish and high. "Oh, *you*."

"Oh, *me*," I say, laughing, too. "But seriously."

"You're coming. I'm cooking," my mother announces, no longer joking, and when Helene stops joking, you stop arguing.

. . .

When I was in eighth grade, like eighth graders everywhere, I was given the assignment to explore my family history by interviewing a close relative. I figured this was my chance to get the answers to the questions my mother had been evading for months. I hounded her daily, right up to the night before the assignment was due. Every time I asked, she said things like, "Why don't you call your dad's second cousin Sascha in Lansing? He was a Communist!" Or "I'm so tired. I've been talking at work all day. I can't say another word. Let's do this tomorrow." And finally, "For God's sake, just make something up."

"Fine!" I said, and picked up my pen. "Helene Strauss Applebaum was born on Jupiter." I scratched my head and pretended to write, drew circles and loops on the page. "Her parents abandoned her, and she grew up in a large family of green aliens, the only one of her kind. When she was thirteen, she embarked on a"—I sketched an alien with long antennae—"a *lifelong search* for her human parents." I looked up at my mother, who was standing in the doorway, and scowled. "I think Mrs. Murphy will love this." I snapped my notebook shut and said, "Hmph."

Helene had been about to leave the kitchen, but she turned and came back, sat down with me at the table, and sighed. "All right, Isabel. But you're going to be disappointed. I'm telling you, I don't . . . Grandma and Grandpa never really talked about Germany. And what do I remember?" She shrugged, answering the question. "A child's memories. Not much of a story. Only bits and pieces. Fragments." She shook her head. "A . . . a room with a red painted toy box. The smell of bread baking. A yellow apron. A cloth doll one of my cousins gave me. I named it Gustav. I thought that was the most beautiful name in the world. But Trude told me it was a boy's name and insisted I change it, and I cried."

"Cousins?" I asked, my heart pounding.

"Mmm-hmm. I had three girl cousins. We played together all the time. They lived in an apartment above their parents' grocery store, and we played hide-and-seek there. There were so many places to hide, so many little closets and pantries. For years I thought, well, maybe they hid." She brushed a little pile of crumbs from dinner into her palm, then got up and dumped them into the sink. Her back was to me now. "I remember when we left, everyone gave me presents and sweets, and I didn't want my cousins to come, because I felt so special. I don't remember anything else." She turned on the water for no reason, turned it off, sat back down. She looked tired, and I thought, with a flicker of resentment, that I was seeing what she would look like when she was old. "Oh, I know who you should interview!" she said. "Dr. Fraser. He's from Utah!" She said "Utah" in a strange, drawn-out way, *Youuu-taw,* as if it were an exotic place you could never go, as if magical elves lived there.

"You know this is a *family*-history assignment, right?"

"Well, I know, but Dr. F has a really neat story! *Mormons,*" she whispered. She smiled brightly at me, turned it off like that. So we were done. I knew I had to give up. After she went to bed, I sneaked off and called my dad, who told me detailed stories about growing up in Detroit after the war. I got an A.

. . .

Hannah and I walk the three blocks to my mother's duplex. Daylight saving time has just kicked in, and the air feels strange and brittle, too bright for 6:00 p.m. When Hannah was younger, she was always so confused by the time change. For weeks she would ask me, "Is it four but it feels like five, or four but it feels like three?" It would take her body weeks to catch up to it, too; there were nights when she couldn't fall asleep for hours, mornings when she would wake up before the birds. "Mommy," she would whisper beside my bed, the night sky outside our window still inky black. "I would like a waffle." She is sensitive to change, cast adrift by it. I should have remembered that.

I look up at the bare trees, the branches clawing at the bright sky. Chris works for the state, monitoring tree diseases. He and his buddies in the Department of Natural Resources can wax poetic on the history of the devastating Dutch-elm epidemic of the early 1970s or the dogged persistence of the emerald ash borer. Chris can hardly walk past a tree without fondling its leaves, tenderly stroking its bark. I used to make fun of him for it, his physical, almost-sexual communion with the trees. *Oh, baby, let me feel your trunk.* Now it's just one more thing I miss. *Baby, don't leave.*

"It's six, but it feels like five twenty-seven," I say now, my old answer to Hannah's question, our joke. She turns and looks at me, her face impassive, a mask. But then she loosens, almost imperceptibly—except I'm her mother, so to me it's a tectonic shift.

"It's six, but it feels more like five fifty-eight," she says.

Most people celebrate the lengthening light. But I prefer the shorter days, the way winter darkness wraps itself around me like a blanket.

"It's six, but it feels like spaghetti," I say, and then Hannah sighs, annoyed, because she's not five years old, and because these days I never, ever get it right.

. . .

"Darlings." Helene kisses me, then wraps Hannah in a long, worried hug. "Where are your coats?"

"It's practically spring, Grandma," Hannah says, her sweetness blinking back on for Helene, and I try not to be jealous. "It's like a hundred degrees out! No coats." Hannah slides past my mother and through the entryway into the kitchen, and we follow. She plunks herself down on the window seat and pulls out her phone, hunching over it like a mama bear guarding her cub.

My mother moved into this duplex four years ago, when she had recovered enough from her stroke and realized that she wanted less space for herself and fewer miles between us. So now she lives shouting distance from Hannah and me on the ground floor of an old brick house, the kind of place real-estate agents describe as charming, which of course means creaky floorboards, ancient pipes, an unpredictable furnace, and drafty windows. Helene transported all of her furnishings from her old house to this one, and her modernist aesthetic is boldly out of place in this century-old shrine to crown molding and stained glass. It looks like a time traveler came back from the future to decorate. Here in these tiny rooms are the thick glass end tables and boxy vinyl couches that once fit perfectly in the open-planned expanse of her midcentury modern house in the suburbs: the same geometrically patterned pillows, the same uncomfortable chrome chairs that look like they belong on a spaceship. Every time I step inside, my childhood greets me with a befuddled wave.

"Hi, Mom." I hand over a bottle of wine and simultaneously remember that she'd asked me to bring a salad. "Oh, crap. I'm sorry. I forgot the—"

"It's all right, darling," she says. "I made one, just in case."

I manage to feel infuriated by this. "Sorry," I say again.

I hear a sound from the living room and then music, and I look at my mother, who has her back to me now, stirring something on the stove that undoubtedly does not need stirring.

"Helene," I say, and she turns to me over her shoulder with her *I'm just a slightly confused little old lady* smile.

Hannah is still huddled over her phone, muttering softly to it. *"McKinley!"* she whispers. *"That is so not true!"* My mother turns back to the stove and hums something tuneless. Hannah chuckles and *tap-tap-tap*s away on her phone.

"Come," my mother says. She drops the wooden spoon into the sink and leads me through the kitchen and into the living room.

And there, perched on the sofa, is handsome Cal, the divorcé from the support group. "Isabel." He smiles, stands.

Lately circumstances just seem to sneak up on me, situations I thought I understood but realize, too late, that I don't.

Cal is wearing a purple button-down shirt and jeans. I'm wearing the shirt I slept in last night. Josie got it for me from the Lake Michigan Bird Sanctuary; it says WISCONSIN IS FOR PLOVERS on the back. I silently resolve not to turn around. The CD Cal has put on is something Hawaiian and trendy; Chris gave it to my mother for her birthday last year. *Perfect,* I think.

I'm ready to kill my mother, who is resting against the doorframe. I've noticed this about her recently, how wherever she goes, she finds a place to pause. Observing this vulnerability makes it slightly more difficult for me to sustain my murderous impulse, but not impossible.

False pretenses. She has brought us here under false pretenses, and I'm not even sure what they are. "Oh, Mom," I say, through clenched jaw. "How fun."

She smooths the fabric of her beige linen pants: slacks, she used to call them when I was younger, and maybe she still does. She gives her thick, caramel-colored hair a pat and lays a warm hand on my cheek. "It's a little get-together," she says.

"Yes, it is." The background music to our exchange is the festive, high pluck of a ukulele.

"I told you to wear nice clothes."

"I thought you were kidding."

Cal looks at my mother, then at me, with an amused sort of scrutiny, like he's got us all figured out. *Smug,* Josie would say. *One of those men who thinks he can teach you all about yourself!* I'm ready to make up an excuse and flee (by backing out of the room) when he walks toward me and takes my hand.

"I'm really looking forward to this evening," he says, with no obvious sarcasm, which seems suddenly like more than we deserve. His palm is warm and dry. *Give me your paw,* I used to say to Hannah when she was little and we were crossing a street. The phrase comes to me now, unbidden. There is something generous about all of this, suddenly, a feeling underneath logic, a shift. He holds on to my hand for another comforting second, then lets go.

. . .

I never really knew my father. I mean, I knew him; I know him. His name is Jack. Hannah and I have dinner with him every couple of months. He lives in a condo in Herman, a sprawling exurb forty minutes west of here, with his wife, a retired dental hygienist named Sheila, pronounced "Shyla."

After the divorce, I spent every other weekend at his apartment, and on Tuesday nights we would go to Riddle's for pizza together, until my sophomore year of high school, when I managed to convince both him and my mother that I had way too much homework to continue that tradition. As far back as I can remember, he was distant, sour as a pickle, and delicately nursing a festering grudge against my mother.

Early on, just after they separated, he would try to plumb me for details. *How's she doing? Does she go out much? Does she go out with anyone in particular? Does she seem happy?*

I would take a giant bite of my mushroom-and-olive thin crust and roll my eyes. "I dunno, Dad," I would mutter through my mouthful. "She doesn't *seem* anything. She doesn't tell me anything. Ugh."

And my father's face would grow pinched and tight, his forehead furrowed and his mouth set in a peevish frown. "Well," he said to me once, "I could never get past that wall of defensiveness and anger, and it looks like you're turning out just like her."

I suppose it's possible my mother mourned the divorce in private, when I wasn't around, but I'm pretty sure she just breathed a huge sigh of relief and never looked back. There were empty spaces in our house after my dad moved out, but she filled them with work and friends and me—at least, I think so; I think I filled that space. She was the office manager at the Fraser Feldman Medical Group, a dermatology clinic downtown. She got home at six thirty, and she heated up Lean Cuisines for us or threw together meals involving far too much canned tuna and/or frozen corn. (I was in college before I realized that not all vegetables came from a bag with a huge green man on the label.) She played cards with her single lady friends every Saturday night: her gay divorcées, she called them cheerfully, without subtext. And every night she kissed me and told me I was the best thing that ever happened to her. She didn't cry when my father moved out. She cried when I went off to college. She cried at my wedding. She cried the first time (the first five times, actually) she held Hannah.

So, Cal: Cal squeezing my hand sweetly and smiling at my mother like he wants to know more about her? Ladies and gentlemen of the jury, I will allow it.

"Excuse me for a moment," my mother says, and heads back through the hallway.

Hannah, still in the kitchen, lets out a high-pitched, blood-curdling scream. Just after my heart stops but before I can race in to stanch the blood flow, she comes rushing out to me.

"Mom mom mom mom! Can I run over to Chloe's please please please just for five minutes she got a new puppy A PUPPY oh my God can I PLEASE?" Hannah's hair is loose and long and uncombed, her eyes bright and pleading. She tilts her head at me. "Woof?"

"No!" I say, because of course she can't leave her grandmother's house where dinner has been made and company invited and the table set for four. And then, "Yes." Because Chloe lives just two blocks away, and Hannah is not asking if she can get a tattoo or toss back her first shot of whiskey, and am I really the kind of mother who says no to puppies? And also, if I'm being honest, because every no these days has the potential to become a dull and endless battle, the cause of another snarl of disdain, another reason for Hannah to turn away, and sometimes I just don't want that; sometimes, right now, I just can't. "Yes. Okay. Go on. Tell Grandma, and be back in a half hour." I lay my hand on her head for a second. "Got it?"

"Got it," she says, three-quarters pleased, one-quarter mocking, which is a good ratio these days. "I *got* it!" She tucks her blond hair behind her ears and smiles at me with the face of her father and she's gone.

"I'm Cal," Cal says to the space where Hannah was, holding

out his hand as if to shake hers. "It's a pleasure to meet you," but just like before, it's gentle.

"Hannah, say hello to the nice man." I shrug at Cal. "I'm sorry."

"My son is thirty-five," he says.

"Kids, huh?" And why do I feel as if Cal has just seen me naked?

"Well, now," he says. "Shall we arrange our chairs in a circle?"

It takes me a second. Then I clap my hands twice. "Tonight we're going to try something different," I say, my hands on my hips. "Tonight we're going to arrange our chairs into a trapezoid!"

Cal giggles—the real, live giggle of a human male, so rarely heard. It catches me completely off guard. "And then," he says, "we'll load up on cookies and grouse about how much we despise our former spouses!"

"Spouse grousing!"

"Mate hating?"

"How miserable we are!" I exclaim, caught up in it. And then we stop short, because I've cut a little too close to the bone, and we both know it.

"How Miserable We Are," Cal says, more quietly now, "is the title of a musical I've been working on."

A ping sounds deep down within me, a submarine's sonar echoing somewhere unexplored. Is this a man who could make my mother happy? Is there such a creature? "I would see that," I say.

Helene brings out a plate and sets it on the low glass table in front of the couch. "Crudités," she announces. "I like to say that word. *Croo-dee-tay.* But it's really just raw vegetables!" She's nervous, I realize, and I understand that it's my filial duty to make this work: that this is the reason I'm here. Unfortunately I haven't showered in two days, and I haven't had a social exchange with anyone over the age of twelve in weeks.

"We were going to name Hannah *'Crudités,'*" I say. "Helene talked us out of it."

"Ah, Hannah's better," Cal says. "There would have been so many other Crudités in her class." He takes a polite bite of a baby carrot. What is it about him and carrots? "My son's name is Peter."

Helene sits down next to Cal on the couch and turns to him. Is she batting her eyelashes?

"Hmm," I say, liking this man more and more. "Really? *Peter Abbott?*"

He flashes me a smile, quick and conspiratorial. "No. It's Michael."

My phone plays a few notes from *The Twilight Zone,* a text from Hannah: *Can I stay at Chloe's 4 dinner I know u will say no but the puppy is soooo cute! I luv u pleez can I? pleeez?*

I pass the phone to my mother. "Oh, let her," she says.

OK, I type. *u can but u will need 2 make it up 2 Grandma. & b back by 8. don't b L8 or u will meet a dire f8.* If Hannah and I could just text, our relationship might be perfect. Although I can also entertain the possibility that she gets my messages and just rolls her eyes.

During dinner, which is a surprisingly tasty pasta primavera (*did* she order in?), the talk turns to Relationships in Transition, as it was bound to do.

"It's been very civil," Cal says. "My lawyer tells me that in the cleanest cases, both parties approach the divorce as if it's a business transaction." He wipes his mouth and then takes a sip of water. "And we have. Truly, we've treated each other with utmost respect, much as we did throughout our marriage.

Catherine—my ex-wife—is doing very well, I think. She would be shocked to hear that I'm . . . struggling." At that word, the crack that exposes the depth, he grows quiet, reddens a little, smiles.

"A business transaction is easier when there's not an eleven-year-old girl in the mix," I say, more vehemently than I had intended.

Cal nods. "I would imagine."

"Hannah's with me half the week, with Chris the other half. But the days rotate, so sometimes he gets the weekends and sometimes I do." There's a pair of tongs in the salad bowl I don't recognize, clear plastic with blue-tipped handles. When did my mother get new salad tongs? "Sometimes I wake up in the middle of the night and I have to go into her room, because I don't know where she is."

"Divorce was harder back in the day," Helene says. "But it was easier in some ways, too. The mother kept the kids, and the father sent the checks. I think maybe it was better for the children. Well, it was better for you. None of this confusion. Joint custody was unheard of."

"Unless you were talking about who got the marijuana," I say.

My mother gives me a look, and Cal laughs.

"Mom, this is yummy," I say, and she points to a spot on my T-shirt in response. "No," I say, smiling. "That was there before."

My mother—perfectly put together as usual, well coiffed, her makeup, as always, applied carefully—gives me a look and changes the subject. "Isabel is a very talented photographer," she says.

"Indeed, I am! I like to take photographs of babies nestling in oversized teacups." I spear a pea with my fork and hold it up. "Or sometimes I dress them in little green pea costumes and arrange them as if they're peering out of gigantic pods."

"Sounds whimsical," Cal says.

"Oh, and then I also have a series I'm working on of cats wearing bonnets." I don't know why I act like this around my mother.

"Isabel, stop it." Helene sets her own fork down and straightens her necklace, a string of gigantic, shiny yellow beads. "I'm just sharing with Cal that you are . . . interesting."

I haven't taken a photograph of anything except Hannah since college. But it's true that I loved photography, way back when, loved the way shadow separated light, the intersection and overlap of angle and curve, inanimate and alive. And color! How a burst of azure would stand out unexpectedly in a background of emerald green. But whatever. The things we love when we're twenty, we replace them with things that weigh more, that require care and feeding: the things we are obliged to love.

"The talents your parents nurture in you," I say, looking at Helene. "I think that if you're lucky, they become hobbies, and if you're unlucky, then you pursue them seriously as an adult." Helene is staring at me as if I've just grown scales. "I mean, how many gymnasts do you know? Who's a ballerina? Who ends up doing that?"

Nobody says anything for a minute (and, really, what did I expect?). There are the sounds of chewing, swallowing. Josie managed to follow her passion without deluding herself, more or less. Then again, she and Mark didn't have kids.

Before she died, she was working on a project in which she reimagined famous works of art from a strange, possibly brilliant, but definitely confusing feminist perspective. There was a Rodin Barbie and a three-foot-tall Hello Kitty Mount Rushmore. Her theory was that when you see a work of art flipped on its side, you ask questions of it that wouldn't have occurred to you otherwise. ("Like *What the fuck?*" Chris said later, gazing at those four pink-bowed, unknowable, yet still-vaguely-presidential kitties.) All but one of her artworks is gone from our house now, packed away in the basement. I keep the smallest one next to my bed, though. It's a little painting of the Mona Lisa as a bearded man in an Italian soccer jersey, looking for all the world as if he'd just scored a goal, or possibly missed one.

I get up and go into the kitchen to refill the pitcher, running the tap until the water is icy cold. I hold my wrists under the stream for a minute, let it chill my pulse.

What if you make the right choices? What if you shelve those immature and solipsistic pursuits in favor of the grown-up occupations of family and career—happily, you do it without regret, in love, looking forward—and then those fall apart? You turn around and you're staring at the moonscape that used to be your life.

"Are you an avid bird-watcher, Isabel?" Cal asks as I walk back into the living room. I pour water into his glass, then my mother's.

"Excuse me?"

"Your shirt," he says. The lines around his eyes deepen with his smile.

"Oh!" I can't tell where my comfort with Cal comes from, but I'm no longer embarrassed to be wearing old jeans and this ridiculous shirt. "Well, we had a robin's nest in one of the bushes in front of our house last year," I say, sitting back down. "When those birds first hatched, I would go outside and watch them all the time."

"So, then." He nods. "You are."

"*Uggch,*" Helene says, that familiar sound. "Birds are horrible creatures. Filthy. Those beady, reptile eyes." She shoos an imaginary sparrow away from her face with her good hand.

"Oh, I don't know," Cal says. "I've gone birding a time or two, years ago. It can be very serene."

"When the robins were just a day or two old, I would go out and chirp at them." I make a little tweeting sound. "And they'd look up at me with their blind, bulbous faces, and they'd open their beaks like they thought I was their mama. But after another day or two, they figured it out, and then they ignored me."

"Like life," my mother says, "except the baby birds grow up and ignore their real mothers." Helene reaches over and gives me a little squeeze.

"Sorry, Mom, did you say something?"

. . .

After dinner, my mother and I are alone in the kitchen while Cal is gathering plates in the dining room.

"He's nice," I whisper to her. "I like him!"

"I'm glad, honey. I do, too." She rests her hip against the edge of the sink and adjusts her enormous necklace. "He could be a . . . diversion. A little confidence booster."

"Oh! Okay. I guess so." The idea of my mother having a casual fling is, of course, disgusting to me, but I try to roll with it. "I guess I thought he might be more than that?"

"Well, that's not up to me."

"Oh, Mom, of course it is!" Maybe all these years of being single have made her feel powerless. Or maybe she's stuck in the prefeminist world of dating, where the men make all the rules.

"Huh." She smiles. "That's sweet, but . . ."

We're standing inches from each other. Up close, her skin is pink and powdery. The wrinkles around her eyes and mouth make her face look delicate and lacy, like a pastry. She smells good, too—melony. I'm suddenly filled with tenderness toward Helene. "He'd be lucky to have you, Mom."

Dishes and silverware clink together in the dining room. Helene looks at me like I've lost my mind. "Izzy," she says, "honey," then bites her lip.

Cal breezes into the kitchen with an armful of plates, sets them carefully on the counter. "Ladies," he says, then goes back out for more.

My mother leans toward me and whispers urgently in my ear. "This whole evening makes a lot more sense now! He'd be lucky to have *you*, sweetheart. Not me."

My mouth falls open, and the room suddenly feels a little tilted, which, now that I think about it, the real-estate agent might have mentioned. "Helene!" I whisper back, just as fervidly. "He's a hundred and six!"

"Pretty well preserved," she says, rinsing a cup.

Cal comes back in with the last of the dinner plates, which he sets down gently. My mother's kitchen is warm and small. There is a threadbare pot holder hanging from a metal hook near the sink that says I LOVE YOU, MOMMY. ISABEL APPLEBAUM, FIRST GRADE.

Cal steps away from us, backs up against the Formica-topped table, puts his hands on a chair. "I have to confess something." He looks genuinely abashed. He's going to tell us he's married, still married, newly married, and all of my mother's sincere efforts will have been for nothing. Oh, God. What an ass. But how was he supposed to know this was a setup? How could he have known he was a pawn? For the second time this evening, my emotional compass spins and spins.

Helene turns off the water and looks at him expectantly.

She's not wearing shoes—she likes to kick them off under the table—and her stockinged feet on the kitchen floor look bony and translucent, little foot skeletons.

"I brought dessert," Cal says. "But I left it in the car."

"Well, that's nice." My mother cups her bad hand with her good one, the way she does.

"And it's ice cream." Cal smiles, twinkly and embarrassed, and I think again how he might have made my mother laugh, and then I wonder about his lips, the way his skin might feel. What his warm hands could do.

And now I'm so confused and unsettled that I hear a strange little mewling chirp, which has come from my own mouth. "I'll go get that ice cream," I say, "if you give me your keys? Maybe it's not completely melted."

"I think it probably is." Cal reaches for his coat, shrugs it on. "I'd like to go out and get more."

"No need!" My mother opens the freezer and starts rooting around. "I think I might have some in here. Remember last Thanksgiving, when I served that low-fat butter brickle? I don't think I ever finished it. . . ."

"I'll go with you," I say to Cal, surprising myself.

"Well, all right. I'll tidy up in here," my mother says, and as Cal holds the door for me, Helene stays behind, in the kitchen.

If I turn around, I know that I will see her grinning, pleased with herself. And if I look for more than a second, underneath the satisfied smirk I'll see all of the wide-open hope she holds for me, her bottomless desire for my happiness, the way her sorrow mirrors mine. And I am a lot of things, but I'm not a glutton for punishment. So I keep walking. Cal is right behind me; I can feel his footsteps. I don't turn around.

· · ·

Meehan's Market at night is almost deserted. Its upscale clientele apparently has better things to do than shop for unusual gourmet items at 8:00 p.m.

In the car on the way over, Hannah sent me a text: *can I sleep here 2nite? Lucky is soooo cute i can't be away from him!!!! if U don't let me sleep at chloe's we will have 2 get a dog!!!!!!!!!*

"This is it," Cal says. He takes a pint from the freezer shelf and examines it. "Once you try this, you'll never be able to enjoy any other kind of ice cream."

"Oh, good," I say. "I'm always looking for opportunities to stop enjoying the things I once loved."

Cal hands me the pint. "Hmm," he says. "You are dark."

My cheeks heat up. "I know. Chris hates that about me. I'm sorry. It's a . . . bad habit." I feel like sticking my face into the ice-cream freezer to cool it off.

Cal takes the pint of ice cream from my hand and points to the label: DEEP CHOCOLATE EXTREME. "This one's phenomenal." He reaches in and grabs another pint. "I like dark." He closes the freezer door, and it fogs up.

I turn to look at Cal. We're next to each other, close, so that when I turn my face, he's near enough to examine, near enough to kiss. His eyebrows are wiry. The lines around his eyes that looked distinguished from across the dinner table are just wrinkles up close, worn tracks on his face. His eyes are greenish. On his lower lip there is a small dot, like a freckle, but blue. There is a tiny spot just under his chin that he missed with the razor, less than a centimeter, and the stubble growing there is gray.

He's taking my measure, too. I know it. And he sees the same signs of deterioration, I suppose, if he's inclined to look for them, but better disguised. My skin probably looks pretty good; it usually does. But I used to have thicker eyelashes. Fuller cheeks. An entirely different neck.

We're just marching toward the end: slow steps, fast steps, faster. Probably there is no point in trying to connect. It takes so much effort to let someone in. Maybe there was reason for it ten, twenty years ago; maybe then it made sense to try to drum up a partner for the long journey. But now? It will only end soon, and in heartbreak. It always has; it always does.

"My mother is trying to set us up," I say.

"I'm flattered."

"How old are you?"

"Fifty-nine."

"Are you as nice as you seem?"

"It depends whom you ask."

"Do you realize that this ice cream is seven dollars and fifty cents a pint?"

"Yes." He drops the two pints into the green basket he's carrying. "I need bread. Do you mind if we make one quick detour before we check out?"

And no, I don't mind. The light above us flickers, bright and unforgiving. The freezer's fan gives a little *thump* and then hums into action. I'll stay here wandering the empty aisles of Meehan's Market with this kind man for a few more minutes.

———◆———

Seven

Six months after Josie died, Mark decided to move out of his parents' house. He thought they would insist he hold on to his childhood home, but, Mark told me, Mr. and Mrs. Abrams immediately agreed that he should sell it.

"Of course you have to get rid of the house, sweetheart," his father said to him over the phone from Florida.

"Of course you do," his mother echoed. They were each on an extension, elderly Jews in stereo. Mark repeated the entire conversation for me, flawlessly imitating his sweet parents.

"Your good memories will go with you," Mr. Abrams said.

"And the bad ones you can leave behind." Mark's mother swallowed a gulp of her ever-present Fresca. "Remember Larry Bachman?" she said. Mark was about to tell her he had no idea who Larry Bachman was, but it turned out she was talking to his father anyway.

"Oh, sure. Larry."

"He sold the condo after Janet died. He got less than he paid for it, remember? But it didn't matter. He had to get out of there. He's dating Marilyn Epstein *and* her sister June now!" Mr. Abrams laughed appreciatively. "Both of them!" Mrs. Abrams repeated.

They were ten years older than Helene, in their early eighties (Mark was their late-in-life miracle, as they frequently reminded him) and living in a retirement community in Boca. They had become experts in the field of loss.

I went to the house on a warm Friday afternoon to help Mark. The FOR SALE sign was poking out of the front lawn like an unusual species of tree. LAKEVIEW REALTY, it said. EXCLUSIVE HOMES FOR FAMILIES. CALL TRINA COHEN-PUGH FOR SHOW-INGS. Trina Cohen-Pugh was the best real-estate agent in sub-urban Milwaukee. She'd gone to high school with Mark and me, a year ahead of us. She'd been editor of the school paper, the star of the cross-country team, and the president of the debat-ing society; she'd graduated from Northwestern. In high school, everyone thought she'd be the first female president. But who knows, she might have ended up sitting behind the desk in the Oval Office thinking, *I wish I were pricing bungalows right now.* Anyway, if Trina Cohen-Pugh took you on, you'd be closing within the month.

Mark said once that the weirdest thing about living in your childhood home as an adult was sleeping in your parents' bed-room. You were your parents, he said; not that you felt like them, but that on some molecular level you actually were them, waking up on a Sunday morning in a king-sized bed with the sun coming through the white curtains at exactly the same angle as it did when you were five and would pad in from your bedroom early and quietly slip into the big, safe space in the middle.

Josie took a swig from her beer bottle and snorted. "That's so sweet." She was slurring a little. *Thassosweet.* She put her hand on Mark's. "But no way. Noooo way. It's not the sleeping. Let me tell you." I was looking at Josie, but I could sense Mark next to me, nervous. "The weirdest thing about living in your husband's childhood home as an adult is fucking in his parents' bedroom!" She let out a throaty laugh, and Mark pretended to be fascinated by the edge of his chair.

In the fading light of that Friday afternoon six months after she died, I walked through the front door I'd walked through a thousand times, and everything was familiar to me: the green slate tiles in the entryway. The big silver mirror in the living room. The worn Formica countertops in the bright yellow kitchen. The smell of the house, like coffee and toast and a pot of noodles overboiled in 1981. Layers of years accumulated, one on top of the other.

It was messy, though, disheveled and grimy in a way Josie never would have tolerated. Dishes were piled up in the sink, newspapers scattered on and around the kitchen table. The sofa in the living room was pulled out and made up for sleeping, white sheets and a light blue fleece blanket messily thrown over it. Mark had ended up on the couch the night after the funeral, he said, and he hadn't moved back into their bedroom. That couch was thirty years old at least. There was a deep depression in the middle of it, a canyon, and I could see the outline of bedsprings through an exposed corner of the mattress. It didn't look like a place to sleep. It looked like a punishment.

"Welcome to the House of Usher!" he boomed, throwing his arms wide, as if he'd rehearsed it, and then he hugged me and said, softly, "Thanks for coming, Iz." I waved him away. "I mean it. There's no way I could have started this without you." He handed me a beer.

"I know. I'm glad . . . I mean, you know I wouldn't have let you go through this alone."

The truth is I had tried sending Chris in my place, but he'd refused. "You have to do it," he said. "You have to get your head on straight." He was fed up with me by then; I knew that: the way my sadness was a suit of armor. How securely I kept him out.

"Hey, Happy Yom Kippur," Mark said. It was our joke, what the non-Jews of Milwaukee had been saying to us since we were kids. *Happy Yom Kippur! Have a good one!* It was late September, three days until the Day of Atonement, in fact. We were smack in the middle of the Days of Awe—ten days of introspection and repentance, and if you're lucky, and you've introspected and repented enough, at the end of it your name gets inscribed in the Book of Life. Although neither of us believes that.

"I'm feeling introspective as hell right now," Mark said, clinking his beer bottle to mine.

"Me, too," I said. "And I'm repentant as shit."

We were blowing hot air. Nonbelievers are the worst. The window is slammed shut, but there's always a crack where the cold air gets in. Anyway, who was I kidding? Helene's history, my history—it's etched in my soul. I secretly suspect there might actually be a God, and if so, he's mean as a hornet.

We wandered around the house, Mark and I, like clumsy tourists, poking our heads into rooms and closets. We walked through the living room, with the crystal candlesticks Mark had given Josie for their fifth anniversary, the photographs on display of the two of them: in Paris, in front of a tent in northern Wisconsin, on the urban shore of Lake Michigan. I shook my head. "Not here."

We traipsed up the stairs and past their big bedroom, and we paused at the door of his childhood room, which Josie had converted into her art studio. It was draped with canvas and still full of supplies and tools, buckets of clay and bottles of paint, as if she were just in the middle of an afternoon's work, as if she'd just gone downstairs for a cup of coffee. "Nope," I said, and obediently he followed me down the hallway to the bathroom. "Here."

Surely the bathroom was the place to start when you were faced with the task of dismantling your home. Here in this plain, utilitarian room—white tiles, a striped blue shower curtain, a sink, a toilet—what ghost could possibly haunt us here?

We got through four things: a half-empty (*half-full!* sure!) bottle of basil-apricot facial scrub. Two little, mostly used-up containers of Humidité, an antifrizz serum Josie swore by (although it did not work). A comb. A bottle of Zealexifor, a low-dose antidepressant Josie had begun taking a few years ago. She'd been on one before that called Ebulizor, and before that, briefly, one called Dynamizole, until Zealexifor seemed to do the trick. The names were so goofy and obvious. Their sheer absurdity could cheer you up.

We used to make up our own. We'd send e-mails to each other when we had prep time between classes: *Oh, I'm a little down today; I forgot to take my Gladiprene. I'm way too cheerful right now! I need to up my dose of Despairizeme! Despondizac! Hopelesse!*

I stood close to Mark in their tiny bathroom and watched as he picked up that little orange pharmacy bottle, then set it back down gently on the shelf and placed his palms flat on the edges of the sink. The sound he made came up from a place inside him no one else was ever meant to know: a howl from his cracked heart. "Oh, my God, Iz. Oh, my God."

I'd seen him cry before. But not like this. Sorrow contorted his face, pulled and twisted his features with raw force. Time had not mitigated his grief; six months had done nothing to relieve his pain.

I wished Chris were here. I wished he could see Mark's face, could understand how, if you loved Josie, you would never feel better. You wouldn't even want to. "Come on," I said, putting my hand on my friend's forearm, gently pulling him away.

We ended up at one of our old haunts, a dark, overpriced, self-conscious English pub called the Pig's Knees. There was a statue of a Buckingham Palace guard in the doorway, and a huge television set over the bar that was always tuned to a soccer game. I led Mark to a little booth toward the back of the place. The bartender nodded to us. He'd seen us here in various formations over the years: in twos, threes, fours.

Mark shoved his hand through his hair and immediately began drumming his fingers on the nicked, dark brown table between us. "It's not always this bad," he said. "You know I'm not always this wrecked."

"I know."

"Only ninety-four percent of the time."

"That's good!" I said. "Six percent unwrecked!"

"Nobody understands," he said, even though I did; I also understood, fleetingly, that Mark was flourishing in isolation, although negatively, like a poisonous mushroom or a blind cave fish. He swiped at his cheek and blew his nose in a napkin. His face was stubbly, the skin under his eyes dark. The handsomeness of his features was smudged, altered. "There's a schedule to this, apparently. Six months. I'm supposed to be healing by now." He leaned in. "I am not . . . healing."

He was distant from me, lost in the particular way each person goes his or her own kind of crazy: sleepless, obsessive, hungry, crushed. *I'm here, too!* I wanted to say. *I'm sad all the time.* But what good would it have done? I just nodded.

"I'm finding some solace in alcohol, though," he said. "That's an unexpected benefit."

"Keep up the good work with that," I said.

He rubbed his eyes, looked down at his hands. "Maybe the worst part is how hard things had been between us," he said, "before she died. We would have worked through it. I know that. But now it's just this open wound."

I waved my hand in the air, shooing the whole idea away. I knew how hard it had been. I knew more than Mark. "Of course you would have worked through it," I said. "Of course you would have."

"Sometimes when I can't sleep I go to that place near the bowling alley," he said.

I took a sip of my beer, a thick, brown English swill. It tasted like something dredged from a river. The only places near the bowling alley I could think of were sleazy, gentlemen-only establishments with blinking neon boobs in the windows. *"Mark."*

"No, God, Iz, I'm not that far gone. It's just a little Milwaukee dive. I can't sleep, and I get in my car, and I just drive for a while, and then I go there. And I just have one or two drinks. I don't have a death wish." He winced. "I just go there some nights."

"You could come over to our house," I said. "Always. No matter how late it is. You know that, right?"

The Pig's Knees was pretty deserted, but it was never empty. A beefy man in a shiny green soccer shirt was sitting at the bar, watching the game, occasionally pounding his pink fist on the counter and shouting "Oi!" or "Yellow card! Yellow card!" Two women sat at a table a few feet away from us, sharing a greasy plate of something. They were using lots of napkins, pressing them on top of their food, sopping things up.

Mark looked at me for a moment that stretched out too long, like he had just lost his ability to calibrate social interactions. "I need to tell you something."

A lightning bolt of awkwardness struck me on the top of my

scalp and traveled right down my body. I felt my head tingling, my face flushing, my fingers becoming trembly. My body knew before the truth settled over my brain. It was a stage of grief, wasn't it? The inappropriate transfer of affection to your dead wife's married best friend? *Oh, no,* I thought. *No no no no no no.*

Chris and I were stuck in a thick and murky swamp of discontent. We talked about separating all the time. You would think that once one person brings up the subject of separation, the marriage train starts to hurtle down that track, unstoppable. But it doesn't; not quite.

He said it first, in the middle of a fight.

"You refuse to understand me!" I yelled, or "You have never understood me!" or perhaps "You only understand my feelings when I'm feeling what you're feeling!" There was a certain refrain to these arguments.

"You take all your crap out on me," he murmured back, low and dark and growly. Chris never yelled. The angrier he got, the more quietly he spoke, until sometimes, when we were fighting, I would have to ask him to speak up. *Wait, sorry, what was that about shellfish?* "You take it out on me," he continued, practically whispering, "and I'm just supposed to stand here and be grateful to be married to someone with so much passion. Lucky me."

"My best friend is dead!" I wailed. "It's like you forget that!"

And then he looked at me, and icicles formed in the air between us, and he said, "I don't want to do this anymore, Iz."

"Fine," I said with a shrug. I didn't want to fight anymore, either.

He shook his head and slumped into a living room chair and if I didn't know better I might have thought he was about to reach for the remote at the end of a long day. "I really don't want to do this anymore."

"Okay," I said. "I *heard* you." And then I understood what he was saying.

There is a peculiar kind of terror you feel when the person you are closest to—for better or worse—begins to formulate the idea of a life without you. I could practically see the vision he was creating, right there in front of me, of a life alone in a cozy apartment, of Hannah on the weekends, of girlfriends and baseball games and books and friends. A medium-sized dog. A game of darts at a bar on a Friday night. It actually looked pretty appealing. I felt something pulsing and hard rise up in my throat, and I swallowed.

"No," I said, squeaky and pitiful. "You don't mean that." I was a tiny version of myself, the tiniest one, a *matryoshka* me.

Anything can be said in a marriage; anything can be unsaid. We weren't going to separate. I knew that for certain, and I was wrong.

"I'm sorry," I said. Fear squeezed my vocal cords into a kinked hose. I almost said, *Even though I don't know what I'm sorry for,* but I managed to stop myself.

Chris closed his eyes. "Forget it," he said. "It's okay. Forget it." I stood there for a while, hovering over him, until it became clear to me that he wasn't going to say anything else, and then I walked into the kitchen to start dinner. I may have been mistaken, but after a while, I thought I heard the soft sound of my husband snoring.

· · ·

"Listen," Mark said. "I, uh, asked the bartender at that dive on a date . . . a couple months ago." He looked at me with a twitchy, embarrassed smile. "She's twenty-five. I think her name might be Brandy."

Relief flowed through me like water. "That's a good name for a bartender."

"It's not Brandy," he said. "It's Simone."

"That's good, too."

"She said no." He shrugged, in a resigned, old-mannish way. "She said she doesn't date clients. Isn't that funny? I know she meant customers, but she said clients, like she works at a law firm or something."

"The bar," I said.

"Ha." Mark started drumming his fingers again, then caught himself, stopped abruptly. "She has that kind of face that looks like it was carved from a bar of soap. Like you couldn't imagine her ever having a bad day. Whatever. I was glad she said no. I would have said no to me! Crazy insomniac alcoholic old guy blubbering about his dead wife."

"Sexy," I said. The words *dead wife* lingered. The image came to me of the beach a few miles from my parents' old house, where every July, a mass of alewives washed up on Lake Michigan's shore. There were thousands of them, a herring massacre, their tiny, rotting bodies shiny and silver and sparkling in the sun.

"Do you want to know how I asked her out?" He glanced down at the table and touched one of the grooves in the dark wood with his fingertip. He had taken off his wedding ring a few weeks ago; if you looked closely, you could see its ghost, the thin pale line of skin where it had lived. "I said, 'Um, you'd never want to get dinner with me sometime.'"

I laughed. "That's an unusual pickup line," I said. "Grammatically unusual."

"She just looked at me like I was the saddest thing she'd ever seen. Like I was an injured bird. Like I was a dead puppy. A sad, drunk, dead puppy."

"She probably thought you were an emigrant from the Czech Republic."

Mark nodded. "And/or Slovakia."

The owner of the Pig's Knees, a guy from Racine who pretended to be British, came over with a basket of fries for us. "Right you are," he said. "Your chips, mates." He set it down. "Cheers."

"It's okay if it's too soon," I said.

"It's never too soon for chips, mate," Mark said. He saluted me with a french fry.

"For dating."

One of the women at the nearby table looked over at Mark and smiled. I noticed that she was wearing a thick coat of lip gloss, but then I realized it was probably just the grease. I could see that, despite his failure with Simone, Mark might be very attractive to women now. In public, at least, he wore his sadness like a rumpled shirt. He made you want to come over and fix the collar.

"Iz." Mark grabbed my hand from across the table. "There's a little more." He let go of my hand abruptly, left it stranded in the middle of the table, five pale, shipwrecked fingers.

I looked at his face, and I had the sudden memory of something that happened when we were kids, one day after school. It was dusk, one of those Wisconsin midwinter late afternoons when the sky and the snow turn a ghostly lavender for a half hour, and then it's completely dark by 5:00 p.m. Mark was standing in the front hallway of our house. His mother had just pulled up to collect me and take us to Hebrew school. Mark hadn't rung the doorbell, because I'd seen them driving slowly up the street in their unmistakable old brown station wagon and I'd opened the door while I went to get my coat. They never honked. Mark's mother didn't believe in disturbing the neighbors. (My mother didn't care.)

Mark walked in just as Helene was finishing a sentence. I'd been telling my mother about a new kid who'd moved into the neighborhood, a blond girl named Ellie Krakowski. Ellie and I had been assigned to do a science project together, and I was describing it to Helene. It had something to do with magnets, or maybe gravity; I don't recall, but I remember that I was pretty excited about it. Ellie, I told her, seemed nice. We were in the seventh grade, so I was twelve. I definitely remember that.

"I'm glad you have a new friend, honey," Helene said from the kitchen as I made my way toward the front closet. She was emptying the dishwasher. Plates and silverware clattered and clanked. "Krakowski," she said. "Krakowski. Just make sure her family didn't put our family into the ovens."

She just lobbed it out there, as casually as some parents, I imagined, admonished their children to look both ways before they crossed the street or to bundle up in the cold. With Helene, specific family stories were off-limits, but grim admonitions about gas chambers were perfectly fine. Every time she said something like this, the blood rushed to my face. What kind of family ended up in ovens? Whose mother talked about it like this, like we'd better invest in good running shoes that are easy to tie, because our neighbors were probably coming for us with pitchforks any minute?

I had, until that moment in our foyer, been able to keep this particular habit of Helene's a secret.

Ugh, my parents are so embarrassing, kids were starting to say to one another at school. *My dad wears black socks with shorts! The other day at the mall my mom called me "sweetie" in front of all my friends! Ugh, they're so embarrassing!*

But really. *Make sure her family didn't put our family into the ovens?* It was so much more than embarrassing. It was bright and primal, practically alive, something veined and hissing in the attic: a genetic mutation of familial shame and tribal terror. Although I wouldn't have said that then.

I stared at Mark, paralyzed. He stared back. His mouth dropped open a little bit. *Into the ovens,* I thought. "Um, my mom's baking bread?" I muttered, hoping he would think he'd just misheard, and then I looked down, waiting for the humiliation explosion in the form of Mark's inevitable guffaw.

He pulled off one of his heavy gloves with his teeth, then eased the other one off with his free hand. His puffy nylon jacket squeaked as he moved. "Hey, Iz," he said. "I've been reading the *Lord of the Rings* trilogy. It's so cool. It's all I can think about, even when I'm not actually reading. My mom says she called me for breakfast three times this morning and I didn't hear her, I've been so distracted. Come on, let's go."

. . .

The bartender was putting out clean pint glasses. The soccer fan was shouting obscenities. The girls at the table a few feet from us were finishing their oily lunch. Mark and I had more than just memories of Josie in common, more than just the deep puncture wound of her loss. We had loved each other for a long time.

"What is it?" I asked.

"One of the, um . . ." He stopped talking, took a sip of his beer, and smiled at me.

"Well, that's good to know!" I said.

"No, listen, one of the, one of your . . . Andes called me the other day. You know how you and Josie used to call them that? You used to laugh at them?"

Mark always chided Josie and me for making fun of the

Andes. He never understood that mocking them was our only defense. "Oh, no, Mark, we weren't laughing. Well, okay, we were. But only because they were—"

But Mark wasn't interested in hearing my explanation. "Andi Friedman," he said. "She called me."

Andi Friedman was the most purposeful of the Andes, and the one who seemed to have the most differentiated inner life. I could give her that. I'd see her alone sometimes, striding down the hallway in her heels, *click-click-click,* lost in thought. On Monday mornings, when the three of them would sit together in the lounge and scroll through their phones, sharing photos they had taken over the weekend, *Oh, my God, that guy! I know, right? How was I supposed to know he had a girlfriend?* Andi Friedman seemed to listen more than the other two, to absorb rather than constantly emit. She sat still. She was not the prettiest or the sparkliest. But if you had to choose which of them to be trapped with in a mountain cabin in a snowstorm, you would probably choose her. Or if you were trapped with all of them for an extended period of time, you'd eat her last. Plus she had not been there with us, on that trip to Lake Kass. Although later, she was just as culpable. She'd had just as much to say as the other two.

"Andi's grandparents and my parents used to go to Beth Shalom together." Mark was still talking about her. "They knew one another pretty well. Isn't that funny? She was really sweet. She said her grandma told her to call me, but that she had wanted to, ever since Josie died." Mark fiddled with his glass. His knee had begun to bounce under the table, thumping a dull, repetitive rhythm against the wood.

"Her grandparents and your parents," I said. I took another sip of my horrible, horrible beer.

Mark grew still, and then he looked at me with pity. There is nothing worse than pity from the pitiful. "We went out for dinner the other night," he said. "We went to that new Vietnamese place on Brady. We, I . . . I don't know, Iz. She was . . . nice. She was so nice. It was just good to be out with someone who . . . I don't know. It was easy. I like her." He shrugged, as if that last part were a question. "I like her a lot," he said.

And there it was, the image of Mark and Andi, a vision I didn't want, but I was having it: Mark's mouth on her bare neck; her smooth, traitorous face flushed with pleasure.

"I don't want to know this," I said, clipped and furious. "Is this why we're here? Is this why I came to your house, why you cried over Josie's hair-care products? I don't need to know this." Now I was blind with rage. A bright red scrim appeared in front of my eyes; I thought, *Wow, it's not just an expression, you do see red.* "I'm so happy for you," I said. I was out of breath. My tongue was a slab of meat. I tried to slide out of the booth. I wanted to make a swift and elegant exit, but I was so clumsy. Instead of sliding, I scuttled along the bench like a crab, *thunk, thunk, thunk,* until I was out, until I was standing at the edge of the table. "I'm delighted," I said, my voice high and loud and embarrassing, the tears already starting to pool up behind my eyes.

"Izzy, don't. Please don't. I'm . . . this is so hard. You can't feel worse than I do." Mark put his hands up to his stubbly cheeks and rubbed.

"You know she just wants to save you," I said. "You know there are women who want to do that. That's all she wants."

"Iz."

I understood that Mark and I were in a competition I would never win. The betrayal of my dead friend spooled out in front of me like an unraveling skein of yarn, and I had the feeling, right then, of losing something that was already gone.

. . .

Cal calls me the morning after our trip to the grocery store for ice cream, our strange and jolly evening with my mother.

"My son tells me there are rules," he says, by way of hello. "A requisite three-day waiting period before I'm allowed to call you. But I don't think that applies when you're nearly sixty. Time is of the essence!" He laughs to himself, that easy sound I already know I like. "So I'm calling right now to see if you'd like to go out with me. On a date."

It's Saturday, and too early for this phone call. I'm standing at the stove, listening to the sizzle of pancake batter on the frying pan, waiting for it to bubble. I'm wearing my fuzzy pink robe, my green monkey slippers—the kind of getup that says *married, done trying.*

Hannah just got home from her sleepover, grouchy, with dark circles under her eyes and a wild, tired look on her face. She's thumping around upstairs now, music coming through the ceiling. *Girl, you look so fine fine fine. Say that you'll be mine mine mine.* This is the same song that was playing in the car the other day, the one Hannah asked me to stop singing along to: "Mom. Please. Ew. This song is *heinous.*"

Come over right now, I want to say to Cal. *Can we just skip all of this? Come over.*

He walked me home last night, kissed me sweetly on the cheek at my front door in a pool of light. I went inside and I poured myself a glass of grapefruit juice, splashed some vodka into it—Chris's, a birthday present from his father—and I stood in the middle of the kitchen and I said, out loud, to myself, to an empty house, "Well, Isabel, how do you feel?"

And the answer was stirred. Gently stirred. Pleased to be the object (finally, again) of someone's affection. I was happy, if I let myself admit it, happy for the first time in months, like I was being given a chance. . . . And also, if I was being completely honest, I felt a tiny bit like I'd been kissed on the cheek by Dr. Carlsson, my old orthodontist, who used to like to talk about the trip to Alaska he and his wife had taken in 1976. He would jabber endlessly about it—*the elk! the moose! the midnight sun!*—to his captive audience as he tightened the wires in my mouth, his dexterous fingers working around my canines and bicuspids, his face always so near and intimate, every detail held close for my examination: the spotty brown sun damage on his cheeks, the hairs in his nostrils quivering as he breathed. This is the price you pay for expertise. The rough planes of a lived life. Attraction, repulsion. Cal's kiss was maybe just a little bit like that.

Hannah clomps down the stairs and throws herself into a chair, drops her backpack and Clucky, the rubber chicken she sleeps with, on the floor next to her, and rests her elbows on the table, her face in her hands. Chris will be here soon to pick her up, my poor nomad, itinerant victim of her parents' failure.

"I would like that," I say to Cal, quietly, the phone tucked between my shoulder and my ear.

"Are you free this afternoon?" he asks. "I have some ideas."

"Yes." It's a sweet secret now, a tiny jewel nestled among the lint and old Kleenex in the pocket of my robe. "This afternoon."

I end the call and set a pancake in the shape of a teddy bear down in front of Hannah, round ears and a slightly misshapen face, into the middle of which I've placed two chocolate chips for eyes, a smiling row of them for a mouth. I know the risk I'm taking and brace myself for a sneer. But she looks at it and grins, delighted. Then she looks up at me and dials back her smile. But it's still there.

"Thanks, Mama," she mutters. The tender skin under her eyes is so dark it looks bruised. Is she wearing mascara?

I turn back to the stove, busy myself with the pancake batter. Hannah and I are slipping back into the cogs of our Saturday morning routine—a functioning twosome, but still, after all these months, I feel Chris's absence like a presence, an object. It's there in the chair by the window that stays tucked under the table, the gallon of milk in the refrigerator that always ends up going bad before we can finish it, the extra pancake batter.

"I'm starving!" Hannah says, and for a second I envy her hunger, how easy it is, still, when you're almost twelve, just to want something. I make more teddy-bear pancakes, bunnies, snowmen, a fat H. She devours them all.

"Hey." I slide another one onto her plate. "How was the dog? Lucy? Was she so cute?"

She tips her head up to me, her body still hunched close to her food. Her hair is a tangled mess, and there's a dot of syrup on her chin. She looks a little feral. "Not *Lucy*," she says. "Lucky. Annoying. Unlucky. Barked all night."

"So you probably didn't sleep much," I say.

She glares at me full on. "I didn't sleep at all." She touches the back of her hand to her chin and wipes off the syrup. "Whatever. I wouldn't have slept anyway."

"What do you mean?"

Hannah rolls her eyes. I have to stop myself from backing away from my child.

"Do you think I *ever* sleep? Do you think I, like, lie down at night and just close my eyes and, like, dream about princesses?"

When she was little, four or five, Hannah used to crawl into my lap in the mornings, her hair sticking up in tufts, her little body warm from sleep. She would rest her head on my chest and whisper, "I stayed awake and played in my bed *all night*! I did not sleep one wink!"

"What do you mean?" I ask again.

"I haven't been sleeping!" she says, the high, frantic voice of my little girl, and she starts to cry. Without warning the tears are just rolling down her cheeks, a flash flood. "I can't sleep! I keep thinking it's like . . . dying." She takes a ragged breath and looks at me like she's drowning, and I'm just standing here, balancing a teddy-bear pancake on a spatula like an idiot, like a clown, doing nothing to save her. "You fall asleep," she says, "and where do you go? You're gone. It's like . . . it's like you're practicing to die!"

Well, okay. I have the urge to cut up this pancake and feed her. Actually I want to chew it up and drop it into her mouth like she's a baby bird. "Sleep," I say, as gently as I can, "is what every living creature needs." At least, I think it is. Do ants sleep? Spiders? "It's really . . . Honey, it's the opposite of dying."

She shakes her head, holds out her hands in front of her to stop me from hugging her. And I wasn't even going to hug her! Because I knew she wouldn't let me. And now I'm just hacking through the underbrush: Why wasn't I going to hug her, anyway? Because I'm so accustomed to her rejections that I've given up? Should I have tried? Are those hands held up in defense just showing me that she needs me even more? My maternal instinct is buried underneath an unexcavated pile of clutter, along with the missing check I wrote for her field trip to the Art Museum and the bike key I lost last year.

"Sweetie," I say. "You have to sleep."

She gets up from the table with a clatter of dish and fork and a snort of disgust. "Oh, okay," she says. Her hair brushes my arm as she breezes past me. "Okay, I'll do that."

A month or so after Josie died, we took Hannah to a psychologist, naturally. Dr. Melody van Kamp was a middle-aged woman whose practice advertised specialties in adolescence and grief counseling and, peripherally, pet therapy, about which I always wondered: With, or for? She met with Hannah alone a few times, and then with Chris and me.

"She's doing really well," Melody told us. The sun streamed into her cheery office, which smelled like Lysol and was decorated with pictures of dogs, cats, and, oddly, chickens. "She's not hiding anything. Hannah is open about her feelings, and that's marvelous. And she's not defensive, either. A lot of children have their claws out at times like this." Melody smiled encouragingly at Chris and me. We were perched on opposite ends of a long couch. Chris was studying his thumbnail, and I was trying to catch his eye, because it seemed that Melody van Kamp had confused Hannah with a different child. "Of course, you never know, with adolescents," Melody continued. "Anything could come up for her at any time. They can seem fine for a long stretch and then go rabid with no warning!" She laughed and gazed out the window. "But that's parenthood, right?"

Luckily, our insurance covered these sessions.

· · ·

Hannah has gone back up to her room. The doorbell rings: he's right on time. Even this is a new and jarring development, Chris a tentative visitor in what is still, technically, his own home.

"Come in, come in!" I yell, feeling generous. And because he still has a key, he does.

He walks through the house quietly. In the kitchen, he leans toward me for what I think, with surprise, is going to be an uncomfortable kiss, but which he intends to be an uncomfortable hug, so that, after some maneuvering, our shoulders collide, my forehead bumps into his cheek, and then Chris pats my back twice and quickly moves away.

"Awk!" Josie used whisper to me in weird social situations, an echo of what we sometimes write in the margins of students' essays. *Awk! Awk!* The embarrassed cry of the flightless dodo.

"Hannah will be right down," I say. "What are your plans?" Before last night, my plans for today were to clean the bathroom, buy some groceries, call my mother, and breathe. I think about Cal, and the amazement of my day opens up before me. With a swoop of my arm, I offer Chris a seat at the table, a pancake. He sits, unsure of what to make of me. I set a plate down in front of him.

When I was in middle school and would come home upset about something, a fight with a friend or a bad grade, Helene used to say to me, "The worst has already happened to us." It was mortifying, of course, but it was also a perversely comforting sentiment. "The loss of our family," she would say, "is in our bones." You could make serious hay with that one. She still trots it out occasionally. I want to explain it to Chris now, although I'm certain he wouldn't understand. *I have a date,* I would tell him, *with an older gentleman. And here is a pancake in the shape of a bunny!*

"Life goes on," Helene sometimes says, "but only if you're lucky."

"We need to do a few errands." Chris's knife makes a hideous screech against his plate. "Take Mrs. Reinhoffer to the vet." Mrs. Beverly Jean Reinhoffer is our cat, of whom Chris has full custody. I never liked her and was glad to see her go. Over the last few months, the absence of Mrs. Reinhoffer has, at times, been my sole consolation. She used to jump onto my lap and dig her claws into my thighs if I tried to move her. Also, she had the habit of finding me, wherever I was in the house, and throwing up. "And I want to pick up that part for the dishwasher. I can try to fix it when I drop Hannah off on Tuesday."

"Thank you," I say.

"I know we were just at the vet," Chris says, "but Mrs. Reinhoffer needs shots."

"Okay." Does Chris think I care how many times Mrs. Reinhoffer sees the vet? I really don't care about that cat. "Oh, listen, by the way." I slide another pancake onto his plate and pull out a chair for myself. "Hannah has not been sleeping well. She says she's scared to close her eyes. She thinks it's like dying." Morning sunlight plays across the kitchen table between us, reflects in Hannah's abandoned glass of orange juice. I feel, for a brief moment, proud of this intimate knowledge that I possess about our daughter, something private and delicate and mine. In this endless, silent jockeying for position that neither of us would admit to, I am, for one shiny, ugly moment, on top.

And then Chris looks at me in complete confusion. "I know," he says. He sits up a little bit straighter in his chair. "I know. This has been going on for weeks. Maybe a month. How . . ." His eyebrows are about to skyrocket off of his forehead. "Iz, how did you *not know* this?"

I look down at my monkey slippers. They sneer back at me. *Stupid human.* "She just told me."

"We've been listening to a relaxation CD I got from the library. I bought her some lavender oil for her pillow. I was going to talk to you about signing her up for a yoga class at the rec center."

"Okay, that's great," I say. "Good. Lavender oil. Excellent."

"I don't . . ." He looks out the window and waits a few seconds. The sleeves of the shirt that I bought for him are pushed up on his arms. The hair that I used to run my hands through needs a trim. "This is kind of a big thing you've missed, Iz. Our daughter is terrified to *sleep.*"

"Yes," I say, fidgeting in my chair, the proximity of our bodies still reflecting the harmony of five minutes ago, not the defensive anger that's boiling up now.

Hannah has turned on the music again upstairs. It's a different melody, but a similar bass line thuds down to us, deep and intrusive, the soundtrack to a low-grade panic attack.

"I know that now," I say. "Is this really the time to rub my face in it? When Hannah needs our help?" I see that I am still holding the spatula. "Good for you, that she's confiding in you. Maybe next time she shares such a *big thing* with you, you could let me in on it."

"Jesus," Chris says, his voice soft and maddeningly calm. "Uh, I think—"

"What?" Is he asking me to make him more pancakes?

"Your pancakes are burning," Chris says, gesturing toward the stove with the slightest tip of his chin.

And, yes. They are.

. . .

Chris and I met just after I moved back to Milwaukee, fifteen years ago. I was living with my mother and working part-time as a receptionist at the Fraser Feldman Medical Group, where Helene was the office manager. I got the job through sheer nepotism and hung on to it the same way.

The doctors (that's what she called them, reverently: *the doctors*) loved Helene. She was the smiling face of their practice, efficient and organized and compliant in an old-fashioned, *may I bring you some coffee?* kind of way. I was less efficient and more bored and incompetent, still trying to get over the shock of adulthood. (My favorite thing to do was to say, when people asked me to validate their parking, "You're excellent at parking!") But Helene loved having me with her. She introduced me to everyone—patients, consultants, drug reps, valets—with outsize, wildly misplaced pride. *This is my daughter, Isabel. My darling daughter!* She would pack us identical lunches or treat me to a bagel and soup at the café on the first floor of the building; she'd schedule our breaks together, because she was the office manager, and scheduling breaks was her job. Although I complained about it to Mark—*It's too much! She made me wear her sweater today! I was doing some filing and she complimented me on my alphabetizing skills!*—I actually loved working with my mother, basking in her judgment-free love, gossiping about coworkers, stealing gum and M&M's from her purse. Still, I worked on my résumé during downtime and was counting the days until I could find a teaching job.

Chris limped in on a sunny Monday morning, the first appointment of the day. (Well, there were no windows in the office, so for all I knew the morning sun had given way to dense fog or a tornado or a dust storm; the Fraser Feldman Medical Group was a climate-controlled pod in the heart of a downtown high-rise.) He had a huge brace on his knee, his wrist was wrapped in an Ace bandage, and a large white piece of cotton gauze was taped over his right eyebrow. He was tall and sexy in a wounded way, my favorite kind. He propped himself up on my desk with one elbow and exhaled, smiled at me, and then winced.

"Wow. What the hell happened to you?" I said.

He laughed, then winced again. "It really hurts to smile."

"Oh. Psychiatry and Mental Health are down the hall."

He looked at me, baffled. "No, I . . . I have an appointment with Dr. Feldman. He's taking out my stitches."

"Sorry," I said. "I was just kidding. Because you said, you

know, that it hurts to smile, so I . . ." I was always doing this, cracking dumb, inscrutable jokes in the presence of handsome men. It was as if I were programmed to alienate, as if somewhere deep down I wanted to be single forever.

"Ha," the handsome man said, shifting his weight. "My appointment is at nine. Christopher Moore."

I nodded. The office was empty. My mother was in the back, and the doctors hadn't arrived yet. "Please have a seat," I said. But Christopher Moore didn't move.

"I was playing basketball," he said. "I went for a layup and took an elbow right above the eye. I went down like a bag of bricks." I could tell he wanted me to be impressed.

"That's impressive," I said. I thought sports were stupid, but I managed not to say that. What I did say, after an awkward silence, was "We're having a special this week, if you happen to also have syphilis. Two for one." Then my face got so hot I could feel it turning red: a boiled tomato, a roasted pepper, a steamed, dying lobster.

"Noooo," Chris said, scrunching up the unbandaged side of his face in confusion. "I'm good. Thanks." Then he walked away slowly toward the rows of empty chairs.

Forty-five minutes later, as I was replaying the whole exchange for the three-hundredth time, Chris hobbled out of Dr. Feldman's office and stood in front of me. He cleared his throat. "My syphilis is cured!" he announced. A woman in the waiting area visibly flinched and stared at us. "Would you like to go out with me?"

. . .

"Daddy!" Hannah whirls into the kitchen, carrying her pillow, throws it at Chris. "Mama made teddy-bear pancakes. Do you want some? She could make you some!" *Let's be a family!*

Chris pulls her into a hug and kisses her on her head, and the ease of affection between them feels like shards of glass in my chest. "She already gave me some. They were good. But we have to go, Banana. Mrs. Reinhoffer is in the car, and she's probably mad as heck by now."

"Heck!" Hannah says. "Do you mean hell?" She grabs her backpack and Clucky. "What's she doing in the car?"

"We need to stop at the vet," Chris says, and I notice he's not meeting anyone's eyes now. "Mrs. R is due for her shots."

"Oh, goody! Annabelle! I love her!"

I slide the burned pancakes into the sink, run the hot pan under cold water just to hear the hiss. "Who's Annabelle?"

"Dr. Lundy. Our vet!" Hannah says. "She's so great. We love her. She's going to let me help with some of the animals, she said. Like when they come in for shots, they need someone to just pet them and keep them calm? She said I could come in and do that sometime. Right, Daddy?"

"Yep." Chris himself looks like he could use some sedation right now. "We've got to go now, Hanners." He looks at me over her head. "I'll be back Tuesday after school. With the part for the dishwasher. Okay? Bye."

Eight

A few hours later, twenty minutes before Cal is supposed to arrive, I pull my robe tight and sit down with a piece of paper and a pen. I can't do this. I realized it this morning as the front door slammed behind Hannah and Chris, and the smell of burned pancakes lingered in the air. I can't. And so, dear Cal,

I have a cold
I have a cold sore
I have a tapeworm
I have a twelve-year-old
I have issues
I'm old
I'm sad
I have a little lower back pain
I'm not looking for a relationship right now
I'm looking for a relationship right now
I need to focus on me
I need to focus on cake
I'm a shell of a human being
I'm so self-absorbed that I managed to overlook my daughter's
    debilitating insomnia

I think my (ex?)-husband might be dating a veterinarian named Annabelle
This will never work, because you're too old and I'm too asshole
The Holocaust

I set my pen down and examine the list, cock my head to blur my vision just a little, let the letters skid and slide and transform into their component blue lines and dots and squiggles before my eyes: mysterious, unintelligible.

And then, with my remaining seventeen minutes, I go upstairs, brush my teeth, and get dressed. I even put on a little makeup.

. . .

"My mother is eighty-nine," Cal says in the car on the way to the nursing home—the assisted-living facility, as he scrupulously calls it.

"Eighty-nine is the new seventy-four," I say, meaning it.

"For some people." Cal taps his horn at the car in front of us, whose driver is lolling at a green light, texting. "But she's . . . she's eighty-nine. Anyway, thank you again. This will only take a few minutes, and you really should feel free to wait in the car. This is awkward, and there's no reason for you to—"

I cut him off by putting my hand on his knee. "Cal, it's fine. I'm happy to come in with you." He smiles and pats my hand, then moves his back to the steering wheel. "I've always wanted to meet your mother," I say.

"I know. I'm sorry I've kept you two apart for so long."

When Cal walked in the door fifteen minutes ago, I could tell something was wrong. I'd come downstairs and was eagerly waiting for him in the living room, even as my own emotions left me with a feeling of psychic whiplash. But I had exorcised my demons, at least for the day, left them impotent on a scrap of paper in the kitchen, and now I was just looking forward to see-ing Cal. I even briefly considered seducing him. I had a hunch it would be easy, although I had never actually seduced anyone before.

I invited him in. I thought for a second that he'd been here last night, but then I remembered we'd said goodbye outside. We walked into the living room. There were things I hadn't noticed just a few minutes ago: a bowl of soggy cereal on the side table next to the couch, a pair of Hannah's socks in a ball next to the TV. The afternoon sunlight cast a theatrical beam on a tumbleweed-sized clump of dust in the corner. "My house needs a little attention," I said. "Don't look at anything too closely." *Including me.*

"Okay," he said. He sat down on the edge of my favorite chair and stared at his feet, sighed softly, then looked up at me with big, sad, regret-filled eyes.

Shit, I thought. *So soon.* Such a quick turnaround from this morning. I sympathized, though, even as I felt stung; after all, I'd composed that list. What would his excuse be? *I don't want a woman who's sixteen years younger than I am; I want one who's thirty years younger? I'm not looking for anyone quite so still-married?* Well, I wasn't going to let him be the one to end this . . . whatever it was . . . first. I'd salvage a scrap of dignity from the wreckage.

"Um, Cal," I said, a little shakily. "I'm so sorry, but I'm not really up for—"

"Isabel." He cut me off. "I spoke with my mother this morn-ing." He paused and glanced around the room as if he were just realizing where he was. "She's elderly. Obviously." He smiled, or possibly winced. "We speak every morning. Today she seemed . . . well, she wasn't herself. She seemed a bit disoriented, or maybe just unusually sad. I tried to convince myself that she was fine and that you and I could still spend the day together. But I'm afraid I do need to go check on her."

My system flooded with a relief-shame cocktail. I took a breath, delighted that I wasn't being rejected, then quickly adjusted my face into a sympathetic frown. "It's okay," I said. "Of course! Some other time!"

Cal shook his head no and said, "Yes," as if he'd suddenly confused assent with negation. He was troubled, flustered, the opposite of the calm and assured man he'd been the other two times I'd met him. The sands shifted; my perception of him altered in ways I couldn't figure. I felt my chest click open one tiny notch. And then I offered to come along.

. . .

My hand is still on his knee in the car, which I realize, too late, was a poorly planned gesture. What will I do, just keep it here until we get to the nursing home? In fact, I have no idea where we're going. What if it's forty-five minutes away? What if it's in Detroit? Maybe I'll just leave my hand here forever, dead-weight, heavy and growing increasingly sweaty, on Cal's sharp knee. Finally, desperate, I snatch it away, pretend to cough and cover my mouth.

After a few minutes of silence, during which I contemplate what a mistake it is for me to ever leave the house, we finally pull into the parking structure of Lutheran Manor, Assisted Living for Seniors.

"We have arrived at *Lyootheran Manor!*" I announce in an English accent, and luckily Cal laughs. It's a beige, defiantly bland rectangle of a building, pocked with tiny windows. If you didn't know better, the Manor could be a plain old apartment building built in the 1960s, a brick-and-concrete fortress against whimsy.

We drive down into the bowels of the parking structure. "The Manor is very charming, isn't it?" Cal says, as he pulls into a space next to a pillar.

"Rather."

Cal walks around the car and opens the door for me, just like nobody ever used to do. "This will be more fun," he says, "than a colonoscopy."

. . .

Chris introduced me to his parents for the first time on his mother's sixtieth birthday. Chris and I were newly in love, and my heart was wide-open. His parents were hosting a party at their country club. When we arrived, the champagne had been flowing for quite a while.

"Isabel!" Chris's mother flung her bony arms around me. "Isabel Applebaum! Christopher has told us sooooooo much about you." As a result of vigilant, military-style maintenance and the diet of a squirrel in February, Ginny Moore is the size of a sapling. Her hug was like being poked by the spokes of a broken umbrella. "Your name sounds like a poem! IZZZZabellll APPLEbaum!" She trilled it. *"It's dactylic!"* she whispered, and kissed me on the cheek with an actual *mwaaah,* then moved on to hug Chris, who looked like he was being asked for directions to Neptune.

Chris's father, a tall, graceful man with a crinkly Robert Redford grin, handed me a party hat and blew a festive paper horn in my face.

I laughed and looked around the Lakeshore Country Club party room, at the sprays of white roses and lavender irises and the beautiful tables and the slim, bejeweled ladies draped lightly on the arms of their portly men, and I felt weightless, free. These were people who drank champagne and told stories about golfing. Did they carry burdens? Probably. But did those burdens involve the lingering, inherited terror of imminent loss? I felt certain they did not.

Chris had told me that his parents were snobbish and reserved, inaccessible, emotionally hobbled by their devotion to complicated rules of propriety. But none of that restraint was in evidence at Ginny's party. Chris's mother touched my arm, and his father brought me a glass of white wine, and I could practically see our loving connection arcing across the divide. *That Isabel,* they would say to Chris later. *She's one of us!* That was the moment I decided that if Chris and I got married, I would take his name. It wasn't that I thought that changing my last name would erase the murky, old-world echoes of disruption and loss; I wasn't deluded. It was the sound of it, the way it seemed that Chris's last name could round out my edges, smooth me down to a polished gem. Isabel Moore. I was through being dactylic.

But Chris was right, of course. That day was just a tipsy aberration. As it turns out, Ginny and Edward Moore might as well be extras from the cast of *Ordinary People.* They skulk about their well-appointed home in suburban Chicago in brooding silence. You can go a whole weekend with them, and the only sounds you'll hear are the wingbeats of magazine pages and the clink of ice in their glasses.

In the fifteen years since that party, the most effusive I've ever seen Ed and Ginny was when Chris and I told them we were getting married. We were staying with them over Memorial Day weekend and had just finished a very light lunch on their deck. I was fantasizing about bread when Chris broke the news.

"Ah, well done," Ed said quietly, and popped out of his seat to get a bottle of champagne, while Ginny raised her wineglass and said, "Hear, hear!" Later that day I overheard Ginny stage-whisper to Chris, "It's just that we always pictured you with someone more . . . *athletic.*"

All of this slides through me now, a decade and a half of ambivalent connection to Chris's family, the pinpricks and knife wounds that eventually became, through some benevolent, gravitational pull, hilarious: How Ed wandered away in the middle of toasting us at our wedding. That they sent Hannah a fruit basket for her fifth birthday. How Ginny insists on things about me that aren't true: *You don't like the theater! You're allergic to mascara! You never eat cheese at night!* These stories, repeated, were threads that wove Chris and me together.

The thought of having to accumulate a new history with someone makes me feel uneven, as if my legs are two different lengths. I take a deep breath of stale air and steady myself for a second against a Honda Civic. Just when I think I've dug down as far as I can go, a new layer appears, silty sediment underneath the rock.

"I should tell you something about my mother," Cal says, pressing the elevator button in the parking garage. "She's . . . opinionated."

I picture a frail old lady in a magenta tracksuit, ranting about the Democrats. "Noted," I say. "I promise not to start a kerfuffle with her."

Cal doesn't bounce anything back to me. He just nods, and I feel foolish and a little chastised. How is it that, at forty-three, I still can't read the room? We're inside the overheated building now, walking down a carpeted hallway that smells like macaroni and disinfectant. It's long and wide, with rubber bumpers on the sides, like a bowling alley at a child's birthday party. I have the urge to stop in my tracks and pivot, to head straight back down the hall and out the broad, pneumatic door through which we entered.

But Cal reaches for my hand instead. "'Opinionated' may be the wrong word, actually. She's . . . she can be kind of hateful. I probably should have warned you earlier, but honestly, I didn't think you'd need to know quite so soon."

We pass the dining room, empty; the TV room, where seven or eight people sit in wheelchairs in front of a game show; and the recreation lounge, which is decorated to the hilt with blue and green streamers and balloons and a huge banner strung across the wall, HAPPY 95TH BIRTHDAY, BETTY! The lounge, like the dining room, is completely empty, a ghost ship.

We take the elevator up to the fourth floor, where, Cal explains, the more independent residents live in small apartments until they're unable to live on their own. It's like the day-care center Hannah went to when she was two: children progressed from classroom to classroom as they got older, from the Bunny Room to the Dolphin Room to the Penguin Room. This is just like that, except not at all.

Cal drops my hand in front of apartment 447 and knocks, more of an alert than a question, since he has his key in the lock before his mother has a chance to say *Come in* or *Don't*. He turns to me, raises his eyebrows, and smiles in a way that reminds me of the look on Hannah's face at last year's spelling bee, right before she started to spell "psychology" with a *c*.

Vivian Abbott is sitting in her small, warm living room in a blue armchair, her back to us, staring out the window, as if she had been sent from central casting: Old Woman, Waiting. There is an intermittent clicking noise that I at first attribute to the heating system. As it turns out, she's staring not at the scenery but at her computer screen, typing.

"Goddammit," she says, turning to us. "I was in the middle of a sentence." She holds up a hand and waves to us. "Cal, what are you doing here?"

"Hi, Mom." He walks over to her, leans down, and kisses her on the cheek. "You sounded a little funny when we spoke this morning. I wanted to come check on you."

"You're a good boy," she says. "And you always have been." She sets her computer down on the table next to the chair, then stands and pulls her lavender cardigan around herself. Even here, aged and frail in the independent-living unit of Lutheran Manor, Vivian Abbott is a beauty. Her eyes are bright blue and clearly appraising as she looks me up and down. Her skin is pale and delicately lined, softening her fine, sharp features. I wouldn't have guessed how old she is. She looks slightly younger than Cal.

"Hello, darling," she says to me. Then, to Cal, "Is she Michael's friend?"

"No," Cal says. "Isabel is my friend."

"My goodness," Vivian says.

I walk over to her, and she takes my hand in hers. Her palm is dry and papery. With her left hand, she pats my upper arm. I want to hug her. How can Cal say she's hateful? I guess we just cling to our old misunderstandings, those early injuries.

"You have very unusual features," Vivian says, squeezing my hand. "Such thick hair and dark eyes. Are you a Turk?"

"Mom. Isabel is not a Turk."

"Are you sure?" she asks me. "I'm sorry, but I don't trust Turks. I had a cleaning lady who was Turkish. I don't need to tell you what happened there. Well, I don't trust Spaniards, either,

for that matter, so I can't be a bigot, even though Cal says I am."
She smiles sweetly. "I'm just happy to hear you're not a Turk."

"Oh, Mom," Cal says. "And I'm just happy you're feeling
okay."

"I certainly am." She winks at me, and I wink back. "You are
darling. I can see why Michael likes you."

"We brought you some cookies," Cal says, handing her a bag
I hadn't noticed he'd been carrying.

"Pecan Sandies. My favorite! How is Michael?" she asks me.

"He's fine, Mom. He's in San Francisco, remember?"

"Of course I remember! He's out there working for that
Internet security company. We Skyped last week. He looked
so handsome. I'm just wondering if you've spoken to him *since*
then." She waves her hand dismissively at Cal and clucks her
tongue. "Elizabeth," she says to me, "my son brought you all the
way out here just to show you that I'm not in full possession of
my faculties. Well, I am."

"Mom," Cal says. "That's not why . . ."

She waves him away again and will now make eye contact only with me. "We'll enjoy these cookies. Pecan Sandies, my
favorite. Would you be so kind as to go into the kitchen and get
me my sterling-silver serving platter? It's in the cupboard over the
sink. I would do it myself, but I might get lost on my way back
from the kitchen." She puts her hands on her hips and juts out her
chin imperiously, like a much-younger woman, then, exhausted
by all the effort, eases herself back down into her armchair.

In the cupboard over the sink there are three plastic cups, a
butter knife, and a bottle of antacid. I'm searching the rest of the
spotless kitchen, quietly, for the serving plate, when I overhear
Mrs. Abbott say, "If not a Turk, then what? Sicilian?"

"No, Mom, she's Irish," Cal says loudly, for my benefit. *"Black
Irish."*

This is the weirdest situation I've ever been in, including the time a squirrel tried to climb up my leg in the park.

"Oh, I know black Irish," Vivian says, "and she's not that. She's has lovely skin, though."

I feel a little puff of pride. I do have lovely skin! This is why you go on a date with a man who is almost twenty years older than you are: so that his elderly mother will compliment you behind your back.

"She's a little heavy in the hips, though. Pretty enough, but not *too* pretty," she continues. "That's important. Catherine, you'll forgive me for saying, was too pretty. Too pretty for you, too pretty for her own good."

"Mom, please, shush."

"What? A plain Jane will treat you better!" She's practically shouting now. "It's common knowledge, Calvin."

"I don't think I've ever had a Pecan Sandy before," I announce, carrying out a large green plastic plate shaped like a Christmas tree. "This was all I could find. Sorry." In fact, I did find the silver platter she was looking for. But it was too pretty! Ha!

Cal looks at me like we're both disappointed fans of the losing team. I wink at him.

I sit down and bite into a cookie. "They are well named."

"Is it the taste, or the grainy texture?" Cal says.

I make a face at him, try to make it look like I'm eating sand and also that I forgive him.

"Well, as long as you're here, I'll tell you," Vivian says with a sigh as she reaches for a Sandy. "Marie over in four fifteen had a stroke, and they moved her down to the first floor. She's a young one, too. Seventy-nine."

"I'm sorry," I say. "Is she a friend of yours?"

"That's not the point, is it?" Vivian snaps. "And no."

It goes on like this for a while; hours, possibly, although

according to the clock only twenty-three minutes. Addie Warner in 445 took a fall the other day and did not report it to the nurses, can you imagine? Was it really a Mennonite holiday last week, or were Mr. and Mrs. Messerschmitt across the hall angling for special treatment from the staff?

Finally Cal stands up. "Mom, thanks for the visit, and I'm glad you're okay," he says. "I will see you on Saturday. I have to go now." For an awful moment I think he's leaving me here. Then, for the second time today, he reaches for my hand, pulls me up. "Isabel and I have something arranged for this afternoon."

Mrs. Abbott looks up at her son. Her face is as open and vulnerable as a baby's, her pale lips slightly open, her eyes bereft. *Don't leave me, don't leave me.* She might as well be saying it out loud; her gaze is so naked and pleading that I have to look away. All I want right now is to leave this too-warm apartment, this old woman who has nothing to do with me, her sour, calcified, aching need. My hand is in Cal's as if it belongs there. I am the opposite magnet pulling him away, going, going.

"I'll be back on Saturday," Cal says again.

Vivian Abbott's expression hardens. Still sitting in her blue armchair, she runs a bony hand down her pants, swooshes off cookie crumbs, pats down her hair. "Well. Fine. Knock before you come in," she says. "And next time wait for an answer."

Nine

I didn't think of them as babies. They weren't. They were pieces of me, though: secrets, sweet hazy dreams, the thrumming anticipation of surprises. I guarded them tenderly, selfishly, and so when they were gone I grieved them like amputations, silent deaths, down, down, deep at the center of me.

After two of them, we got Hannah, warm and fat and loud, throbbing with life, oblivious to its alternative, but then, a couple years later, another one lost, and then another one almost two years ago, and by the end of it, for sure, a part of me was broken, just shattered, gone.

When I called my mother after the last one, she said, "I always hoped that maybe, after everything that happened, we would be spared."

"Ridiculous," I said, sobbing. "Say something useful. Make me feel better."

"I wish I could," she said.

Chris held me and said, "We can try again . . . if you want to," and that was sort of helpful, but I felt almost as sorry for him as I did for myself, at least partly because procreational sex with an anxious, grieving woman is a pretty dismal affair. There are frequently, for example, tears, and I don't know for sure, but I don't think you can mistake those little half-suppressed sobs for moans of pleasure no matter how badly you want to.

Mark said, "Oh, man. Oh, wow. I'm so sorry, Iz. I'm really sorry." There was a long pause, and then, "Here, let me go get Josie. Here, here she is. Here's Jose." And that was helpful, because he got Josie.

Josie said, "I'll get you drunk," and that was the most helpful of all.

We met at Heinrich von Raaschke's. It was Oktoberfest. For some reason we thought this would be a good idea. It was unseasonably warm, and you could sit outside in the Bierhaus's biergarten, which was cozy and strung with lights and smelled like apple cider.

"I love the way everything's a *garten* in German," I said, pulling my chair out and sitting down. "Biergarten, kindergarten."

"I think the two should be combined," Josie said, "into a kindergarten where beer is served."

"Or a beer garden where children are served."

"You mean like children are served alcohol," Josie said, "or children are served as food?"

"Food."

"Yes." She unfolded her napkin and glanced around for the waitress. "Everyone knows five-year-olds make the tenderest cuts of meat."

"Their little thighs and their butts," I said, thinking of Hannah, who was already in fifth grade. And then, without warning, I started to tear up.

"Oh," Josie said. "Oh, Izzy."

I squared my shoulders and waved away her sympathy. "It's all right," I said. "I'm just crying because when you eat a five-year-old, the portions are so small."

Josie nodded. "And it's like, do you order two, or do you just order one ten-year-old?"

I blew my nose in my napkin. Noises rose up from the people around us—boisterous laughter, glasses clinking, silverware scraping. "I'm so sad," I said.

"I know."

This was the thing about Josie and me, how we understood each other: goofy jokes skating on the surface and the truth of what lay underneath, the complicated architecture of it all. It was how we loved each other.

"Goddamn," she said. "Where is Katie?" She was our favorite waitress. And we had been coming here for so long that we not only knew the servers, we knew which sections of the restaurant they worked. When the biergarten was open, Katie had the back half, Leni the front.

"Here I am, ladies!" Katie waddled up to our table. It had been a while since our last visit: she was hugely pregnant.

"Oh, my God," Josie said.

Katie laughed and crossed her arms over her chest. "I guess I haven't seen you two in a few months. But don't worry, I won't go into labor until after I bring you your drinks." She paused for dramatic effect, then leaned down conspiratorially. "I'm actually only six months along. It's twins!"

"Congratulations," I said, and smiled like my face was being pulled apart. I'd been through this before. After my first miscarriage, I saw a pregnant woman sitting on a bench eating a sandwich, and I burst into tears. After that, except for work, I didn't leave my house for a week. But you can't live that way. So I taught myself how to fake it—smile, smile, smile—and it turned out not to be that hard. Practice makes perfect.

"Don't you already *have* two kids?" Josie asked, aghast, and I loved her.

"Yep, sure do." Katie rolled her eyes. "Fertile Myrtle, that's me."

I swiped at my face with my napkin and looked away.

Josie stood up then and swooped around to my side of the table so fast the silverware rattled. "Oh, my God, I'm so sorry! I just realized I forgot something at home. I forgot my, um, my stuff . . . that I need. We have to leave! Is that okay with you, Iz? Do you mind? Can we go? I'm sorry, Katie." I nodded and stood, ready to bolt.

Katie was already calmly clearing our water glasses. "Oh, gosh, don't worry about it," she said, a little distracted, holding the glasses with plump, swollen fingers, efficiently moving on to her next table, because this was her job, and no matter how much she liked us, paying customers were the ones who tipped. "Come back soon!" she called. She blew a stray hair away from her face. "Come back before these darn babies are born!"

I walked quickly, ahead of Josie, through the biergarten and around the building to the parking lot, where our cars were parked next to each other. The early October evening was humid, almost tropical; in a couple of weeks, the autumn cold would move in, icy and dank, and these last warm gasps would be a memory.

Josie steadied me with both hands on my shoulders and stared at my face like a lover. "Crap on a cracker," she said.

"It's fine," I said. "I'm fine."

"That pregnant bitch," she whispered.

"I know! So rude, how she flaunts it."

"Let's go for a drive," she said. "My car."

Josie was always good at navigating, compensating for my innate directional inability. She drove everywhere, unless we didn't care if we got lost. The compromise, though, was that she got to make the rules. "Where should we go?" she asked, and turned left out of the parking lot without waiting for me to answer.

"Why don't we go to the maternity ward at St. Luke's and admire some newborns," I said. "Or let's see what's going on at the Mommy and Me class at Gymboree."

"Hmmm," Josie said, pretending to consider my suggestions. "No. Let's do something illegal!" She slapped her palm on the steering wheel.

I turned to her. My whole life, anytime anyone suggested doing something even slightly dangerous—going for a ride on the back of a motorcycle, swimming in a lake with no lifeguard on duty, taking a particularly large bite of something—I would hear my mother's voice: *You're my life.* Helene staked her claim against the risk takers, the gamblers, the brave. *We don't do that,* she would say. *Please never do that.*

And then came Hannah, and I understood. I was so risk averse when she was a baby that some days just crossing the street with her in my arms seemed fraught with peril. "Jose, you know I don't—"

"I'm kidding, I'm kidding," Josie said. "I know you don't. And I know where I'm taking you."

She drove through downtown, veering east along mostly deserted streets that were familiar but nevertheless confounding to me. I relaxed against the back of the seat and let her drive. An empty plastic cup rolled around on the floor at my feet. Josie's car was the manifestation of her id: a familiar mix of candy-bar wrappers and packs of spearmint gum and empty Diet Pepsi cans and napkins, a few stray student papers, and a medium-sized purple stuffed mouse and a small stack of art magazines in the backseat. It smelled like her, coconut shampoo and vanilla oil, sugary, a little burned. I had been with her when she bought this car, years earlier, almost new. The end of it was just a few months away.

We drove for about twenty minutes in relative silence, the kind of peaceful quiet you don't really note as unusual until it's pointed out to you—how rare and peculiar it is to feel comfortably alone without being alone. I thought about Hannah, home with Chris. It was nine o'clock. She was almost eleven years old, but she still liked to fall asleep in our bed, and then, hours later, one of us would carry her to her own bed. Sometimes she would wake up just enough to mutter something—*Mom* or *Thirsty* or *Where's Clucky?*—but mostly she would just stay asleep, slumped over and heavy on Chris's shoulder or mine.

By the time I focused on where we were going, we were there.

She had taken me through the city and out of it, into the dark heart of the suburbs. We were coasting down one of the beachfront lanes in Porcupine Bluff, a wealthy enclave. This was a private road; NO TRESPASSING signs were posted all the way down the dark hill toward the lake. We *were* doing something illegal! She parked on a little promontory overlooking the water, sandwiched between another NO TRESPASSING sign and a NO PARKING one.

"Jose!" I said.

"Come on, you love it here."

I did. We'd been coming here for years, although less often recently. Technically, you could get ticketed just for being here, but the suburban police force was an inconsistent entity. Some nights they would be out in force, lights flashing, sirens blipping, power mad and bored, with nothing better to do than order a couple of giggling women off the rocks. Other nights you could roam the wild, dark, deserted beach and feel like you were somewhere else completely—the rocky coast of Maine, or Mars.

We got out of the car and scrambled down the gradual slope to the sand. Once we were underneath the rocky outcrop, there was a little stretch of sand where we were invisible to anyone walking or driving by on the road above. Other people must have known about this spot, and the NO TRESPASSING signs seemed like they would be catnip to teenagers. But this beach was rare and untouched, the sand blown smooth and perfect. We'd never seen anyone down here besides the occasional jogger or dog walker.

Josie stood a few feet from me, staring out at the calm water. "How can this be private property?" she said. "How can twenty or thirty suburban homeowners claim this beach? Is Lake Michigan theirs, too?" She spread her skinny arms out wide as if she were reclaiming the land for all of humanity.

I shrugged. The moon was tiny and dim behind hazy clouds. The night sky, muted by those clouds, was a dirty shade of pewter. The waves thwapped against the shore, water and earth perennially fading into each other.

"We should take the kids on a field trip here," Josie went on, riling herself up. "Oh, my God, Iz. How about that? An illegal field trip!"

It was hard to know when she was kidding about a thing like this. The Claire Whitley incident at Lake Kass was long past. Josie never wanted to talk about it—not once—and so, eventually, I had stopped trying. But it had peeled away a fine layer of her, and what was underneath was a little strange and raw. Three or four of my students had come to me just since the start of the school year with reports of Josie's off-the-wall comments. "Don't listen to every single thing your parents tell you," she had said a few times, and, "Learn it for the test, you guys, and then go ahead and forget it. You will never need to know the history of the cotton gin."

"I think that's a fine idea," I said. "Maybe we could take them to a bar after, and buy them cigarettes and condoms."

She laughed, an appreciative little *heh,* and shoved her hands into the pockets of her jeans.

I slipped off my shoes and walked to the edge of the lake. Josie followed. The freezing water lapped up onto our feet. Josie yelped and jumped back, but I liked the shock of it, the icy pain and then the bone ache, the way it pinned your focus. I moved back only when I couldn't stand it anymore. And then we stood there, just quiet again in the soft darkness, for a few minutes.

"No more babies for me," I said. I hadn't even known I was thinking it until the words came out of my mouth. But I heard the truth of them—that it didn't matter if Chris and I tried or didn't, if I kept on wanting or just stopped, raged against the unfairness of the universe or managed to find peace. This was finally the end of it. I felt a wave of sadness rise in me, flood my lungs, and I squeezed my eyes shut to it. I let it have me. I was done.

"Hannah . . . is spectacular," Josie said.

"I know it," I said. I wasn't even thinking about Hannah. I was thinking about how I had been pregnant four days ago. A Monday. I was thinking about how you could wake up in the morning in one place and then go to sleep that same night somewhere else. It was like traveling to another continent.

"Do you want to know something?" Josie said.

"Hmm?"

"It has nothing to do with this. Is that okay?"

"Yes, please."

It was windy this close to the water but still warm, wetly cloying and a little fishy. It felt like we were being breathed on by an enormous dog. Josie pulled an elastic band from her pocket and gathered her hair into it. "I'm not telling you this so you can fix it, or to distract you from what you're going through." She looked at me. I nodded. "This is just something I've wanted to say for a while. Okay?"

With her hair pulled back, her face looked small, childlike. I nodded again. Was Josie going to tell me she was pregnant? She and Mark had never wanted children, but these things happened. Was this what she had to confess? I wrapped my arms around myself, my lonely body. Smile, smile, smile.

"Sometimes I think . . . sometimes I feel pretty sure that Mark and I aren't going to stay together." She spoke quickly, then bent and picked up a small stone and chucked it into the water.

I thought, *What?* and, on its heels, *Oh, of course.* Miscarriage, mismarriage. Nothing stays. I released a breath I hadn't realized I was holding. "I don't get it," I said.

"It's not that I don't love him. I mean, of course I do. Of course I love Mark. Who doesn't love Mark? But sometimes I feel like I'm not meant to stay married to him." Josie started walking, still barefoot, down the shore. I fell in next to her. "I don't even know," she said. She hadn't rolled up her jeans against the water, and the bottoms were wet, indigo. "There's nothing keeping us together, you know, the way you and Chris have Hannah. And some mornings I wake up and he's still sleeping, and he's snoring, or whatever . . . I can smell his breath, or his hair is greasy, or he rolls over and farts in his sleep." She laughed, shuddered. "It's all so disgusting! People! Are so disgusting! I know it's not just him. But I think, I don't want to be a *witness* to this, you know? I don't want to spend my days next to someone just . . . charting the decay."

"Wow," I said. "Tell me how you really feel." We were nearing the end of the beachfront before it angled up sharply to the road, where we would turn back.

"I know. It's just . . . do you remember Teachers' Convention last fall?"

She knew I did. Teachers' Convention was the highlight of our year. A few weeks into every fall semester, we went to Madison for two long days of keynotes and focus groups and breakout sessions about everything from how to teach math to girls and how to keep at-risk boys from dropping out of high school to Integrating Drumming into the Teaching of Algebra and Curses, Cursive! and Grammar: Whom Needs It? Some of it was interesting, even enjoyable . . . but that wasn't why we attended Teachers' Convention. We went for the nights.

When I was growing up, I figured that my teachers existed solely to expand our young minds. Maybe they had interests outside of school—spouses or families or, more likely, cats—but if they had lives, they lived them, I presumed, in a minor key. Their nonschool hours were just filler, a place to sleep and maybe a microwaved meal for one until they—dedicated altruists, all of them—could bound back into the classroom where they truly belonged. If you'd shown me photos of Teachers' Convention when I was a kid, I would have gone hysterically blind.

Those two nights in October were an orgy of raucous complaining and drunken revelry, foul-mouthed ranting, sloppy flirting, and hilarious, alcohol-fueled gossip marathons. Transgressive desires that lay dormant during the school year surfaced during those two nights. For the unattached or the ethically unbothered, those desires were made literal, although the women outnumbered the men, so there was an extra buzzy, competitive edge to it. Teachers' Convention was a massive steam-vent, a wild party, and we giggled over the memories of it until June.

"Do you remember that social studies teacher we hung out with?" Josie continued. "Alex Cortez?"

Midmorning on the first day of the convention, Josie had gone to a session on current events, while I debated the finer points of close literary analysis with six elderly fussbudgets, three of whom sported what we called the Wisconsin perm. I'd come out flushed with a clearer understanding of how the Brontës used weather, and Josie had come out with Alex.

We all had falafels together on State Street. I accidentally dropped one on the sidewalk. Alex was a handsome, married high-school social studies teacher from Middleton whose wife was an environmental lawyer specializing in lawsuits against windmills, and until this moment on the beach, that was the last time I'd thought about him.

"Well, we struck up a sort of . . . friendship," Josie said, a little dreamily. "An e-mail thing, just back and forth, the two of us. A lot of back and forth. A lot."

We were standing at the edge of the beach now. The wind was picking up a little, blowing away the night clouds. Solid darkness had settled in. The moon was higher and fatter. Josie was barreling through this confession. I knew not to interrupt.

"We kissed once. And believe me, I feel terrible about that! But it was just a kiss. That's all. It was nothing." She looked down. Her lips twitched in a secret little smile she could barely contain. She was lying. "We talk about everything, though. That's what's amazing. Lori—his wife—was pregnant when we met, remember?" I didn't. "And they were thinking about moving to Madison, they were tossing the idea around, and Alex was really decisive about it. One day they were thinking about moving, and then, a few weeks later, they moved. I mean, can you imagine Mark doing that? First he'd have to spend two months making a flowchart of all the pros and cons of moving. Then he'd have to spend another month researching moving companies." Right before my eyes, Josie was molding Mark's talents and quirks, the imperfections and habits that made him Mark, into her own unappealing little sculpture. It was like I was watching her work. "Well, I mean, nothing happened," she said again, to the lake. "But, Iz, I think something could. If we lived in the same city. If we let it. There's just this energy between us. Alex is so different from Mark. He's, like, bold and eager and straightforward. He's the anti-Mark." She looked at me, her eyes bright. "And he paints! In his spare time. Which of course he doesn't have that much of, since the baby was born. And he has two older girls, too, Maya and Elena, so his work's cut out for him! But he's a painter. An artist!"

I turned slightly away from Josie; I couldn't keep her gaze. I clasped my hands in front of me like I was praying. I had the unaccountable feeling that all the days of my life were like the pages of a book fluttering away from me in the breeze, that I was blank, without history.

Was this how easily the ties of a marriage could be loosened? I didn't adore Chris every day. I didn't! Sometimes I looked at him and saw nothing more than a random collection of disgusting habits and dirty socks. The way he slurped his cereal. The dry spit on the corners of his mouth when he woke up. How he cringed when I got angry or upset, as if all emotions aside from gentle amusement and mild annoyance scared him. Sometimes he was unfamiliar to me, alien, a strange choice made by someone who used to be me.

Josie rocked a little on her feet. "Would you say something, please? This is really embarrassing. I'm suddenly really embarrassed."

I had the thought that, if Josie and Mark split up, I would be one of those friends who took sides, who discarded one for the other. And I would take Mark's side. I would be a terribly loyal friend, I realized suddenly, to Mark. I squinted against the wind, against my rising fury. "This is so fucked up," I said to Josie, and then regretted it a little, but not completely.

She gasped. "Oh. Yeah, okay. I'm sorry, Iz. I'm sorry I said anything. I'm an idiot." She glanced at my belly, then quickly looked away and shook her head. Her ponytail bounced like a cheerleader's. "I'm really sorry." Her voice was small and sad. "My timing sucks." She jammed her hands into her pockets again and started walking. "We should get going, huh? Let's go."

I waited for a few seconds, let her move several paces ahead of me. It didn't take us long to get to the other end of the beach, and we climbed back up the rocks, Josie ahead of me, quick as a goat. I had to concentrate hard on the slight, uneven incline, stepping from stone to stone, wobbling a little, righting myself. My body was off-balance, just like after my first three miscarriages, my center of gravity realigning. Josie waited for me at the car. I was out of breath. She wasn't.

"I wish we could forget this ever happened," Josie said to me over the top of the car.

Just before I opened the door, I scanned the dark street, half hoping to see a police car's flashing light, to hear its siren revving up. I was wishing for a dramatic end to this, but there was nothing. It was just us and the warm, black, empty night.

· · ·

My mother picks a bit of fluff off of her scarf and adjusts herself in her chair. A weak, liquid March light seeps in through a wall of windows. From somewhere nearby, there is the sighing, rhythmic shush of an oxygen machine. We're in the kind of waiting room that stops time.

Behind the desk, two receptionists, both wearing pink sweaters, are speaking into their headphones. "Does it itch?" one of them says. "Tuesday, Tuesday," the other says. It reminds me of an assignment I give my fifth-grade students every year, where they have to write poems from bits of overheard conversation.

Helene looks around and sighs, then plucks a yellow foam ball out of her purse and begins squeezing it rhythmically, like she's been taught but rarely does. Printed on the ball in jaunty, bright red type are the words SQUEEZE ME FOR STRENGTH! With her good hand, she reaches up and touches her hair.

She looks around the open-plan room, the rose-colored chairs clustered in little groups to give the illusion of cozy sociability. "I've spent too much time in waiting rooms."

I called in for a substitute so I could keep her company at this appointment, where she will find out how much more of her strength is likely to come back after the stroke. These last couple of months her progress has slowed, like a train coming to a halt. She drags her right foot still, especially when she's tired, and her right hand is so weak she can't open a quart of milk. At her last few appointments Dr. Petrova has started saying things like "Yes, but under the circumstances" and "Well, all things considered," little linguistic inoculations against further hope.

"Isabel," Helene says. "Thank you for coming with me today. I know you had to give up a personal day." She picks up a magazine from the side table, then puts it down. "Then again, I gave up my youth for you."

"Oh, Mom. Doctors' appointments always make you so sentimental."

"You're all right," she says. "But do you know who I really love? Hannah."

"I know."

"Why are you keeping her from me?"

We had, of course, come over for dinner two nights ago. And the two of them had gone to a movie together last weekend. "I'm punishing you for things you did to me when I was a kid that neither of us remembers."

She smiles and takes my hand, then presses the squeeze-me ball into my palm. "This damn thing," she says, "is just an attempt to keep me from dwelling on my troubles."

"What troubles?" I ask, thinking we're still just joking around, trying to make each other smile here in the hushed waiting room of the hospital—the architectural equivalent of a clenched stomach. I'm a little distracted, thinking about Cal, the visit with his mother, and everything that came after. I feel a blush rise to my cheeks and hope my mother doesn't notice.

"That I won't regain any more strength. That I'll be limited for the rest of my life. That I'll always need help. Your help." She shakes her head. Her hair is sprayed hard, the way she likes it. She's wearing a turquoise scarf knotted around her neck, little gold hoop earrings, and a long, soft, camel-colored sweater with small shoulder pads and pockets. She looks like she's ready for a ladies' luncheon in 1985. "That I'm at a steeply increased risk for a second stroke. That it will happen some night when I'm alone, and it will be so much worse than this one, and I won't be able to call for help."

I stare at her, speechless. Sometimes I just want to crawl into the lap of the person who has loved me the longest and the best—and how is it possible that this is the same person who is looking at me now as if I'm the only one who can save her?

The other day on my way out the door I caught a glimpse of myself in the hall mirror: heavy-lidded brown eyes and thick, slightly uneven eyebrows in desperate need of grooming; long, inelegant nose and lips that curve up at the ends; wavy, uncooperative dark hair with strands of gray shooting up at the crown like popped wires in a burned-out lightbulb, and I had the strange and fleeting feeling that in that moment I was both Hannah and myself: I was staring at the face Hannah sees when she needs her mother. This was the face that came to her when she had to get a signature on a permission slip or when she wanted a grilled cheese sandwich, when she hated me or woke up from a bad dream or wanted to know if she could use the microwave, when she missed me in the middle of the day at school and no one else would do. And even after twelve years, the idea that I am someone's mother stunned me.

"Mom," I say now, without really thinking, "why don't you move in with us?"

"Oh!" she says. "Oh, no. I don't think so, sweetie. Thank you. No."

"Why not?"

A man zooms by in an electric wheelchair. A woman wearing lavender scrubs gets out of the elevator, singing to herself. My mother doesn't say anything for a while, and then, "Do you remember Bob Feldman?"

"Of course." He was one of the dermatologists she used to work for; my own indulgent employer, briefly, fifteen years ago.

"He had another heart attack last week. Joanne from the office called to tell me about it."

"Oh, wow. Is he okay?" I'm still, for no reason, squeezing the yellow ball my mother gave me.

"I don't know." She picks up the same magazine from the side table and flips through it. "He might be, he might not be." She raises one eyebrow at me meaningfully. "He moved in with his daughter six months ago, and now he's practically dead."

"But I still don't . . ." I stop myself. The hazy, diffuse morning sunlight is still trying to make its way through the windows, but it's losing the battle to the fluorescent lights. Helene rummages through her handbag. A snoozing woman a few seats away gives a little snort and wakes up; the woman next to her touches her arm.

"I'm starving," Helene says. "Do you want a granola bar?"

"Not really."

A nurse comes out of the office and stands in the arched doorway of the waiting area, holding a clipboard. She looks up. "Mrs. Kaczmarek? Grace Kaczmarek?"

"That's not us," my mother says, as if I'd thought maybe it was. She hands me a little package. "There are two bars in here," she says. "Open it up for me and we'll share."

I take the package from her and tear open the foil, hand her one. And I bite into mine, forgetting, for a second, that I'm not even hungry.

Yesterday, after Cal and I left his mother's apartment, we got back into his car. The slam of the doors echoed like a clap of thunder in the cavernous parking structure. "I was going to take you bird-watching," he said. His voice was a little gloomy and defeated. It didn't match the kind, optimistic man who'd pulled into this parking spot an hour before.

I had the briefest flash that maybe Cal was a serial killer, although if that was the case he was a mellow, nonthreatening one, the sort who introduces you to his elderly, racist mother before offing you. The kind-eyed, gentle type. Still, how well did I know him?

"Bird-watching!" I said, studying his face for signs of evil.

"Remember? That shirt you were wearing, and you told me about the baby birds . . ."

"I've never been," I said.

"I have," he said. "But not for many years. So I thought . . ." He leaned across me and went for the glove compartment. He had a nice smell, a little gingery.

"Are you going to kill me?"

"What?" He opened the glove compartment.

"Oh, phew!" I said.

He looked at me. He was holding a pair of binoculars by its string.

"I thought maybe you were a serial killer," I said.

"You're a strange lady." He held the binoculars up to his face and looked at me through them. "Even stranger close up."

I reached over and covered the lenses with my hand. "So . . . your mom's nice," I said.

Cal laughed. "I'm really sorry. For what it's worth, she's had a hard life. My dad died when I was seven. And my sister, Mary Claire, has had kind of a rough go of it, so that's been very hard on my mother, too. . . ." He trailed off.

"Did she remarry?"

"Nope."

"She still wears her wedding ring." I had noticed it, back in her apartment, a small diamond set in a thin gold band, sliding around on Vivian's bony finger.

"Yep."

"All this time?"

"She's hard-core. She's taught me a lot about grit. And loyalty. And she won't be around for much longer, so . . ." He studied the binoculars. "And yet she makes me feel like garbage."

"I hope Hannah says that about me someday."

And there was that laugh again. I thought, *I would not get tired of that laugh,* and then I blushed, even though I had only thought it.

"Anyway, Isabel Moore," he said, his voice regaining a little tug of hope. "Are you in the mood for a drive?" He pulled a little paperback from the pocket of his car door and held it up for me. *A Birder's Guide to Southeastern Wisconsin.* The receipt was sticking out of the middle of the book like a floppy, waving hand, and my face went warm, there in Cal's chilly Prius, at the understanding: that he had bought the book for us, for our afternoon, for this date.

. . .

Chris and I went out for the first time on the Fourth of July (which, in retrospect, may have confused my susceptible heart—fireworks on a first date!). He called me early, told me not to have dinner, that he was packing a picnic for us. I was so nervous, I didn't eat all day. But Chris was twenty-seven, still just a boy, his psyche not yet forged in the fires of other people's needs, and so our picnic consisted of a bunch of grapes, a large wedge of Swiss cheese, and two bottles of wine. I guess he thought it would be romantic. I was starving by the time we got to the park and spread out our blanket, practically feral with hunger. About five minutes after I'd wolfed down all of the grapes and half of the cheese and guzzled two paper cups of red wine, my stomach started groaning and gurgling in painful protest. It was an excruciating drive home. Traffic was bad.

I made Chris wait in the hallway outside my apartment. I was mortified. I decided I would never see him again, just to spare myself further humiliation.

"I feel like we know each other really well now," he said later, still smiling. We were in my tiny kitchen. He slipped a piece of bread into my toaster and made me a cup of tea. I had the first inkling of his generous soul, of the way he would try, in our years together, to gentle me out of myself. That night he kissed me in the kitchen, and I am not lying when I say that we could hear the pop of fireworks from where we stood, distant but unmistakable.

. . .

"So, what do you think?" Cal said.

I nodded. "A drive would be nice." I had the strange, discon-nected feeling of Chris falling away from me, of my husband, still my husband, floating in space, bright light and color, beyond my grasp.

. . .

Cal entertained me with bird facts on the drive—*Guess which birds have the biggest brains relative to their bodies? Crows. There are between one and two billion birds in the world. The chicken is the clos-est living relative to the Tyrannosaurus rex.* He was so delighted with himself, I couldn't help but get caught up in it.

"Guess what a group of chickens is called?" he asked.

"I do not know."

"Go on," he said. "Guess."

"A bucket?"

"A peep!" He grinned at me, then set his eyes back on the road, careful.

We were already there by the time I realized where we were going: the perennial plight of the directionally impaired. We pulled into the gravel lot and I looked around, and the famil-iarity of the place felt at first like an unpleasant memory, the creeping, disorienting sense that something is wrong before you know what it is. The Lake Kass Science Learning and Exploring Center building was a brown shack to our left, the trail that led to the lake on our right.

"Oh!" I said.

"Here we are!"

I swallowed the fully formed lump in my throat and got out of the car. Yesterday's unusual warmth had been blown off by a crisp wind, and it felt like early spring in Wisconsin was sup-posed to feel: brisk and sharp, just inching past winter.

"Have you ever been here?" he asked. "It's so close to the city, but it feels like you're miles and miles away."

"I, uh . . ." It seemed like the entire weight of our bright, shiny, brand-new gem of a relationship rested on my answer. "Maybe once."

Cal led me across the parking area to the trail, still brown and patchy from the winter, then down a gradual slope to where marsh grass edged the lake. It was like stepping back into a photograph. Even the light was the same, bright and clear. The air smelled wet, muddy, alive.

We strolled along the lake for a few minutes. Tiny waves splished against the shore. A school of minnows darted beneath the surface. It was the kind of lake that lulled you into forgetting about the treachery of water.

I remembered Kyle Gilson falling in, how he flailed in the shallow water, the drama of it. *Oh, my God, he's going to die!* We still thought, back then, that our lives would unfold in a series of close calls and funny anecdotes.

Cal paused, craned his neck. He pressed the binoculars up to his eyes. He was wearing a light blue windbreaker that flapped like a flag in the breeze. "I haven't seen a single bird," he said. "Has something dire happened? Did we miss the apocalypse?"

Just then a large Canada goose flapped above us, a fat flying bowling pin, then dipped low and plopped into the water. "It's the goose of doom!" I said.

He handed me the binoculars. I hung them by their string around my neck. He moved, almost imperceptibly, closer to me. His arm brushed against mine. "I like you, Isabel. I'd like to get to know you."

What should I have told him, there on the shore of Lake Kass on a chilly spring afternoon? That I still sometimes slept with my not-exactly-ex-husband? That I may have been partly responsible for the death of my best friend? That I grieved: hopelessly, constantly, fruitlessly, passionately? It seemed like the most important parts of me were also the worst.

I stopped walking and touched Cal's arm, turned so that I was facing him. We were practically the same height. Cal Abbott is not a tall man. It annoyed me, briefly, that a fifty-nine-year-old man could look as handsome as he did, as appealing. He reminded me of a retired tennis pro, or a just-past-his-prime James Bond. If I were a forty-three-year-old man and Cal were a fifty-nine-year-old woman, I'd have my hand on her arm just to make sure she didn't stumble. But here I was, admiring Cal's face in an entirely nonsolicitous way.

He had an amused little smile on that face, the same one from the first night in my mother's living room, like he knew what I was up to. But he didn't know anything about me. I was not a girl who made the first move. The first boy who kissed me became my boyfriend for two years. The fourth boy who kissed me became my husband. I leaned toward Cal, tipped my face to his. He put his arms around me lightly.

The kiss was easy, like we'd been married for twenty years, and also new, because it was new, Cal's unfamiliar lips, the skin and bones of a face I hadn't touched before. I put my cool hands on his cheeks. My fingers grazed the thin skin of his forehead. More than the kiss, I was moved by the strangeness of his face.

We separated. I let my arms drop to my sides. That smile crept up his face again. But it was less sure of itself.

My stomach dropped a little, and my heart thudded. Sometimes it was hard to tell the difference between thrill and panic.

"I brought my class here once," I said. "One of the kids fell in."

"I feel like I would have heard about that if it had had a tragic outcome." He motioned to the water, shallow and calm.

"You could drown in a bathtub!" I said. "But no, we rescued him."

"I used to take Michael here when he was little. We would camp over there." He pointed to the wooded area across the gravel road. "I always slept closest to the tent flap, in case Mikey got up in the middle of the night and wandered into the water."

"You and Michael, just the two of you?"

"And Catherine."

I shrugged and then, for no reason, laughed. Cal pulled me back into his arms and kissed me again, on the lips for a moment and then, unexpectedly, once on the cheek like a punctuation mark, and his face was still strange to me, but a little less so.

We walked around the lake for a while longer, then headed onto the wooden dock that stretched across the water. Something had been recalibrated between us: our bodies had been magnetized by the admission of desire. Cal held my hand loosely. Our feet clonked like little hooves on the wooden boards. The air was sharp and delicious in my lungs. It felt good to breathe, which was no small thing after so many months when it seemed like I couldn't take in enough air, like my lungs were sponges saturated with sadness. The afternoon had me feeling bold and exhilarated, in the same way that caffeine does—as if I were about to receive a phone call or an e-mail with excellent news. The memory of Josie floated near me, as it often did, but it was cleaner than usual, somehow, less punishing. I had a friend, and she died.

A pair of black ducks paddled by. Cal squinted at them. "Mud hens."

"Mud hens," I said, a little giddily. "Mud hens! I thought they were North American flap-winged feather dusters!"

"What?" He cocked his head and gazed at me as if I were an overly articulate, troublesome five-year-old.

"Mud hens are not a real *thing,*" I said. I don't know why I thought Cal was fooling me with a fake bird name, but I was convinced of it. "Mud hens," I said again. "You made that up."

Cal's blue windbreaker made a little *flit-flit* sound as he raised his arm to shield his eyes from the sun reflecting on the water. He squinted at me in utter confusion, and I had the sudden and vertiginous feeling of being whisked far away from him on the current of my own foolishness.

"No," I said quickly. "I didn't mean—"

"How strange that you think I would make that up." He reached into his pocket and handed me the bird book with a little flourish. "Allow me to prove you wrong."

Page 47. There they were. Mud hens, cross-listed as the American coot, which, if I'd pointed it out to Cal, probably would have put the nail in this coffin.

"Welp," I said, handing the book back to him. "You're right. There they are."

We were a few feet down the dock, the water lapping against the wood. On the other side of the lake, a small group of people huddled by the edge, peering down at something. There were four of them, three tall and one short, all wearing bright spring jackets: a nylon bouquet of crimson, lime green, yellow, and magenta. The tallest one crouched down, put an arm around the little one, and pointed to the water. I couldn't make out their genders or their features or the relationships to one another. They were just a little cluster of humans investigating something. We hadn't come across any other people out here, either, I realized: just a goose, a mud hen, and those four people in the distance.

Cal leaned close to me and lifted the binoculars from around my neck. The intimacy of it surprised me: his fingers on the back of my neck, his warm breath. He raised the binoculars to his eyes and aimed his gaze across the lake. "A flock of Great Northern Suburbanites. Flightless, brightly marked."

He was trying—to repair a minor rip in the fabric? Or to bring the afternoon to a gentle and permanent conclusion? I had no idea. Maybe he was remembering what it had been like to be here with Catherine, twenty years ago, when he knew the woman he was with, and his family was whole.

The wind whipped up from nowhere, a sudden sharp gust. It was hard to breathe again, just like that. The tallest human across the lake, the one in the lime-green jacket, looked up suddenly and waved at us. I waved back.

"The last time I was here," I said, "my friend almost got one of our students killed. She . . . the little girl, Claire . . . she was deathly allergic to bees, and she got stung. My friend was the teacher in charge of the medication. She was supposed to have Claire's EpiPen with her at all times, but she forgot it on the bus." I couldn't say Josie's name. I was using her brazenly, betraying her again. I swallowed a thick lump of shame. She was my excuse for all of it.

"But she was all right?" Cal said.

I shrugged. "The little girl? Yeah. She was okay."

"The idea of being responsible for so many people." He blew a little puff of air. "Well, I always felt that I chose the right line of work, wrangling nucleotide chains rather than human beings." Cal worked for the university, doing research on type 1 diabetes. He didn't talk about it much, but I had Googled him, of course. He had won a big award a few years ago, and an NIH grant. "I like that my work is quantifiable," he went on. "That, at least in my lab, when it's just me and the DNA, I'm not at the mercy of anyone's emotions."

I nodded. Jim Ambrose, the sixth- and seventh-grade science teacher at Rhodes, was always saying things like that. He's rumored to have exclaimed once to a classroom full of stunned eleven-year-olds: "Your wife might cheat on you, but science will never let you down!" And at the staff holiday party a few years ago, he cornered me in the hallway as I was about to leave. "Poetry!" he scoffed. "Poetry won't cure cancer!"

The wind rippled the waves. I began to feel as if Cal and I would remain here forever, that this was my perilous, desolate fate: some minnows, a goose, an American coot; strangers waving to me from the other side. There seemed to be only one way out of the muck. "Could we . . . leave?" I said.

Cal nodded. "Where do you want to go?"

I pretended to think for a minute. "To your house?" I tried to pull off a confident grin, but my lips twitched.

A decade flew off of Cal's face. He caught his balance as the ground shifted, and he discovered that he was standing somewhere happy and unexpected. "Yes," he said. "Of course."

In what strange, postapocalyptic world was I propositioning a man? I knew that there were women who had sex without immediately pledging their undying devotion to their partners like delusional swans. There were women who could do this. Probably lots of women. I had never been one of them.

Sex tangled up my circuits, rewired me. For one month in college, I went to movies and restaurants and parties and bars with Chad Hansen, appreciating his quiet sense of humor, his big lumberjack body, the slow way he spoke, how his meaty paw dwarfed mine when he held my hand, his extensive knowledge of venison. I liked him, although he often told me that I reminded him of Woody Allen and once suggested that his boss at the bar he worked at was trying to Jew him down. We enjoyed each other's company (for the most part), but we were foreign-exchange students to each other, with an end date stamped on our relationship.

There was a band I liked coming to Madison in early January—Charm School—and I wanted to go with Chad. But after that, I was going to break up with him. I had rehearsed my speech. *We were meant to be temporary.* I knew that. I knew it until one bitter cold night in December when we slept together.

Really, when I think about it, it happened because it was so very cold out. His landlord was stingy with the heat, so we crawled into his bed to get warm, but it was early in the evening, not time to sleep yet. The sex was slow and sweet and lingering, and afterward we were both really much less cold.

After we had sex, he lay next to me and touched my face like a sculptor, with awe. I decided right then that I loved him, Chad from Waupakakee. I would get over our differences: the way he beeped me on the nose whenever he thought I was getting too serious, how he sometimes put on headphones while I was talking, how much he loved video games that involved shooting animals, how he told me, without my asking, which specific forms of exercise would target my trouble spots. But it made sense to me. That's what sex was: *making love.*

Ten months later, after a big fight ("Isabel, you don't always have to say every single thing you're thinking!"), Chad looked at me with his big, dopey blue eyes and said, "Iz, what are we *doing?*" And I woke up from my sex trance and thought, *Good God, I have no idea.*

So now, with Cal, I couldn't claim ignorance. I knew there would be a cost.

. . .

The drive back to Cal's house seemed to take half the time it took to get to Lake Kass, our nervous energy like a tailwind. Cal kept trying to make sure I was comfortable, turning the heat up, then down, then off, changing the music from opera to Bob Dylan to "Darkness on the Edge of Town." *Is this okay?* he would ask, before altering the environment again. *Better? Okay?* I had the fleeting and uncomfortable thought that I was seeing a preview of his moves in bed. He tipped the air vent toward me, then away, one hand on the wheel, and all of his jangly vigilance made it easier for me to pretend I was the calm one, the instigator, the believer that this was no big deal.

His house was a small bungalow on a street of small almost-identical bungalows. Most of them were white or gray, with the occasional light blue or green outlier. Some of the houses were slightly nicer, built with the special kind of light-colored brick that gave Milwaukee its nickname, Cream City. Josie used to elbow me whenever she spotted a particular type of attractive local guy, the kind you could tell had grown up here: beefy, pale, sometimes sporting a mustache, and never an ounce of fashion sense, but still strangely, undeniably sexy. *Cream City,* she would say, and I marveled at her ability to turn something so neutral into something so lewd.

Cal's house was one of the nicer ones, brick, neatly land-scaped, with freshly painted white trim. Its distinguishing feature was the bright orange mail slot set in the front door.

We walked up the front steps together, and he stood back as I walked in. We hadn't spoken for the last ten miles of the trip, both of us too nervous to keep the conversation going. We were two people who hardly knew each other about to reveal our flawed selves.

"Here we are," Cal announced.

"Here we are." I heard Hannah's voice in my head, her worldly disdain for the frailties and stupidities of adults: Here we are. *Duh.*

Cal stood behind me, laid his hand on the small of my back. The nerve endings in my body migrated to where his palm rested lightly, and all I felt was the pressure. If we did this, it would mark the path toward the end for Chris and me. It would be—I knew myself; I knew this—irreversible.

I had known this man for about a day. You could get carried away by passion when you were young, and the repercussions would come later. This was different, reasoned and careful. This was a repercussion appetizer.

His front door opened into a small entryway and from there directly into the living room. The room was neat as a pin, and a study in shades of green—forest-green rug on a hardwood floor, dark green pillows carefully arranged on a nubby, oatmeal-colored sofa; moss-green wool blanket folded over a leather armchair. The house had a faint, sweet smell to it, and I couldn't quite tell if it was fresh air or cleaning product.

Everything was at right angles in the room, all of the edges sharp, the corners crisp. It was a page from *Tidy Bachelors Monthly.* I looked around to try to find any details that might have indicated that a woman had been here anytime in the past several years. And then I realized that I had no idea what I was looking for. Between Chris and me, Chris was the one who had the eye, who knew which colors softened a sunlit corner, how to drape a blanket over the side of a sofa so that it looked like an inviting place to rest. When he moved out of the house, everything that had been easy and flowing stopped and petrified a little.

Cal led me into the kitchen, and we sat down across from each other at the small, square table. The last of the afternoon sunlight angled in through the windows, soft and pinkish. In his warm, dimming kitchen, I thought I saw, for a second, exactly who Cal was: the sorrows and joys of his past linked up and settled into his features, his lined eyes, his straight nose, his lips. He was, for that moment, ageless. And in that delusion there was, maybe, the faintest fluttering of something like love.

The kitchen was unsurprisingly neat, no dishes in the sink, just one lonely white mug in the drainer, and I decided that there hadn't been a woman here in a long time, if ever. My relief was followed quickly by suspicion. Why had there not been a woman here? What was wrong with this man? The small pantry behind him was half open, the only thing amiss in the whole house so far. Four boxes of pasta were lined up next to one another on the edge of the top shelf, a herd of rotini lemmings about to jump.

Cal clasped his hands together and rested them on the table, gazing at me, and I had the odd feeling of being in a job interview. *Thank you for considering me for this position. I'm a people person! My weakness is that I am too conscientious.*

"Would you like some wine?" he asked. "Or tea?" He looked around at his kitchen as if he were seeing it for the first time. "Actually, I don't have any tea," he said.

"I'll have tea."

He smiled, the lines around his eyes crinkling. "Isabel, if we're . . . well, this isn't how I normally . . . I don't really know how to do this."

"Neither do I," I said, and the air between us got a little lighter. He stood, walked behind me, and I felt the hair on the back of my neck stand up, but he just turned on the light and sat back down. I ran the palm of my hand over the blond wood of the table, smooth as butter.

He pulled his chair in and leaned toward me. "You are very beautiful."

"Shut the fuck up!" I said. And then I snorted.

Cal's eyebrows lifted in surprise. My whole body heated up like a convection oven, sudden and swift. I felt my cheeks go pink. Cal was a gentleman, a grown-up, and I was an idiot-child.

Helene was always telling me that I needed to learn how to accept compliments. A few weeks before Chris and I got married, she sat me down in her living room and made me practice:

You look gorgeous.

Thank you!

Your dress is so beautiful.

Oh, thank you!

You and Chris are perfect together.

Thanks, thanks, thank you so much.

It didn't stick.

Cal shook his head. "I'm sorry. I don't quite ..." He shrugged, helpless. We were worlds apart. And I had rendered him speechless.

I smoothed my hair, realized it had been several hours since I'd checked my face in a mirror. I licked my lips, which were a little chapped. "So, you really like pasta, huh?" I said.

"Ah ... pardon?"

I pointed to the cupboard behind him.

"Oh. Well, it's a staple." He looked at me, a little bit desperately, and shrugged. He leaned back in his chair, his body language putting more space between us. I held on to the edge of the table and willed myself to keep looking at Cal. "I'm sorry. I think I'm kind of free-falling here." I stood, finally. "I should probably go. I'm really sorry." The words were a spell; I was overcome, suddenly, with remorse.

Cal eased himself up from his chair with an athletic grace I hadn't noticed in him before. He moved toward me, and then he was standing next to me, close, and he put his hand on my shoulder, just his hand. And I leaned into him, and I wished he were Chris, and he pulled me into his arms, maybe wishing I were someone else, too—Catherine or someone just like her, and I didn't know for certain, but I was pretty sure I wasn't that woman.

The gingery smell of him was stronger here in his own house, like something spicy-sweet that he cooked often, that clung to him and became part of his own scent. His cheek was rough against mine. That was the thing I had always loved most about men, a face next to mine, and no matter how recently a man had shaved, there would always be a little friction.

Cal let go, and we stood facing each other. He laid his hand on the table, near mine. "It's okay," he said softly, with a sincerity that almost felled me. "It's okay if you want to go, but I would like it if you stayed."

Eleven

———

We stood in the fading light of his spotless kitchen. It seemed like everything important in my life happened in a kitchen, accompanied by the background music of a refrigerator's hum. Why wasn't I an astronaut or a mountain climber? No, this was my big moment, witnessed by a sink and a stove, a three-armed espresso machine and an expensive-looking blender and approximately fifteen cans of soup lined up neatly on a bottom shelf and all those boxes of pasta.

I was filled with such a baffling blend of sadness and desire that I could hardly stand, lust and loss pulsing through me like my own blood, like life.

We were so near to each other. When you're two inches from someone's face you can't just stay where you are. You either have to pull away or close the gap. And right up until I did it, I didn't know what I was going to do.

I had the clearest image of Chris and Annabelle, the veterinarian. He was peeling off her latex gloves, smiling at her, tugging the thin rubber off her fingers, one by one, and Annabelle, the veterinarian, the good-hearted lover of animals, comforter of puppies, curer of cats, smiled back, ready. I saw them in a bathroom, Chris gently removing her white coat, turning on the bathtub faucet. As soon as she came home from work she would need to step into the shower to get rid of the faint smell of antiseptic and animal fear that clung to her. I didn't know a thing about her. In my mind she had brown hair, brown eyes, milky skin. And there was Chris, his naked body next to hers in the shower now, hot water pouring down on both of them, and he wrapped his long arms around her compact, nip-waisted, naked, animal-loving body, and he was free of guilt, guilt-free, and I wanted that, right then, to be free of guilt also; somehow, impossibly, that's what I wanted.

Cal was wiry and muscular, but not the same kind of muscular as a young man, more comforting, attainable: a runner or a bicyclist, possibly, but still, fifty-nine, and probably as happy to spend a Sunday morning lounging around the house drinking coffee as to hop on the bikes and go for a long, vigorous ride.

He was waiting for my answer. Stay or go. A man like Cal would be done with you after so much teetering indecision, all of this too-early exposing of hurts and divided loyalties. *A game,* he would think. *I'm too old for games.*

. . .

Two weeks before Chris moved out, during a bleak and dirty February cold snap, we sat in the overheated office of Dr. Gwendolyn Grieco, finalizing the terms of our separation. Although I wouldn't admit it, there was still a part of me that thought that this was all an elaborate setup, a desperate long game Chris was playing to try to get me to come around, to fix myself, to change.

I went along with the arrangements. I had even gone with Chris the week before to DomestiCity to help him pick out plates and cups and silverware for his new apartment, as if we were registering for our wedding, only backward.

We strolled companionably through the aisles. A man pushing a cart rushed past us, a little boy wriggling in the child seat.

The man was on his phone, his cart stacked high with packages of diapers. "I am hurrying," he said. "I know, I know. Just wrap her in a towel or something."

Chris and I looked at each other and laughed. In a way, it felt like we were on a date. It felt like we were on the most romantic, high-stakes date ever. How far were we going to take this? Who was going to give in first?

He picked up a tightly folded fleece blanket and examined it. I looked around at the shelves of linens, plain and patterned, thread counts high and low, the infinite possibilities. I was almost jealous—that he was buying all these new things for his apartment, and I was stuck with our old green towels, linty with memories, our chipped blue cereal bowls, remnants from the ancient civilization of our marriage.

We wandered into the kitchen-goods aisle. I held up a white dinner plate with a border of little yellow flowers and green leaves. "Oh, I love this one," I said.

Chris stopped, pushed his hand through his light hair, exactly the same way Hannah does, pausing to think more clearly as if they're shaping their thoughts, hand to head. "We'll get through this, Iz," he said, there in the middle of Kitchen Furnishings. "I think we will. We just need to be in different spaces for a while, a little bit separate, a little air between us." He was quiet, calm. "And, worst-case scenario, if we can't . . . if we don't . . . we'll already have our own places."

I ignored him and continued filling his cart with water glasses and dishcloths and napkins. "You'll need this," I said, tossing a huge roll of paper towels into the cart. *And this, and this, and this.* It was unbelievable, a lark. Someone else's life.

But the evidence, like so many rolls of paper towels, was piling up around me. Chris signed the lease on the apartment. He called some friends, X-ed out moving day on the calendar. On that Monday in Dr. Gwendolyn Grieco's office, thirteen days before the move, I was finally, just barely, starting to believe it. But even then it still seemed more like a weird and painful part of our marriage—as if moving out were a precursor to moving back in, a thing we would reminisce about, years from now, with a kind of exhausted pride: it would be something we had survived.

Dr. Grieco was youngish, pretty, with olive skin and straight, reddish-brown hair and serious black glasses that were constantly slipping down her nose. She was vulpine, a little pointy faced and sharp, but this didn't take away from her attractiveness. She wore no makeup other than red lipstick, and I was pretty sure she was a little bit in love with Chris. She was always saying things like "You two must have been friends before you started dating. Surely, Chris, you chose Isabel from a cast of available characters" and "Chris, how do you deal with the inevitable attentions of other women?" And to me: "I can see that it's hard for you, Isabel, to be the less ... outgoing half of the couple."

"I feel like she's always angry at me," Chris said to Dr. Grieco. She jotted something down on her yellow pad and nodded encouragement. *Handsome man,* I imagined her writing, *articulating feelings!* His voice was infuriatingly measured and deliberate. He turned to me. "There's so much darkness in you, Iz. I don't know. I didn't see it before. Was it always there? Maybe we only worked as a couple when things were easy," he went on. "It started with the miscarriages, and then ... well, we just couldn't get through this. Josie died, and I tried to be there for you, but you pushed me away so hard...." He paused and rubbed his hands over his face like a much-older man. "We were supposed to weather the storms together, but we couldn't ... You're not who I thought you were."

Josie's death had torn off my skin, had exposed me, my muscles, my veins, my pounding, aching heart. So maybe I looked a little different these days, a little bloodier. But this was me. It always had been.

The dry heat in Dr. Grieco's office gave me the strange sense that I was outside my body, drifting somewhere a few feet away.

"Good, Chris!" Dr. Grieco said. She gazed at him tenderly. *Horrible woman,* I thought. My eyes fluttered closed, then snapped open. "Sometimes," she said, "in a marriage, it becomes clear that the couple you were when you first fell in love is not the couple you are today." She clipped her pen to her yellow pad and set them on her lap. "And the question is, do you come together and grow, as this new couple?" She held her hands together. "Or do you allow yourselves to move apart from each other?" She moved her hands apart to demonstrate, as if she were hosting an educational show for preschoolers.

I half expected Chris to raise his hand and yell, *Oo, I know, I know!* Move apart!

"I get it," he said, "that moving out is drastic. But maybe sometimes you have to amputate the limb to save the body."

Was I the limb, or the body? I heard a soft, growly noise, and realized it was coming from deep in my throat.

"Chris is moving out of the house," Dr. Grieco said, pushing her glasses up. Her nose was like a child's drawing of a nose, a small triangle in the middle of her face. No wonder her glasses wouldn't stay up. She pressed her lips together and looked at me sternly, and I wondered for a second if she could read my mind. "We've already talked about how this might affect Hannah," she said.

Hannah. That very morning she had stormed out of the bathroom, a human apocalypse, waving her toothbrush and screaming at me. "I need a new one! I need a new one *right now*! Yours was *touching mine*! I'm not using this one. It's *disgusting*!"

Dr. Grieco smoothed her brown skirt over her lap. "But it's also very important that you both understand what this means," she went on. "That you are stepping away from each other in a big way. But distance can also give us perspective."

I tilted my head at her. I felt muffled and gauzy, but at the same time hyperaware: the scritch of her pen on paper, the careful way she modulated her naturally high, reedy voice to make it sound lower, more serious. The hum of the old-fashioned electric clock on her wall. Chris's deep breaths. *This is the moment our marriage ended,* I thought, as if I were both present in this moment and also looking back on it from far off in the future. But then again, we were still connected, alive. Maybe that was the best you could say for any marriage. So who knew?

"The good news is," I said, "now I can finally embrace that decorating theme you hate. Nevada brothel."

There was a long moment of silence. "I don't hate it," Chris said, finally. "I just find the blinking red lights distracting."

Dr. Grieco nodded and furrowed her brow at the same time. "It's good that you're still able to find humor in this difficult situation. Mmm. Not everyone can."

Hell, we'd been joking about it for months. *You can have that ugly lamp if you move out. Please, please take those curtains. You can have Hannah! Ha-ha-ha.* It was the pinprick of light in our darkness. It was the trip to the circus the day before the world ended. It was another reason it had taken me so long to believe this.

Dr. Grieco smiled a vague, approving smile. She had no doubt done this before, ushered two people peaceably toward the finish line. She was good at it: calm, repetitive, reassuring. She would go home tonight, open up a bag of salad, turn on PBS, and not give us another thought. She fixed her gaze on me, then Chris, and then on her watch, in a practiced choreography.

"Looks like our time is up!" I said, before she had the chance to say it herself. I stood, seized by the desire to upend her expectations. Dr. Gwendolyn Grieco didn't know squat about distance or perspective. She didn't know anything about us. I turned to Chris. "Do you want to go get some dinner?"

He waited a beat, then smiled at me the way he used to, like I could surprise him, and not just in a crappy way. "Sure," he said. "Why not?"

. . .

The night before he moved out, I lay in bed and extended my right arm toward the middle of the mattress, feeling for him. He was asleep, rolled up into a ball on the edge of the mattress, like a potato bug. Against logic, we were still sleeping in the same bed. We had been so gentle with each other in the days since our appointment with Dr. Grieco, solicitous and hushed, like two very respectful roommates, one of whom was about to die. *There's no script for this,* he said to me more than once, as we surprised each other with kindness. *We're making our own rules.*

He stretched in his sleep and moved toward me. His leg brushed against mine. I could see him in the annoying glow of the streetlight right outside our window, the one that never allowed our room to go completely dark, even through the blinds. His fine, messy hair; his light eyelashes; his handsome features. He especially resembled Hannah in his sleep, all the tight worries of the day loosened from him, although never completely gone. His pale, familiar face.

"Why are we doing this?" I whispered, but his breathing was deep and even. Our separation was like a tumbleweed now, rolling along, unstoppable, gathering debris. My heart felt thunderous and shaky. I tried to calm myself, to match my breathing to his, but every time I thought I had the rhythm down, I lost it.

The furnace cycled off and created a kind of unexpected silence, where you didn't even realize that just seconds ago there had been noise. Chris mumbled something in his sleep and rolled again, his leg moving abruptly away from mine.

. . .

The morning Chris moved out, the actual morning, was February 14. When he realized what day it was, he sat down on a kitchen chair and covered his face with his hands.

"I'm sorry," he said quietly, his voice muffled by his fingers. Guilt came off of him like heat; he was radiating it. "It's Saturday," he said, which, of course, I knew. "It was the only day the guys could come," which I also knew. "I didn't realize."

"It's fine," I said. I was also sitting at the kitchen table, force-feeding myself cornflakes. I swallowed a mushy lump. "It's actually perfect."

He moved his hands away from his face, and I saw, before he turned away, that his eyes were wet, his face stricken, and I scooped up another soggy spoonful of my cereal and thought, *Good*.

The doorbell began ringing a few minutes later. Jack Halloran was first, one of the guys Chris played pick-up basketball with on Sunday mornings. He was a urologist who had cheated on his wife five years ago with a drug rep at a medical conference in Houston, and, although his wife, Michelle, never found out, he lived with his guilt by doting on her with an almost-psychotic focus. Gary Sanchez was next. He had three kids and worked with Chris at the DNR, and he confessed to Chris that although he loved his children, he frequently regretted having them. Then Dave Milkowski, another of Chris's work buddies, whose extensive history of juvenile shoplifting convictions had been expunged from his record when he turned eighteen. Then

Kurt Grunsmeyer, another basketball pal, a forty-one-year-old serial monogamist who referred to all of his ex-girlfriends as "crazy bitches." Finally Henry Tan, Chris's college roommate, about whom, a few years ago, Hannah had written the poem, "Henry Tan, the nicest man," which he was. Henry's rescue greyhound, Zola, peed all over our old living room rug when Henry and his wife were in the hospital having their twins, and Henry, instead of paying to have it cleaned, bought us a new, more beautiful rug.

They were men I knew well, men who had come over to our house countless times, in various configurations: with their wives, with their kids, for dinner or brunch, to watch basketball. They came over now, one by one, and each of these men, whose intimacies and vulnerabilities and mistakes I guarded, was a stranger to me.

"Uh, hey, Isabel," they said. "Hey." They stared at my feet as if my eyeballs had migrated there. "Hey, uh, so. You okay? Okay. Good. Okay."

They would help Chris lift some boxes and lug them out to the U-Haul and then up a flight of stairs to his new apartment; they would carry out a blue chair from our living room and the old futon from the basement and a bookshelf and, later that day, they'd drive with him to Wegman's DIY on the other side of town to pick up a kitchen table and a dining room table and a desk, and these men I'd known for so many years, they would be like the futon from the basement and the chair from our living room and the bookshelf: they would be Chris's now. And if Chris and I ever got back together? I probably wouldn't even want to see that furniture anymore.

I made blueberry muffins, because I didn't know what to do with myself, and because we had agreed that most things in the kitchen would stay, even though, in truth, Chris was the better cook, the one with the vision: I mostly just scrambled eggs or waited for water to boil.

I baked muffins while the men lugged boxes. And maybe a tiny part of me thought that the guys would see the muffins and stop in their tracks. *Oh, Isabel!* they would think. *What a dear, good person she is. Chris!* they would exclaim. *We cannot help you with this vain and foolish task!*

Not that Chris wouldn't move out. Just that Henry and Dave and Kurt and Jack and Gary wouldn't want to help him anymore, that they wouldn't be so *eager* to help him.

I set the muffins out on a plate on the dining room table, and in between trips, the guys ate them, still warm, and either they were too embarrassed to thank me, or they thought those muffins had just appeared there magically, courtesy of the muffin fairy.

Later that day, Valentine's Day, moving day, Chris called me from his apartment. He had been planning on coming back for one last box of books and some clothes, but Gary and Dave had been able to fit these things into Gary's minivan, and so, Chris said, there was no need for him to come back, and anyway he would see me the day after tomorrow, to pick up Hannah.

"It'll be okay," he said. I heard Kurt's deep, jovial voice in background, echoing through Chris's new apartment: "Where do you want this piece of shit?"

"Yup." I stood in the middle of the living room, which didn't look so much empty as confusingly rearranged, like one of those games in kids' magazines: how are these two pictures different? A shelf of books missing. A spot where the chair used to be. The couch where my friend would never sit. A certain quality to the air.

"Iz, it will be."

I breathed in, out. "Yeah," I said.

"Okay. Bye."

. . .

Cal stood, inches from me, his hand still resting lightly on the kitchen table next to mine. Everything added up to "stay." All these months, I had been learning the singular lesson that sadness was an infinite resource, accumulating like snow in winter. So why not stay, let a bit of it melt?

"I have to go."

Cal backed away. "All right. I'll take you home." And, yes, there it was, underneath the patience, underneath the truly kind exterior of this amused and tolerant human: the rumble of irritability, finally; the exasperation of another man who had had enough.

He walked over to the living room closet, handed me my jacket, helped me into it. "I'll just go grab my keys." He touched my arm, avuncular now, *pat-pat*.

He was someone who would have cushioned the landing. And yet here I was, jacket on. Sunlight streamed in through the windows. "This has been my favorite day since my husband moved out," I said, and a tragic little noise came out of me, a little hiccup-laugh.

"All right," Cal said. "It's all right." He took his keys from the hook. His hand was on my back now as he led me, ever so gently, toward the door.

Twelve

"Iz," Mark's e-mail said. "I still want to do it this year. Will you come?" It was early December. Josie had been dead for nine months.

"I know you and I haven't spoken in a while," he wrote. That was true. We hadn't talked since I'd stormed out of the Pig's Knees in September, after the Andi Friedman revelation. That was how I'd been talking about it to Chris, in those words—the Andi Friedman revelation—like it was the name of some mediocre jazz quartet. Mark had texted me a few times since then, but I never wrote back. Sometimes my righteous indignation was the only thing that got me through the day.

"I know it will be hard without her," his e-mail went on. "But I think Josie would have wanted us to celebrate."

"Bullshit," I typed quickly. "You're the last person who knows what Josie would have wanted. And how's your girl-friend, traitor?" Then I deleted those sentences. I wondered, as I had been wondering for months, how much Mark knew: if Josie had confessed to cheating on him, if he knew about Alex Cortez. "Okay," I wrote. "We'll be there."

Our yearly get-together had started out a decade ago as a path through the tangle of the holiday season. December is tricky for Jews and orphans. Josie's strategy was to employ a military level of productivity, methodically baking dozens of tree- and snowman-shaped sugar cookies while trumpet-heavy Christmas music blared continuously in her kitchen. Chris grew quiet and gloomy, the month of December his yearly descent into darkness, a longing for something he couldn't even name. Mark grumbled and snarked from the minute the Halloween decorations in the stores came down and the colored lights went up. For my part, I thought, *Let's just be together: Josie and Mark, Chris and Hannah and me. Like always.*

Chris and I had never bothered to discuss religion when we were dating. I assumed we'd celebrate all of the holidays with both of our families until we had kids, and then we'd raise them Jewish. It was, I thought, the obvious option when your mother's family had been decimated in Germany. Our team needed the numbers.

As it turned out, this was news to Chris. He had grown up steeping in a Christmas brew of passive-aggressive muttering and silent, seething disappointment, and he wanted a do-over. One year, he told me, his father gave his mother a four-pack of felt-tip pens and wrote on the card, "For the lady who has everything. Best regards, Edward," and his mother took to her bed for two days. Chris wanted, for Hannah, the warmth he had only seen on the Christmas specials—a heart that could grow three sizes, a scraggly Christmas tree made beautiful with a couple of ornaments and a blue blanket and love. Love. That was hard to argue with.

Then again, so was Helene, who, one Passover, as we were leaving her house, handed Chris a box of matzo and said, "You'll get used to it."

So we would get together in late December every year, just

the five of us. Mark and Josie always had a Christmas tree that Mark actively hated. He *delighted* in hating it. "Look," he would say to me, conspiratorially. "It's a goddamn pine tree, and it's *in our house!*" We'd light a menorah some years, if there was overlap. Mark always raised a glass and said, "Here's to the Jews, who put the *s* in 'Happy Holidays'!" We brought each other dramatically awful white elephant gifts: a little figurine of a praying angel; a creepy fish that wiggled its fins and sang "I'm dreaming of a white fishmas"; a sweater for our cat, Mrs. Reinhoffer, that said TEACHER'S PET on it. Mark and Josie doted on Hannah. Over time it came to be the thing we treasured, this little party.

And what would I bring to the festive gathering this year, the first since Josie's death? What would adequately represent the spirit of this holiday season? A bag of dog shit? A horse's head?

"We'll be there," I wrote. "Can't wait."

Mark was hosting it at his new apartment. His parents' house had sold quickly in October, and he'd moved into a big two-bedroom near the lake.

"I want you to know that Andi will be there," he wrote, right after I'd said yes. "Please don't back out. Please just come, Iz."

Andi answered the door before we even knocked. "I saw you from the window!" she said, wringing her hands. "*There they are,* I said to myself, and here you are! How are you, Isabel? How are you?" Her eyes darted from Chris to Hannah to me, and she looked like she might start crying from nervousness. I wanted to lift her pretty shawl, a blue-green silk wrap that hung delicately over her slim shoulders, and strangle her with it. But here she was, looking so desperate and hopeful. I reached for her hand in spite of myself.

"We're fine, Andi," I said, giving her fingers a little squeeze and then letting go. "You look gorgeous." She did; she looked gorgeous. She wore a charcoal-gray dress that hugged her perfect little thirty-one-year-old body, cinched with a slim black belt around her tiny waist. *How is that fair?* Hannah was always saying to me, raging against the injustices of her life. *How is that fair?* When Andi moved, her shawl seemed to shimmer in little rippling waves, like water. Her dark hair was newly short—just to her chin, accentuating her lovely stem of a neck.

I was wearing the black pants and blue sweater I'd worn to school that day. I considered it a victory that they matched.

Hannah gazed at her as if Andi were a travel brochure for an exotic vacation. She tucked a hank of her own long, thick, unruly hair behind her ear and looked at her feet. I put my arm around her, protectively. She shrugged it away.

"I love your jeans," Andi said to Hannah. "I have a pair just like those." And Hannah lifted her eyes to Andi, besotted.

"Let's mosey on in!" I said, and my daughter snorted quietly with disgust.

Chris handed Andi a bottle of merlot and we walked into the apartment. He took it in, surveying the room quickly, like Rain Man, mastering the details. "A photograph of Josie on the mantel," he whispered to me. "Her watercolor on the wall by the hallway. And a little sculpture on the table underneath the window. And no tree. Obviously." I grabbed his hand, laced my fingers through his. We had started seeing a couple's therapist three weeks earlier. "Try to remember that you're on the same team," she had said.

Mark spotted us and moved in our direction, weaving his way around the other guests. Other guests: that was something new. Before, it had always been just the five of us. Now there were some old neighbors, a few of Mark's fellow adjunct English lecturers from the technical college, a couple of teachers from

Rhodes Avenue—Debbie Huddleston, the music teacher; Sanjay Shah, P.E. The Andes were conspicuously absent, and for that I felt a wave of gratitude that bore a confusing resemblance to pleasure.

"Oh, Hannah," Mark said. "I haven't seen you in so long. You look so pretty and grown up!" He grabbed her in a rough hug, more of an awkward wrestling move. "Sorry for sounding like such a dorky adult."

"It's okay, dork," Hannah said, from underneath his elbow. "Hey, it smells like latkes in here."

"Andi has been cooking *all day.*" He looked at me, gauging my reaction; I smiled without showing my teeth, gave away nothing. Let him figure it out. "She really knows how to fry a potato." There was something familiar and unsettling about the way he was talking, a new rhythm to his speech, an overemphasis on certain words. Josie was disappearing from his speech patterns. Andi was moving in. "I'm so glad you're here," he said to us, still looking at me. "So glad."

Chris had admonished me in the car on the way over, quietly, privately, underneath Hannah's music: "This is really important," he said. "Be happy. Or at least act happy. Fake it if you have to." I knew he was right.

"Okay, okay," I said now, trying for a light tone. I punched Mark in the arm. "Calm down, buddy. We're glad to be here, too." Hannah, eyeing me carefully, smiled.

"Are you hungry? There is so much food, it's ridiculous. I don't know how that happened." Mark shook his head and shrugged in mock incredulousness. He was wearing a dark purple shirt and a geometrically patterned tie. He looked less like he had gotten dressed and more like someone had dressed him. His face was clean shaven, his hair neat. He looked fresh. Happy.

There were certain women who cared what their men looked like, who viewed their partner's appearance as a reflection on their own. Josie had never been one of those women. Andi, it seemed, was.

"We're hungry!" Chris said, and Mark escorted him and Hannah over to the table that was loaded with drinks and snacks.

I drifted away and wandered around the large, open living room, tried to get my bearings. I examined everything, the curious integration of furniture and knickknacks from Mark and Josie's old house with things I'd never seen before—their dusky-blue pillows on a new gray couch; their crystal candlesticks sitting on a pretty Arts and Crafts coffee table I didn't recognize. Under the coffee table was an indigo and deep green rug I could not place—was it one they'd had up in their old bedroom? Or was it brand-new, acquired specifically for this apartment, this new life? I pictured Mark choosing it carefully at Namdar Carpets in the Third Ward, near Solitano's, the Italian bakery we liked. Maybe he'd stopped in for biscotti after he picked it out—alone? With Andi? And where were Josie's rugs? Life was a tender accumulation of possessions, quickly discarded.

Hannah sidled up to me. "Mama," she whispered. "This is no good. Can we go home?"

Her hip bumped against me lightly, her arm bounced against mine. Oh, I wanted to leave, too. I wanted to carry her out of there like a koala bear. I wanted, wanted, wanted to go home. "I don't think so, Banana. Not yet."

"Why not?"

"We've only been here a few minutes. We should stay for a bit. Did you get a snack? Something to drink?"

Hannah took a ragged breath. "I don't want anything. And it stinks in here. It stinks like latkes. My hair is going to smell. My stupid hair is going to smell, and I just washed it this morning, and I hate it here!" Her voice was getting louder. Deb Huddleston, midconversation, looked over at us, concerned.

"Shhh," I whispered to Hannah. "Please. Shhh."

"I hate it here!" she said again. "You made me come. Don't you understand? This is all wrong! I want to leave!"

"Hannah, we can't. It's not . . . we can't . . ." I was paralyzed in the face of my daughter's keening need, a Pompeian trapped underneath the flowing lava. "We just can't yet, it's not . . ."

Chris was walking over to us, smiling, holding a plate stacked high with food. When he noticed Hannah's stricken face, my rising helplessness, his smile shriveled into a tight scowl. "Iz," he hissed. "You promised you'd try."

"Hannah wants to leave, actually," I said. "Not me. Hannah." She looked up at me, confused, her eyes teary. In the marital trenches, once in a while even your own child was cannon fodder.

Chris softened immediately. "Oh, Hanners," he said. "Come on." He handed me his plate and put his arm around Hannah's shoulders, led her away.

And so I was alone in the middle of the room, balancing a ridiculously heavy plate of latkes and sour cream and grapes and chocolate-dipped pretzels. The plate was beginning to leak oil; I could feel it seeping onto my hand. I thought briefly about setting it down in the middle of the blue-and-green rug. I looked around at the little clusters of people, the festive murmur and sparkle of it all. A love song by Charm School that I hadn't heard in years, "I'll Pull Out," banged from hidden speakers with their signature, jangly cowbell rhythm. (*We don't need protection/ from our sweet affection/Don't want nothing to come betweeeeen us.*) One of Mark's colleagues from the English Department, a tall woman wearing a velvet jacket and a porkpie hat, was laughing loudly at something Sanjay Shah was saying. A pale, dark-haired woman who looked like Andi—she had a younger sister—was holding court with three men I didn't recognize; probably, based on scruffy haircuts alone, they were Mark's colleagues. I stood there for five or ten minutes, maybe longer. The room was too bright, too loud. I wondered where Chris and Hannah had disappeared to.

And then two things happened at almost the same time. The doorbell rang, and, without waiting for anyone to answer, Kelly Anderson-Jensen and Andrea Brauer breezed into the apartment, laughing at something, their high, good-natured giggles like tinkling bells. But I barely had the chance to register their arrival, because Mark and Andi were heading toward me, quickly, together. I noticed how subtly his tie matched her dress, like a subliminal message flashing between the frames in an old-fashioned movie. He had his arm draped around her. She wore a look of practiced calm on her face. I'd seen her with that expression at school, expertly soothing an agitated child.

My heart started to pound in my chest, a frightened baboon thumping. I thought I might do or say something I would regret. I felt the regret already, like blood boiling in my veins.

"Hey, Izzy," Mark said. "Chris said to tell you he took Hannah out for a quick walk." He stepped closer to me and brought Andi with him. "She was upset."

Andi nodded and raised a hand to smooth her silk shawl across her shoulders, her fingers lingering on the delicate fabric. "She seemed really upset."

My own fingertips were slick from the latkes, my palms shiny with oil. I wanted nothing more than to get rid of this heavy, absurdly laden plate of food, and then go wash my hands. These paper plates were flimsy, not up to the job. Josie would have known better. Or maybe not. Hell, maybe Josie bought these plates, and they, unlike her rugs, survived the move. I shifted it from my left hand to my right, my fingers greasier with each adjustment.

"I know that Hannah is upset," I said. "I'm her mother." Andi had been avoiding me at school ever since September, staring at me when she thought I wasn't looking with her big kangaroo eyes, frightened, curious, ready to hop away at a moment's notice. This was how I knew she and Mark were still together. "Of course she's upset. This is *hard for her.*" My words came out chopped and angry. I looked at Mark, then at Andi. "She thinks we should be mourning, not celebrating." Strictly speaking, I didn't know if that was exactly what Hannah thought. But it was close enough.

At that moment I sensed the Andes. They hung back, huddled a few feet away from us, their laughter clicked down one notch to a sort of high murmur. I turned, just in time to see Kelly catching Andi's eye, a silent exchange between close friends: *What's going on? What's wrong with her?* and Andi, telegraphing back with a little shake of her head, *Stay away.*

I can't explain what happened next, what primal nerve exploded inside me. "How the hell can this be happening?" I said to Mark, and I wasn't sure if I meant the party or the life we were living, the life that should have included Josie, happily married to Mark, or at least happily enough, and growing older and making tragically bad art and seeing everything the way I did, sideways and hilarious, knowing me better than anyone, but instead looked like this, bright and shiny and wrong, Andi instead of Josie, the world tilted on its axis and me, barely standing.

I turned again and Kelly and Andrea were whispering to each other. I handed Mark my plate. "Take this, please." The sour cream was beginning to melt, the watery extract seeping toward the pretzels. My hands were coated with oil. I needed to wash them. I needed to find Chris and Hannah and get out of here.

"Iz!" Mark snapped, and I stopped short, surprised, maybe because I'd never seen him angry before. "Tell me," he whispered, "how is this supposed to work?" He glared and took another step toward me. He was very near me now, too close. There was a little dab of spit in the corner of his mouth. I fought the urge to back away. I smelled his minty shampoo mingled with something sharp and salty underneath it. He still held Chris's seeping plate of food. "Do you want me to be sad forever?"

It was a reasonable question. I had never thought of it that way before. "Yes," I said. Andi looked like she was going to cry again. Off to the side, Kelly and Andrea were moving in, closer, like lions.

"Don't you love how she's decorated the place?" I heard one of them say, and Andi shook her head again, and then I knew that she and Mark were living together in this apartment.

"Yes," I said again to Mark, my voice high and tight and about to crack. "I want you to be sad forever. That's what I want." I turned to Andi, and I could see that she was good, that she loved Mark; in her drawn, concerned face I saw a flicker of how she would grow old, with Mark, with children, how she would be one of the good people who got to be happy.

Mark shook his head and walked away, just like that: *Enough of this.*

I stood up very straight. "Thank you for having us over," I said to Andi, "but we really must leave now," as if we were at some Edwardian garden party. And with my oil-slick hands, I gently lifted her shawl from around her shoulders and ran my slimy fingers along the fine, shimmery blue silk. "This is very beautiful," I said, touching it everywhere, fondling the ends, caressing it, leaving little fingertip-sized grease stains over every inch of it.

"Um, thanks," she said. She would find out later what I'd done—in a minute, when one of the Andes noticed, or later tonight, when she took it off before slipping into bed with Mark.

I turned around. Chris stood there with Hannah, their cheeks pink from outside. He was looking at me, watching me. I met his eyes and knew that he had seen. Well, he had seen me. Probably they both had. I shrugged. *You saw. So what?* I tilted my head at him, defiant.

He sighed, and because I knew him so well, I heard everything that curdled in that sigh, the disappointment, the resignation, the dimming concern, the fading love. And I opened myself up to the cold thing that had been clawing at my heart since Josie died: Underneath the sadness there is more sadness.

. . .

When I try—and I do, in spite of myself—to stitch Josie's unraveling back together in my mind, the first thing I come up with is the incident with Lily Barrett and her cell phone. Horrible little Lily Barrett—we called her that long before the cell phone debacle.

Any teacher who'd had her in a class could attest to the girl's cruelty, her Machiavellian social jockeying, how she was on her way to becoming a dangerously unrepentant grown-up bully if someone didn't intervene. She was the girl who would organize her friends to get up and switch tables in the cafeteria if one of the unpopular girls sat too close. She would send a photo of herself and five friends from a slumber party to the two girls who hadn't been invited.

I once overheard a conversation between Lily and another

girl, Amelia Ricci. I was on playground duty; they were sitting together under a tree.

"I'm so fat!" Lily complained, pinching a bit of skin on her thigh.

"No, you're not! I am," Amelia said, poking her tiny tummy.

Lily nodded sadly. "I know."

We always knew where Lily Barrett had been by the trail of tears in her wake. She worked the periphery, so her friends didn't know from one day to the next if they were in or out. She was sly. Merciless.

Josie had been pacing the classroom when the incident occurred, explaining the Irish potato famine to her students. She was a kinetic teacher, always on the move. She stopped, midsentence, behind Lily, clued by the telltale hunched shoulders, the intense downward focus. Lily was texting Grace Lister, about to hit SEND. *Maddie could use a potato famine,* she had written. *Her butt looks huuuuge in those jeans!!!!* They think they're so clever, especially the clever ones. Josie peered over Lily's shoulders and snatched that phone from her slim fingers before the girl could inflict any more psychic damage.

It gets a little dicey here. The school has a strict no-electronic-devices-during-school-hours policy. So Josie was—and this is very important—well within her rights to confiscate the phone. But according to Lily Barrett, Josie yanked it from her hard, leaned down so close Lily could see the downy fuzz on Josie's cheeks, could smell her vanilla perfume ("She was so close to me, Mommy! I was *actually scared*!" she wailed later, in front of Principal Coffey and her parents) and whispered, "You little bitch."

Nobody heard, not even the kids who were sitting inches away. In the end, it was Lily's word against Josie's. And anyone who's worked in a school knows that kids lie. They do.

Some of them are brilliant at it. It's the only recourse of the powerless.

Later, in Principal Coffey's office, Josie sat up straight in her chair and clutched her hands in her lap, looked around the room in indignation. The Barretts were nice people. Craig Barrett was the director of a local food bank. Beth Barrett was a public health nurse. They had the cowed, defeated air of kind people who had birthed a monster, gentle robins who had somehow hatched a vulture. They held hands. Craig Barrett sighed. Principal Coffey sat behind his desk in a rumpled, light green poly-blend shirt and rubbed his tired eyes.

"I know I shouldn't have been texting, but she called me a name!" Lily growled, glaring at Josie. "A really bad name. *The b-word!*"

Craig Barrett sighed again. "Lily," he said.

"I certainly did not," Josie said firmly. "I did not, Lily, and you know it."

. . .

"I did," Josie admitted to me a few days later. "I absolutely put my lips right up to that little she-beast's ear and whispered it. *You little bitch.*"

It was a Sunday morning. We were sitting at my kitchen table, sharing a cinnamon roll. Hannah and Chris were in the living room, watching SpongeBob. The Lily Barrett issue had been put to bed; Josie had been cleared. Now she set her fork down on her plate and poked at a crumb on the table with her index finger. "I don't know what got into me." She laughed without smiling. "I've never . . . I have never. You know that. I mean, she deserved it, but she's a ten-year-old child." She stared at her fork as if it might explain her actions, or absolve her.

But the fork wasn't up to the task. I chewed slowly, thinking. "I mean . . . they get to us," I said. "It's no secret we all want to say something like that once in a while."

"But we don't. You don't. Do you know anyone who has? The thing is, Iz . . ." She half smiled at the sound of that. "The thing is, Iz, why couldn't I control myself?"

This was a year or so after Lake Kass and well before Alex Cortez came into her life. In the living room, SpongeBob played a trick on Mr. Krabs. Hannah's giggles and Chris's laughter sounded like music.

"Let it go," I said, peeling off a soft hunk of cinnamon roll. "Forgive yourself."

She nodded. I wanted to make this okay for Josie. But I also wanted to move on, to talk about something else, to get up and pour myself some more coffee. I wanted to reassure her, but all I offered was a topical antidote.

The thing was the look in her eyes, a touch of panic: which I saw, noted, and decided to ignore.

. . .

It was not hard to find Alex Cortez in Madison. I Googled him and cross-checked my search with Van Vleck High School, where Josie had mentioned he taught, and right away his home address, phone number, and e-mail address popped up, along with an unfortunate link to ProfessorAssessor.com. ("Mr. Cortez is a *hottie!*" "Sexy accent." "I got a C+ even tho I did ALL the assined work and there was alot of it. A★★HOLE!")

I stared at the tiny photo of him on the website, trying to read Josie's imprint in his face, or to somehow divine their connection. I remembered him vaguely, or maybe I didn't. He had thick dark hair, a squarish face, dark eyes, full lips. He had that private smile a few men can manage, like he knew the effect he had on people, but hey, now, that wasn't his fault, was it? He was a *hottie*. But really, what could a slightly blurry photograph on an amateurish website possibly tell me? Since Josie had died, I'd been simmering with a powerful need to meet him in person, along with an almost equally powerful desire not to.

It was late June. Josie had been dead for three months, which I still sometimes measured in days. My grief was humid and consuming. I dreamed almost every night that she was still alive. Once I woke up in the middle of the night and, just for the briefest moment, I thought that Chris was Josie. *What are you doing here?* I whispered through a sleepy fog. *I've missed you so much.* I reached over to touch her narrow back and was jolted awake by the broad, familiar expanse of Chris's.

One night I woke up and Chris was propped up on his elbow, staring at me.

"What is it?" I said.

"You were crying in your sleep."

I didn't think so. I shook my head and raised my hands to my wet face.

Chris lay back down and turned his body toward mine. The bed creaked. He smelled like clean cotton. "There was this kid I went to high school with," he said softly. "Matt . . . Goodman. No, Gilman. Matt Gilman. He had leukemia freshman year. He was hardly ever in school sophomore year. He died the summer before junior year."

I was in a daze, the sweet, sad mist of my dream still floating around me, fading. Josie, fading. I breathed in Chris's scent. What was he talking about? Matt who?

"And," he said, "I felt like, for months, I just couldn't believe how . . . unjust it was. How we're put on this earth to leave it. I know it's different. I wasn't even really friends with Matt. But I dreamed about him for years."

This was my husband, in the dark, trying to find me. I understood what he was trying to do. I understood his kind attempt to reach me.

"That's when I stopped believing in God. Not that I ever really had, but that's when I stopped. Eventually I decided it's what we do with our lives that matters." He sighed peacefully, a man who had long ago come to terms with these impossible contradictions. Matt Gilman's death had *helped,* had given him clarity. But it hadn't helped Matt Gilman. "Anyway," Chris said. He moved his hand to my bare shoulder and squeezed it.

His touch was cold bone on bone, unbearable. I closed my eyes and waited for him to stop.

. . .

I composed the e-mail to Alex Cortez and stored it for a week in my drafts folder. I finally hit SEND late Sunday night. He wrote back to me twenty minutes later.

> Dear Isabel, I'm not sure I'll have any answers for you,
> but I would like to meet. I think about Josie every day.

I knew what it was like for a teacher with young kids in the middle of summer, the vacation you could hardly wait for that morphed into a black hole. I suggested we meet the next day, Monday. He agreed immediately.

"I'm just going to do some errands," I said to Chris that morning, although he hadn't asked. He was sitting at the kitchen table eating a bagel and tapping away at his computer, working before he left for work. The emerald ash borer was attacking trees throughout the city, and the DNR couldn't get ahead of

it. They were cutting down trees in all of the southern neigh-
borhoods. Chris was mapping the damage, stricken. He took it
personally.

"Uh, we're out of cream cheese," he said, his mouth full. "If
you're, uh, if you're . . ." *Tap tap tap.*

"Going to the store. Yes," I said, cementing my lie. I felt like
I was going to meet a lover. But how could I have explained this
to Chris? *I'm going to meet the man Josie might have been having an
affair with, so I can feel closer to my dead best friend? I need to speak
with someone who loved her, even if that someone might be a bastard?
I'm off to learn some sordid information about Josie, because, did you
know, I think maybe discovering something new about her is the only
way I'll be able to stop being sad for a second?*

I grabbed my grocery list from the counter and scrawled
cream cheese on it. Now I'd have to stop at Engman's on the way
home. "Are we out of anything else?"

. . .

The summer was already unbearably hot, and on the days when
it wasn't ninety degrees, it was raining, an almost-continual bleak
warm drizzle. Alex had asked if we could meet at Wee Bounce,
an indoor playground for toddlers on the outskirts of the city.

"I apologize in advance," he wrote. "This place is probably
a Petri dish for antibiotic-resistant Staph, and I can absolutely
testify that the decibel level will crush your soul. But I'll have my
kids with me, and this is the only place where you and I might
have a fighting chance of claiming a few minutes to talk. Plus it's
air-conditioned and they have a coffee bar."

"No problem," I wrote back quickly, smiling. "I remember
what it's like." I had the disconcerting feeling that I would have
agreed to meet him anywhere: a drug den, a strip club.

Traffic was light, and I began to relax into the drive, that amorphous dream time. I didn't know what I was going to say to Alex Cortez. I wasn't certain about what had happened between him and Josie, but whatever it was, it had been going on for a while. She had mentioned him in the months since her confession at the beach, but always in a false, polished way, as if she were talking about a movie she'd seen or telling a story about an acquaintance. As if she'd never tried to show me her heart. *My friend Alex Cortez. That teacher I know in Madison, Alex. Remember?* She referred to him in the same way she spoke about the nice woman in her pottery class, the friendly barista with the glasses, her dentist. But they'd had an affair, and my hunch was that he'd ended it, cruelly, setting her downward spiral in motion.

Every year I explain to my fifth graders the debate about the art versus the artist: Can you love a work of art if the person who produced it was truly awful? Wagner hated Jews. Picasso mistreated his wives. Dickens was a rotten husband and a crummy father. Most of my students, preteen moral absolutists, come down quickly and vehemently against the reprehensible artist. But there are always one or two—the boy with the alcoholic mother, the girl whose father sends her a check for her birthday and Christmas—who reluctantly raise their hands in favor of ambiguity, of siphoning what is beautiful from an imperfect source.

Would meeting Alex Cortez be like loving "The Love Song of J. Alfred Prufrock"?

Maybe I wanted to tell him to his face that he was a bastard. But maybe I just wanted to weep in his arms.

I pulled into the parking lot of Wee Bounce—a ramshackle little storefront sandwiched between Re-Pete's Secondhand Sports on one side and Good Imported Russian Foods on the other—and slid out of my car into a gasp of concrete heat. Madison is always ten degrees hotter than Milwaukee in the summer, without the breeze off Lake Michigan to cool the relentless midwestern swelter. I was unprepared for it, although I shouldn't have been—the hydrogen blast of it and that quick grip of panic, the feeling of being trapped inside a hair dryer.

I walked into Wee Bounce and stood still for a minute in the lobby, becoming acclimated to the cooler temperature and the soundtrack of rising screams. I paid my entrance fee to a friendly, wide-faced, blond teenager and peeked through the doorway. It was just one vast room, and it was already jammed with careening toddlers, even at nine thirty on a Monday morning. There were four big, bright bouncy castles lining the walls, and in the middle, like a moat, was a carpeted play area surrounded by worn beige couches. In the far corner there was a tiny cordoned-off coffee bar, really just a countertop, behind which another teenager, this one with dyed green hair, rested on her elbows and gazed out into the middle distance.

Wee Bounce was a terrible, terrible place, a teeming nest of horrors, a dungeon of chaos. But Alex Cortez was right: it was nicely air-conditioned. I walked across the lobby and into the main room.

It smelled like vinyl and diapers and desperation. There were so many women, and as I scanned for Alex Cortez I recognized on all of their varied faces that acute maternal focus, the sweaty rigor of it. They were so young, these mothers of toddlers: ten, fifteen years younger than I was. They looked like my students, clear eyed and inexperienced, dear as kittens. They wore shorts and had their hair in ponytails, and they dashed around after their children. *Careful, Eloise! Jackson, stop licking your sister!*

I had the sudden, quick swipe of a memory, there in the middle of Toddler Cage Match, of being at the grocery store with

Hannah when she was two or three years old. She was sitting in the cart, facing me, her fat legs dangling, her face red, and she was howling. I had probably denied her something amazing: a toothpick, a penny, a bottle of Drano. It didn't matter. Sometimes it just went that way, the innocuous, pleasant moment becoming, without warning, deadly.

"I DO NOT LIKE YOU!" Hannah screamed. And I was sweating, frantic, trying to grab a few essential items from the shelves, knowing that the mission had to be aborted. I flew down the juice aisle and tried to dodge an older woman, who stood her ground and glared at me.

"Excuse me," I said. She scowled. I angled my cart away from hers. *Grouchy old bat.*

But she reached out for me and touched my elbow. Hannah was screeching so loudly I thought I might permanently lose hearing; she scrunched her face, paused, and took a cleansing breath, gearing up for more.

"The days are long," the old lady said, nodding. "But the years are short."

Hannah's wails pierced the air. I smiled, and the old lady smiled back. And I thought: *Please, please, get the hell out of my way.*

. . .

I kept searching the room for Alex Cortez and had the fleeting thought that he was standing me up. I was wearing a light green T-shirt, black capris, sneakers—the summer uniform of the fortysomething female. I had smeared on some under-eye concealer this morning and a swish of mascara, and I realized now that I had wanted to impress Alex Cortez, and also that I would not. I felt old and out of place and, worse, shocked to feel that way. As if on cue, a woman carrying a small, crying child knocked into me as she rushed past and murmured, "Oh, I'm sorry, ma'am."

I felt a tap on my shoulder. "Isabel?"

Yes, I did remember him. Not too tall. Extremely white teeth. Straight nose, angular cheekbones. A face so symmetrical and well assembled, he looked factory-made. He smiled at me. *Oh, Josie.*

He held two Styrofoam cups of coffee and led me toward the play area. A little girl trailed behind him and, holding her hand, a wobbly toddler in overall shorts. They were giggling, delighted with themselves, as adorable as ducklings. Alex set the coffees down on a low table and reached out to shake my hand, squeezed it, and my pulse sped up with the knowledge that this stranger knew Josie, too; that he had a piece of her.

"I thought you might need sustenance," he said, and gestured to the coffee on the table.

"Thanks."

The little girl tugged on her father's T-shirt. She looked like a lighter version of Alex, the same face but with red hair, pale skin, eyes so green the villagers would have burned her at the stake a few hundred years ago. "I wanna play, Daddy."

I remembered Josie, at the beach, talking about Alex's children in an overfamiliar way, as if she were a beloved aunt. *And he has two older girls, too, Maya and Elena, so his work's cut out for him!* I smiled at her. "Is this Maya?" I asked.

"Ah, no. Maya's in first grade. She's at day camp this morning." Alex looked at me, and I saw what I hadn't noticed at first: guardedness, nervous suspicion. "This is Elena, and this is my guy, Antonio." He rested his hand on top of Antonio's head with a sweet, tender possessiveness: he loved them all, you could tell; but this one, oh, this one. "Go play," he said. And, to Elena,

"Make sure you hold your brother's hand. Remember there are big kids here, and he's very little." He watched them run off and almost crash into a herd of children, skidding away at the last second, and then he turned to me. "I can't look. It's crazy here. I warned you."

I took a sip of my coffee, which was lukewarm and tasted like ashes. I peeked under the lid, wondering if someone had possibly flicked a cigarette into it.

"It's really bad coffee," Alex said. "It used to be better, maybe? Or maybe when the babies weren't sleeping through the night I was just more desperate."

I took another sip. "No, it's fine. It's good. I mean, caffeine, right? Who doesn't love it?" I thought about setting my cup down, getting a running start, and hopping from bouncy house to bouncy house and then bouncing right out the Wee Bounce front door. *Thank you for the coffee! This was a mistake! Goodbye!*

"I'm very glad that we're meeting," Alex said quietly, "even if it's just so I can tell you in person that I'm sorry I didn't go to Josie's funeral." I started to interrupt, but he shook his head. "I just have to say this," he said. "I'm ashamed to admit that I had planned to lie to you. I was going to say that I didn't find out that she died until weeks later. But she . . . ah, we were in contact, you know, pretty regularly, and . . . Mark. He called me. Two days after she died. He didn't know that Josie and I . . . I guess Josie had mentioned me, as a colleague. He got in touch and he asked me to make some phone calls. So I did that. Isabel, I was stunned. I still am." He leaned forward, elbows on his knees, his eyes intently on mine. He was relieved to have confessed. "I know how close you two were."

I nodded. I felt the first shivers of a perfect, icy rage.

On the drive to Madison, I had considered walking into Wee Bounce and just launching my whole quiver of arrows at him:

You ruined Josie's marriage, you undermined our friendship, you're a liar and a shithead and you're the reason she's gone. But when I practiced my speech in the car I kept getting stuck. I couldn't think of the word for a married man who has an affair with a married woman. It wasn't "infidel," was it? Now, staring into the pool of Alex Cortez's dark, dreamy eyes, it came to me.

I took another sip of my coffee. I began to resign myself to its awfulness, and, simultaneously, I started thinking maybe it wasn't so bad. I glanced at one of the bouncy houses, all the flailing little arms and legs—a huge, multilimbed dragon, trapped in a puffy castle—and wondered if you could mark the exact moment in your life when jumping around on bright inflated plastic stopped being enough.

Alex smiled and waved to his children as they bounced into view. "DaddyDaddylookatme!" Elena screamed, then bounced back out of sight. A hank of Alex's thick, dark hair fell across his forehead as he glanced down to discreetly check his phone.

"This place is pure childhood," I said. "What's the adult equivalent? A wine bar?"

He looked up at me with a polite, quizzical smile.

Josie would have run with it, would have picked up my cue. *A documentary about experimental jazz,* she would have said, *followed by a brief Q and A with the director.* What had she seen in him, besides his absurdly good looks? What about this Ken doll had moved her so profoundly that she was willing to jeopardize everything?

"I've been immersed in my kids' lives for so long," Alex said, "I don't even remember what adults do for fun."

I didn't know it was going to come out of my mouth until it was too late. "Adults," I said, "commit adultery." On the other hand, I suppose maybe I did.

I rubbed my hands up and down my goose-bumped arms

and stared at my pants, a faded black cotton-spandex blend stretching across my thighs. I thought Alex might just get up and leave, might round up his children and hustle them out of Wee Bounce and back into the inferno of the parking lot. I thought, at the very least, he would probably gather his things and move as far away from me as he could.

But he just sighed. "I'm not as much of an asshole as you probably think."

I shrugged. *How much of an asshole are you?* "Before she met you, she was happily married and alive." I knew it sounded ridiculous even as I said it.

"She was alive even after she met me. And do you really think so? Happily married?" The briefest twitch of contempt flickered across his face.

A woman in a pink T-shirt plopped down on the couch across from where we were sitting, blew out a long puff of air, and smiled at us. "Whew," she said. "I don't know who's going to need a nap more when we get home, my boys or me!" She kept smiling, her round cheeks mottled with heat and exhaustion. She was clearly desperate to engage in some adult conversation, no matter how banal. Normally I would have sympathized, but not today. I smiled tightly and wished for some small emergency to present itself to her. *Uh, is that your kid? I think he just ate a Lego.* Alex didn't even bother looking at her, just slid closer on the couch and leaned toward me. We must have looked like a couple, like two parents jealously guarding our moments together. For a second, I wished we were. "Whew," the woman said again, and looked away, embarrassed, pretending she had been talking to herself all along.

"You make it sound like this is some kind of Mexican soap opera," Alex whispered to me. "Do you think I casually broke Josie's heart one day, *ay, Dios mío,* and she killed herself? Did you know her?" I breathed in sharply, and he stopped himself. "I'm sorry. I didn't mean that." He rested his forehead in his palm for a second. "This is . . . this has been so hard."

The woman across from us was now staring into the distance with the blank, practiced look of the eavesdropper. Alex inched even closer to me, brought his voice down another notch. Was this the way he seduced Josie, with this unbearable proximity, this heat? There were faint lines between his eyebrows, a small scratch on his chin. His breath smelled of coffee and spearmint. His irises were almost black. He put his hand on mine, just for a second, then quickly moved it away. "I feel responsible," he said, "but I don't know how responsible to feel. I'm guilty."

"Me, too," I whispered. "Oh, me, too." Mark was trying to drown his sorrows in those early months, pushing me away, lost. Hannah was feverish with grief and confusion, capable only of receiving comfort, and only in small doses. Chris just squinted at me hard from very far away, trying to make me out. But here was Alex Cortez, and there was no distance between us. I felt my whole body loosen, my rib cage unlock, the pull of desire. I wanted to kiss him, or press my forehead against his and just rest there, the two of us. I bit my tongue so that I wouldn't cry.

Alex nodded at me, his eyes a little teary, relieved. And then he pulled his phone out of his pocket. He glanced down at it, cradled it in his palm. "I might be a bastard, but I love my wife. My marriage isn't perfect, but I love her with all my heart." He sighed. "Josie had certain . . . expectations."

Oh, I thought. *Wait.*

"I tried to manage them, and then I couldn't any longer. You know how she was," he said, drawing me farther down this path that had suddenly become a maze. "She would look at you like you were the brightest star. I mean, she thought I was this brilliant artist, this tortured soul. I'm not! I mean, sure, I dabble,

I'm not terrible. . . ." He trailed off for a second. "But it was too much. In the end I was scared of her."

"What do you mean, scared?" My heart started pounding uncomfortably, my body beating out a warning to my brain.

"She talked about moving to Madison, getting a job at my school. She wanted me to leave my wife. It had gone too far. I told her we had to cool it." He cleared his throat, shifted on the sofa. "She didn't take it well."

I just sat there, trying to mask my dread, waiting.

"She, ah, she said she wanted to talk, she wanted to go for a drive." He picked up his coffee, blew on it, set it down without taking a sip. "It started out okay. I told her, we can't take this any further, it was all getting too complicated. She seemed all right with it. She said she understood." He paused. "And then she drove us to my house. She parked across the street and turned off the engine and she said, 'It's time for me to tell your wife. I'm going to tell her that you have been cheating on her.'" He ran his hand through his hair once, then again. "I think I just sat there for a minute, you know, with my mouth hanging open. I couldn't believe it. I thought my chest was going to explode. She put her hand on the door handle and she said, 'Once a cheater, always a cheater,' and I said, 'Josie, I have three kids.' She didn't do anything. And then, after a few minutes, she started the car again and we left."

I remembered the story she had told me about "Roger," her faithless high-school boyfriend, how she had admitted to doing and saying almost the exact same thing. *Once a cheater, always a cheater.* Was this the confession she had been trying to make, telling me the truth about Alex by inventing a fake boyfriend, handsome and shifty as his real-life counterpart?

Alex Cortez exhaled and looked up at the ceiling, as if for

guidance from the god of bastards. "I know she was only trying to scare me. And holy shit, she did." He laughed a little, like he was trying to shrug it off. "Man, I was furious. That was it. Afterward, she kept sending me her weird art, paintings where the men were women . . . the Venus de Milo as a guy wearing a beer hat!" There was mockery in his voice, not a lot but how much does a person need? It was like a sharp slice through soft flesh.

"Yeah," I said, "so weird." I thought about the painting she'd given me for my forty-first birthday, thirteen smiling women gazing rapturously at Tupperware. "Ridiculous."

"Right?" he said. *"Right?"*

I ran my finger along the sharp plastic that edged the lid of my coffee cup. It was a design flaw—you had to place your upper lip right here, on this jagged rim, to drink your coffee. It was just a tiny danger, another risk that came out of nowhere when you weren't looking. "Josie was . . . she did have certain expectations," I said, my voice cracking idiotically, my face pulsing with heat. "Maybe she just expected better from the people she loved. She was passionate that way."

Alex looked at me, a little smirk on his face, like what did I know about Josie's passion? He held the secret map to that country. "Oh, she expected better?" he said. "You think she could claim the moral high ground?" He was still smirking. I could see that Alex Cortez was the kind of person who enjoys proving his point. "Yeah, she wasn't exactly innocent."

A laughing girl tumbled out of one of the bouncy houses and climbed back in. From across the room, a chorus of high-pitched screeching sounded, just for a second, like cicadas. A few feet away, a woman with curly blond hair and a tattoo of a cresting wave on her shoulder scooped up her small boy and said, "It's all right, sweet pea." A young woman in a short blue sundress—a babysitter, a nanny, too young to be even one of these mothers—walked through the front entrance with three little girls. And, *whoosh,* I was free from Alex Cortez's fraudulent intimacy; I emerged, sputtering, from the weak tea of his sorrow.

I blinked and looked around the room, pretended to settle on a point in the distance. "Whoa," I said. "I think Antonio threw up."

"Seriously? Dammit," Alex muttered. He got up quickly to investigate, and I stood and grabbed my purse. I left my Styrofoam cup of horrible coffee growing cold on the low table and headed for the door. I had had enough. I had had more than enough. From the side of a three-foot-high Mount Rushmore, four inscrutable, unblinking kittens watched me go.

———————

Thirteen

When I tell Helene about Cal, she does not offer the sympathetic ear I had hoped for.

We're driving home from her doctor's appointment. Dr. Petrova had reminded her again that improvement after a stroke diminishes greatly over time. She gestured with her hand, a gradual incline followed by a flattening. "You have made an excellent recovery. But there are no miracles," she said, in her no-nonsense, post-Soviet way. This was why we liked Dr. Petrova, mostly. But sometimes it could come across a little heavy-handed. *No miracles! God is dead! Long live Mother Russia! See you in two months.* "I'm afraid you are no exception, Mrs. Applebaum."

"I do the strengthening exercises every day. I never miss a rehab appointment." There was desperation in her voice, pleading, as if by carefully explaining how diligent she was being, my mother could convince Dr. Petrova to upgrade her prognosis. I was surprised by how embarrassed I felt and pretended to study the human anatomy poster on the wall. "But even after all these months," Helene said, "I can hardly hold a pen in my right hand."

"So now you learn how to write with your left hand, hmm?" Dr. Petrova was entering something into her records, tapping away on her laptop. "Something the occupational therapists can help you with. A challenge." The twenty-minute appointment was a minute away from being over.

So Helene was not in a great mood.

"Okay, Mom," I'd said as we left the office. I carried her purse in my left hand and offered my right arm to support her. "It's not what we were hoping for, but where you are isn't so bad, is it?"

She snarled as she gripped my elbow. "I can't drive. I can't read at night anymore. The whole right side of my face droops when I'm tired, like a suitcase." She looked at me, her dark eyes scared, her face pale and old. "Not so bad? Huh. You're not the one who can't open a damn bottle of Advil."

What is the correct answer to my mother's raw attempt to offer up her pain and force me to see her as more than just a wellspring of maternal comfort? *Mommy, hold me?*

. . .

"I went out with Cal on Saturday," I tell her as we pull out of the parking lot.

She perks up a little. "Oh?"

"We drove to Lake Kass and did some bird-watching."

She looks out the window. "Stop it."

"Stop what?"

"I never know when you're joking."

"I'm serious. We visited his grouchy, racist mother in her assisted-living complex, and then we went bird-watching. We watched birds. And then we went back to his house. And then I freaked out and he drove me home."

"That sounds like a nice day."

"I really scorched the earth," I say, turning left down Lake Drive toward our neighborhood. "I kind of . . . made it clear that I wasn't ready. I kind of ran away screaming." *I kind of suggested I'd be up for casual sex and then bolted.*

Helene is silent for a while, considering what I've just told her. She doesn't say anything at all for a long time, and I start to think she's dozed off. "Do you understand," she says quietly, but with a steely undertone that makes me take notice, "that a downhill slide ends at the bottom of the hill?"

We roll through a yellow light. To our left, the street slopes up toward the city. To our right, Lake Michigan flashes blue and silver in the late-morning sun like a wading pool, deceptively welcoming.

"Huh?"

"This is it. This is all we've got. I liked Cal. He seemed kind-hearted. I thought he might be a shoulder for you, but okay, I guess not. But you have a beautiful daughter. And Chris, well, I don't know what's going on there, but I know he's a good man. Maybe you need to focus, to . . . to . . . refocus on those things. I'm tired of you sabotaging yourself. I'm up nights worrying about you. I lie awake." With her left hand, she massages her right. "Well, I can't sleep anyway. But, you know, I'd rather be reading a novel than worrying about my forty-three-year-old daughter." She shakes her head and sighs, and I understand that there's a part of her that would like to wash her hands of me, and even though she never will, the realization feels like a sharp-toothed piranha lurking beneath calm, turquoise waters. We're as entwined as a long-married couple, my mother and I, but if this past year and a half has taught me anything, it's that nothing is permanent, no knot too tight to be loosened.

The blue Subaru in front of me slows gently and puts on its turn signal, and I tap my brake pedal. "Whoa!" I say, then fling my arm across my mother's body. It's an attempt at a joke—there's plenty of room between our car and the Subaru—but Helene doesn't laugh.

I have the sudden memory of driving with Hannah for the

very first time, about a week after she was born. She was properly straitjacketed into her car seat, backward facing, so I had no view of her from the driver's seat. But I knew that she was awake, because she was making those little mewling baby noises that remind you that you are the mammal who would lay down your own life for the tiny, helpless creature in your care, although she is brand-new to you, although she is nothing more than gaping, consuming need, although in twelve years or so she will become surly and unfathomable and mutter *You're so annoying* under her breath after you've told her for the twentieth time to turn off the TV and do her homework, although she will borrow your favorite pair of boots without asking and then casually insult your taste in footwear. But you don't know that yet. And even if you did: you will always be that mammal.

That afternoon in the car, twelve years ago: I white-knuckled the steering wheel like I was driving into a blizzard, even though it was a warm, cloudless afternoon. I heard a sucking noise from the backseat, and I knew that baby Hannah had jammed her fist into her mouth, and it was such a terribly sweet sound that I could hardly bear it. I wanted to pull over and call Chris to come get us. I had to force myself to stay on the road, to drive up to the speed limit. I was shaking with fear, at the mercy of all the other cars on the road, the cell-phone dialers, the drunks, the cell-phone-dialing drunks: an endless parade of peril.

"I don't want you to worry about me, Mom," I say now. "And I know that you're right."

She sighs again. But would it be that easy? To adjust my lens a little? To stop wallowing in all this murky sorrow? To change my attitude, let the sunlight in, fix myself? I glance over at my mother. The late-morning light in the car is unforgiving, illuminating a few broken blood vessels on her cheeks, the centimeter of dull gray at her hairline, the traces of lipstick bleeding out into the wrinkles around her mouth. I have the rest of the day off, and it suddenly feels like it will be a chore to fill the empty hours. "Do you want to go get a little lunch?" I ask. Helene never says no to a little lunch.

"No, I'm tired. I think I'll just go home and lie down for a bit. Can you take me home, please?"

. . .

It's only when I look at things now, more than a year after Josie died, that any of it begins to make sense, only when I work it out in my memory that it looks like a series of actions building up to her death. Perspective, in that way, is cruel.

We were walking across the parking lot together one day after school. The wind tossed up swirls of powdery snow, and the dazzling winter sky was a shock. I huddled into my collar, and Josie pulled her jacket tightly around her. I glanced at her and said, absently, "Oh, cute coat. Is it new?"

She stopped and turned to me, grabbed my arm so that I had to stop, too. Sunshine bounced off the cars, and, facing each other, we simultaneously lifted our hands to shield our eyes, like mimes.

"I stole it," she said.

I stared at her for a second, squinting. "What?"

She gave my elbow a little squeeze and looked down at her coat—soft, camel-colored wool. "I stole it." She raised her eyebrows, daring me to pass judgment. "Yep. I did!" Her cheeks were reddening in the cold. "It was actually an accident, if you can believe that."

"Um, what?" I said again. My brain felt dulled by the chill. "You stole that coat? By accident?"

"I was at Macy's," she said. "Shopping. I had picked this one out." She ran her hand down the sleeve. "Isn't it pretty? I was looking for a clerk. You know how that place can be." She shrugged, as if everyone knew how that place could be. "I couldn't find anyone. I searched and searched, and finally I just got so fed up, I draped the coat over my arm and walked out."

"Josie!" I said. "You have to go back and pay for it!"

"Well, yeah, I probably should. But I'm not going to, obviously."

Janice Van Dyke, the seventh-grade math teacher, walked past us in the parking lot and waggled her leather-gloved fingers in a tired wave. In the busy intersection of Rhodes Avenue and Willow Road, in front of the school, a bus honked.

I had had a hell of a day: an outburst during homeroom; a call from Hannah, who had forgotten her clarinet, and the attendant tears when I told her I couldn't leave school to bring it to her. A skirmish between two boys in the hallway before lunch. There was a load of towels that I'd accidentally left in the washing machine for three days, and I knew that when I got home, it would smell like wet dog and need to be rewashed. (I wondered, often, how many years of my life I'd lost to laundry. Sometimes I dreamed about it.)

"I mean," Josie continued, glancing around the parking lot, "it's not like this is some kind of habit!" She looked, finally, a little sheepish. "Although it *was* kind of a rush."

There is so much between two friends: love and disappointment, resentment and optimism and a very smudged reflection of your own face. Maybe I had a hunch that this moment was significant. But I was thinking, *If I get in the car right now, leave school, and don't encounter too much traffic, I might be able to stop at the grocery store and still make it home before Hannah does.* She had her own key, but I liked to be there when she got off the bus.

Josie looked at me, waiting for something: guidance, maybe?

"Jose," I said. "That is bonkers." I laughed a little. I thought, *She could get arrested.* There was a thick sheaf of essays in my bag, weighing me down. That was another thing. "Don't do it again! Promise."

"Right," she said. "Promise." She nodded, turned away from me, looked around at the emptying parking lot. Her hair flew in her face. "I wouldn't."

"I need to . . ." I motioned toward my car. "I've got to get going," I said. "Seriously, don't do that again!" I leaned in for a quick hug, and then I walked away. I left her there, in the school parking lot, huddled up against the cold wind in that pretty, new wool coat.

· · ·

The day Chris moved out, after he assured me, on the phone from his new apartment, that everything would be okay, and after we hung up, I moved some furniture around in the living room: the couch to where the armchair had been, the end table to the other side. I was trying to make it look intentional, like I just wanted to spruce things up a bit, instead of spare. But the room just felt abandoned, like a twenty-two-year-old's first post-college apartment after her roommate moved out to live with her boyfriend. It looked impermanent, accusatory: *Now how are you going to pay the rent?* Displaced dust bunnies blew around in the hot furnace wind. Finally, the life outside my head and heart reflected the life within.

I swept the floor. I made myself a grilled cheese sandwich and took one bite of it. I thought about the Sunday afternoon a few weeks earlier when I had been too sad to get dressed, how I'd wallowed all day in the old, ripped T-shirt and sweatpants I'd been sleeping in and watched reality show after reality show about home remodeling; how, late in the day, as dusk darkened the house, Hannah had asked me to play Scrabble with her and I'd said, "No, sweetie, not now, not just now," and how Chris had marched into the room, stood in front of me with his arms crossed over his chest, and said, *"When?"*

I opened the refrigerator and found a bottle of beer that he had left behind, one of the fussy little microbrews that he liked. I opened it and took one sip—*undertones of coffee!*—and then poured the rest down the sink.

I sat down on the floor and did a few stretches. I checked my phone, my e-mail. I spotted the kitchen scissors on the dining room table, left there by one of the guys probably, and I walked it into the bathroom and contemplated giving myself bangs. I snipped a few strands of hair. "No!" I said out loud. "No cutting your own hair."

Hannah was at my mother's. She had been there since Friday night and was going to stay for the weekend, then return to the warm, sunny, rearranged bungalow her father had vacated. She was surly and angry, had barely spoken to me in a week. She understood, with all the merciless insight of a twelve-year-old, that this was my fault. I had no counter-argument for her.

"You and I will still be together all the time," I had said to her. I was standing in her doorway as she packed for the weekend. "We'll spend as much time together as we do now. Probably more."

She picked up two dirty T-shirts off the floor, jammed them into her overnight bag, and glared at me. "I don't want to see you *more* than I do now," she said. I could tell that it took all of her self-control not to say something worse, and for this I felt perversely proud of her.

I would still throw myself in front of a train for this sullen, wounded girl. And she wouldn't even have to be in danger, necessarily. I'd probably do it if she just asked me politely. *Good job saying "Please," Hannah! Thump.* "I know how hard this is, honey," I said, fiddling with the hole in the sleeve of my sweatshirt. "I know."

She squinted at me like she couldn't quite make me out, and I remembered that I'd been meaning to take her to the ophthalmologist. "Um?" she said sweetly. "You don't know anything, and could you please go away?"

. . .

After I rearranged the furniture and gave myself that tiny haircut, I decided to go to my mother's house, which had not been the plan. I was going to spend the evening alone, watch a movie, wallow in my sadness without having to put on a brave face for Hannah. I thought I would need the evening to pull myself together, to regroup, to get used to being alone. I imagined myself snuggled up on the couch under a warm blanket with a bowl of popcorn and a glass of wine and a box of Kleenex: not exactly enjoying my misery, but not exactly miserable, either.

What had I been thinking? Had my vision of heartbreak been so stupidly informed by sitcoms and romantic comedies? The silence in the house came alive, grew feral. It was Chris, it was Josie, it was my mother's three girl cousins. What were their names? One of them was Trude. I didn't know the other two. The winter wind through the rattly living room windows was a keening. The world had cracked open, but when I looked inside the broken shell, there was nothing.

I grabbed my down jacket from the hook, threw on my boots, my scarf and mittens. I pulled the door shut behind me.

. . .

When I was eleven, I got lost walking home from a tennis lesson. Our house was just three blocks from the tennis court, and I had made the journey a dozen times, but on that day I was distracted. My friend Cindy and I had begged to sign up for the summer class together, but after two weeks, because practically everything came easily to Cindy and when something didn't she'd become sulky, she dropped it.

But Helene said she'd paid for me, so I had to keep going. I didn't care about tennis, and I was terrible at it. After Cindy dropped, it was just me, a pair of seventh-grade twins named Chrissy and Missy who spoke only to each other, and two boys: Ethan Chase and Sam Ullrich. Ethan and Sam were not particularly mean, but they harbored what was clearly an unexamined resentment toward studious, nonblond girls. (Ironically, Ethan would marry an Italian biochemist. Less ironically, Sam would end up managing a small chain of strip clubs.) When it was my turn to hit the ball, they would call out the teacher's instructions—*Racket back, step, swing!*—but for me they changed it to, "Racket back, step, miss!"

I was so flustered by Ethan and Sam's relentless chanting that I headed home with elaborate revenge fantasies swirling in my brain. Thirty minutes later, I realized I had no idea where I was.

I stopped and surveyed the unfamiliar houses. I had walked thirty minutes in exactly the wrong direction. I took a deep breath. If I turned around and walked thirty minutes in exactly the other direction, I figured I would wind up back at the courts, and so I started unsteadily the other way.

Sure enough, after a tense twenty minutes, I began to recognize my neighborhood again. It was like waking from a dream. The short journey home from the courts should have taken me five minutes; I finally made it in just over an hour.

I pushed open the back door, sweaty and annoyed with myself, and let my racquet and backpack drop to the floor. I hadn't given one thought to Helene on my long march. I had been concerned only about finding my way home. But there she was, standing in the kitchen, wound up in the phone cord. "She's here, Jack," she said into the phone, her voice high and quavery and urgent. "It's all right. She's here!" She was talking to my father. Even at eleven, I understood that that phone call bore the expensive price tag of her desperation.

She hung up the phone and turned to me and found that she was tangled in the cord. She had to do a little rotation to get out of it, a twirl and a dip, and we both laughed, and then she stopped laughing and broke down sobbing, and I stood there, and I was still smiling and my heart thudded with sudden quick terror and my brain was swiped clean by my mother's weeping. I didn't get it. I was here. I was fine.

"I'm fine, Mom," I said. "I'm fine, I'm fine. I got lost. I'm sorry. I'm fine." And she nodded and raced over to me and hugged me, and her arms around me, her body enveloping me, the smell of her citrusy perfume mixed with a sour whiff of fear: the force of it suffocated me. I hugged her back, but I wanted to run. It was all I could do not to run. And when my heart finally slowed and my mind began to work again, I eased myself out of that embrace as gently as I could, as if I were her mother and she were my child.

She was so relieved, she said. She couldn't stop crying because she had been so worried and she was so, so relieved that I was safe. She made me toast with honey, although I hadn't asked for it, and she sat with me at the kitchen table and watched me eat it.

Years later I would understand that relief was only part of the story, of course, and that what I saw that day was the wrenching collision of things unfathomable and inevitable, past and foretold.

. . .

I think about that day often, and I was thinking about it as I made my way over to Helene's, huddled against the cold. We bring it up once in a while. It's a story we tell each other, an incantation: Do you remember when I got lost? Remember that day?

I trudged the familiar blocks to Helene's duplex through the freezing February wind, climbed the wooden steps to her front porch, and let myself in with my key. I could conjure the feelings of that afternoon, even more than thirty years later, how the disorientation of an unfamiliar neighborhood rushed at me all at once, the way the sun felt like it was cooking my scalp, my single-minded determination to turn it all around and get home; and then how my own thoughts were peeled away, in the kitchen of my mother's house, in the face of her distress, and revealed to me as selfish—at least in the regular way of a child, where "selfish" is another word for "unburdened."

I peered into the hallway and tiptoed through the kitchen. "Hello," I said, not too loudly. "Anybody home?" The apartment smelled like chicken soup, my mother's famous Campbell's low-sodium. There was music coming from the living room, the 1950s swanky Frank Sinatra that always made me feel like I was about to be murdered by a saxophonist.

Hannah and my mother were sitting on the living room couch, their heads bent together—my mother's smooth, coiffed hair and Hannah's long dark-blond messy waves, almost the same shade, my mother's a little lighter and, of course, chemically enhanced.

If they heard me come in and call for them, they were ignoring me, but the music was loud and so they may not have; I couldn't be sure and didn't really want to know. Helene whispered something to Hannah, who nodded, and I saw that they were crocheting, or rather that my mother, through compensatory use of her left hand and verbal instruction, was teaching Hannah to crochet. Hannah had the hook, and Helene held a large ball of blue yarn. She nodded as Hannah completed a stitch. It looked like she was making a very long, thin scarf, or a charming baby-blue noose. Hannah laughed at something my mother said.

I had come expecting sadness, but I could tell, even in my own state of it, that it wasn't here. They were so happy together, my mother and my daughter, as they always were, and I felt the familiar twinge of jealousy followed by an equally familiar twinge of relief. "Ladies," I said. "I'm here!"

They looked up at me in unison. "We thought you might show up," Helene said.

"Grandma's teaching me how to crochet," Hannah said. "I'm making you a hat."

"I love it," I said, moved.

"*This* isn't the hat," Hannah said, disgusted. "I'm just learning. This is just practice. When I get good at it, I'm going to make you a hat. Although I might keep it for myself. What did you do to your hair?" She bent back toward the yarn, concentrating.

"Uh," I mumbled, "just, um, maybe bangs, I thought? But then, no."

"Good girl," my mother said to Hannah, ignoring me. "You are a quick study."

I started peeling off layers, already sweating in my mother's warm rooms. "Can I turn the music down?" I asked. Hannah generally preferred the music of baby-faced man-boys singing about how they were the only ones who understood how beautiful you were inside. But for my mother she made an exception.

Helene smiled at me without answering and then turned back to Hannah and gestured toward the yarn. "These need to be a bit more even," she murmured, and Hannah carefully pulled a stitch out.

"All righty, then!" I said. I picked up my jacket and walked back to the hallway to hang it up, wandered into the kitchen and closed a cabinet door, lifted the lid on what was, as I'd guessed, a pot of chicken soup. I caught a glimpse of myself in the hall mirror and noted that I had, in fact, chopped off slightly more hair than I'd thought. I drifted through the apartment and into the spare room where Hannah was staying. Clucky the rubber chicken was tucked in carefully. The novel she was reading, about a pack of attractive, angst-ridden teenage werewolves, was open on the night table. I lay down on the twin bed, moved Clucky. A painful tiredness swept over me immediately. When she was little, Hannah would lie in her bed at night and cry with exhaustion, "I'm so tired!" as if the solution weren't right there, immediately accessible behind her eyelids.

It wasn't better than being home, exactly; I was still me. Now that the music in the living room was quiet, I could hear Hannah and my mother talking to each other, not the words but the tones of it, the rising and falling, Hannah's raspy laugh, Helene's higher one.

My eyes were closing, images popping through my brain: a tennis ball, the front lawn of a yellow house, a carton of milk, a large dog. *You fall asleep,* Hannah had said, *and where do you go? You're gone. It's like you're practicing to die!*

"Hannah!" my mother exclaimed from the other room. "Look at that! You got it!"

I had given Hannah and Helene to each other: my lonely mother, adrift, and my sad, snarling wolf cub of a girl. I had given them to each other. I had done that.

Fourteen

The morning it happened, I noticed a bottle of Diet Pepsi in the refrigerator in the staff lounge as I was making room for my peanut butter sandwich. Josie's initials were scrawled across the label in thick black marker. And I thought, with a twinge, about her Diet Pepsi addiction, about the cans and bottles she'd toss into our recycling bin after we'd spent a weekend together, how they clanked and plonked around in the backseat of her car like a broken xylophone. I saw that Diet Pepsi and I wished for a second that she'd brought one for me, the way she used to. But by then we weren't sharing as much with each other, not beverages, not secrets.

By then I also knew for sure that she was having an affair with Alex Cortez—and not just the emotional dalliance she'd admitted to, not just a titillating but still relatively safe distraction from her marriage, but something real and threatening, something she wouldn't come back from easily. I didn't know when it had started—whether it was before she'd even told me about it, *Nothing happened . . . If we lived in the same city . . . If we let it,* or after that, after she'd absolved herself to me. I suppose it didn't matter.

Mark had called me three weeks earlier, on a Saturday afternoon. Josie was in Chicago at a two-day sculpting workshop. I saw his name on my caller ID and figured he wanted company, the way he sometimes did when Josie was gone for the weekend.

"We're about to go out for breakfast," I said, instead of hello. Chris and Hannah were already in the car. "Would you care to join us?" I was in a sunny mood, attentive to the smallest pleasures of my life, suffused with gratitude. These sudden spells of happiness sometimes came over me during the dull weeks of mourning a miscarriage—an airplane briefly soaring above the clouds. At first I doubted the inexplicable elation, mistrusted the happiness until it skulked away, defeated. But after a time, I learned to enjoy these lighthearted hours, because it turned out the happiness left anyway—whether I chased it off or not. "We'll come get you," I said to Mark. "We'll be there in fifteen minutes!"

"Hang on," Mark said. "Wait. I can't reach Josie. Do you know where she is?" She had told us she was staying with their friends Lydia and Paul in downtown Chicago for the weekend. But suddenly I knew she wasn't.

I had been tearing through the house doing a little last-second cleaning, which meant that I was picking objects up and putting them down in other places, and also straightening the edges of piles of papers. I looked at my right hand, which held Hannah's clarinet case; she had left it, for some reason, in the bathroom. I looked at the suitcase-like black box of it and said, "Don't *you* know where she is?"

"She forgot her charger," Mark said. "She's always forgetting it. I figured her phone would run out of juice, so I wanted to tell her, just keep it off when you're not using it, or borrow Lydia's. Whatever. But I couldn't reach her, so I called Lyd, and she just ... Lydia thought I was crazy. She had no idea what I was talking about. Josie's not staying with them, and she was never planning to. Shit, I feel like I'm in a bad movie. I'm really worried. Do you know anything?"

I had integrated the knowledge of Josie's betrayal, delivered to me on that warm night on the beach just a few weeks earlier. I had allowed myself to walk a fine line, to offer a jagged kind of loyalty to both of my friends, to the generous idea, I thought, that we are all fallible—that some mistakes are worse than others, and Josie's, more of a loss of focus than a broken promise, was forgivable. But now it seemed that maybe it wasn't.

I sat down on the couch. Morning light angled in through the living room windows and made delicate shadows on the wall, a lacy latticework from the leaves of the hibiscus in the corner. "I'm sure it's nothing," I said, and then I said it again. "Maybe you got the details wrong. You probably misheard, and she's just staying with someone else." *Well,* I thought, *of course she is.*

"You're right," he said, without the slightest relief. "Can you think of who else she knows in Chicago? Friends from school or, you know, a friend of a friend or something? I guess she could even be at a hotel."

"Mark, take it easy," I said. "She'll be home tomorrow, and she'll explain it. Her phone is dead, and she's just gotten engrossed in the work. You know how she is."

"Izzy," he said, and he sounded, in that second, like the Mark I met in grade school, and all the versions of Mark I had known since then; there are moments when it all collides like that, when everything is pressed down, condensed as powder, fine as dust. "I just need to know."

I thought about Chris and Hannah, waiting for me in the car. I wanted Josie to be elbow deep in a wet mound of clay, visualizing famous sculptures she could turn into Hello Kitties. I wanted her not to be having an affair with Alex Cortez. I wanted Mark not to ask me any more questions. I wanted to sit with my little family in a booth at Desi's and order pancakes. I wanted to be blameless. But there was no such thing.

"Call me when you hear from her," I said.

. . .

Two days later, Josie came into my classroom early, before the students arrived, as I knew she would. I was reading last week's homework assignments: write an ode to your favorite dessert.

"I'm sorry I put you in that position," Josie said. Her face looked pale and drained. Even her hair looked faded, and it struck me that it was color that made her beautiful. Without it she was just another tired, middle-aged schoolteacher. There were pronounced dark circles under her eyes, as if someone from her fake clay workshop had dipped a finger into the loamy slime and daubed it onto that delicate skin.

I looked up from my papers, one finger on the line where I'd stopped (*Ode to a cupcake: Thou tasty pastry, frosted extra sweet!*) so she'd know I wanted to get right back to work. She hovered nervously, a few feet from my desk. Normally she'd pull a chair up next to me and prop her feet up, or rifle through my top desk drawer for my hidden stash of chocolate.

I met her eyes. *I have no idea what you're talking about,* I wanted to say. Or, *Don't apologize. You didn't put me in a position. I'm not in a position.* I wasn't about to be her confidante. We just stared at each other. She shoved her hands into pockets.

Transgression doesn't suddenly appear on a person's face like sunburn. It doesn't alter the bone structure, change the shape of the eyelids, the curve of the mouth. Josie was just herself. She looked like she had been crying, though, or would start soon.

She shrugged one shoulder, a tiny surrender. I could see her collarbone jutting sharp and birdlike through her shirt. We used to joke that she didn't have enough fat on her body to see her through a long morning. "Oh, Jose," I said.

She took a step toward me, and then the bell rang, and children started pouring into the building. It was my favorite part of the day—the breath between stillness and chaos. Once the phalanx began its invasion, there was no more time to chat.

"I guess we'll talk later," Josie said, over the roar. "Okay?"

. . .

I can't say it started on that awful day at Lake Kass, or that night at the beach when she told me about Alex Cortez, or the morning in my classroom when we didn't finish talking, or at some other crucial moment that passed me by as unimportant. Anyway, I don't think it was a free fall. It was more of an untethering: not a terrifying death spiral, but a slow loosening of the safety ropes.

There were those things she had been saying to her students: *Don't always listen to your parents; learn it for the test and then forget it; sometimes you have to lie to protect the ones you love.* Oh, yes, she said that, too.

There was the Lily Barrett cell-phone debacle, of course; the stolen coat incident.

There was, maybe worst of all, Josie's confrontation with Principal Coffey—because although she may have been right, or at least right enough to be steamed, miffed, and/or definitely disgruntled, everyone knows you don't pick a fight with Principal Coffey. Well, you don't win a fight with Principal Coffey. And even if you win a fight with Principal Coffey, you don't win.

Josie had put in a request for funds from the school's discretionary account, which we all did once in a while, when our classroom materials proved insufficient or outdated: $300 to upgrade a microscope, $325 for a grand, all-school papier-mâché Day of the Dead project, $250 to bring in Global Warning, a local group of middle-aged scientists who performed rap songs about climate change. (*Polar bear nowhere, penguins gettin' hot. / It won't be cathartic if we lose the Arctic!*) By unspoken agreement, these funds were judiciously requested and therefore almost always approved.

Josie had asked for two hundred dollars for a subscription to an online, interactive women's history database and was already filling out the purchase form when Principal Coffey turned her down. The math teachers had gotten together (*What could I do?* Josie said later. *They had the numbers.*) and put in a request for a pricey new software program for a small group of advanced sixth graders—Principal Coffey's pride and joy. "I'm sorry, Ms. Abrams. But of course we'll consider your request next year." He gave her one of his patented sympathetic smile-frowns and, resigned to the disappointment, she was about to leave his office, when he chuckled to himself. "Or maybe you'll have changed your mind by then," he said. "Ha-ha! A woman's prerogative!"

And that, she said, was what flipped her lid, was why she spun around to face him in the open doorway, crossed her arms over her chest, and said to the esteemed principal of Rhodes Avenue, "You, sir, are a sexist ass!"

"I said it in an English accent," she whispered to me later that day, in the front seat of my car. "An English accent! Where did that come from?" She laughed and laughed when she told me this story, loudly enough to compensate for my silence. She couldn't see that her own judgment had tacked off course. It was as if she had been lit by the spark of something wild and wrong.

And so. The day after that outburst, but based on the totality of her recent questionable judgments and behaviors, Josie had been reprimanded, had been given a quiet in-school suspension, where her teaching was to come under direct scrutiny until such time as Principal Coffey no longer deemed it necessary.

But who was to say this wasn't all just part of the glorious roller coaster that was Josie? If you loved the rush, you had to accept the nausea. Her heart was fierce, and she told a good story.

I had first lunch period that day, eleven thirty, which was always annoying, because I was never hungry that early, but if I didn't eat, I'd be shaking by two. When I went to grab my peanut butter sandwich from the refrigerator, I didn't notice that Josie's Diet Pepsi was gone.

I was heading to my classroom when I passed Webber Gale in the hallway. He was spiky haired and small for his age, a snarky little whippet of a fourth grader. He was known among his peers for his outlandish behavior, and he had quite a following at Rhodes Avenue, a cadre of kids who delighted in his transgressions. We had all seen it before, of course; every few years there was a Webber Gale. The most poignant thing about them was that each thought he was a gloriously misbehaving original, the only one of his kind.

They elicited a kind of mass psychological transference: Webb's followers egged him on so that he would do the risky thing—sneak into the girls' bathroom, steal a stack of lunch trays and chuck them into the bushes outside the cafeteria, leap from the top of the monkey bars—and get in trouble for it, and they would get to experience the vicarious thrill of it all from the safety of their desks, or the lunchroom, or the ground.

I liked Webber. Once, when the other kids were out at recess and he was sitting alone on a bench in the office (because it is not okay, Webber, to run through the hallway yelling, "MON-

STERS ARE ATTACKING!"), he told me: he didn't always want to be bad, but he had his reputation to consider. He was just a skinny kid, overcompensating.

So it was no surprise that he stole Josie's soda and chugged it before music class. The surprise was that Josie had brought a rum-spiked Diet Pepsi to school.

Ken the custodian discovered Webber in the staff bathroom, staring at himself in the mirror. "What are you doing, son?" Ken asked.

Webber's reaction time was slow, his eyes bloodshot. Ken was suspicious even before it took Webber a full sixty seconds to come up with an answer. And that answer was a loud burp, and only by the grace of Ken the custodian's quick reflexes did Webber Gale not then smash his forehead into the edge of the bathroom sink as he stumbled forward.

Ken steadied Webber Gale and walked him to the office. "I don't know how it's possible," Ken reportedly told Principal Coffey, "but I know sauced when I see it, and this little guy is sauced."

Webber started crying. "Mrs. Abrams's soda made me feel funny," he sobbed. And then he threw up.

In short order, these things happened: Josie was ordered to the office, where she quickly confessed to ownership of the Diet Pepsi, while insisting that it was a terrible, terrible mistake— that there was a regular, untainted bottle of soda sitting at home on her kitchen countertop, *which is no excuse,* Josie whispered, raggedly, wretchedly. *I know that.* Webber's parents were called (simultaneous to, I imagine, a hushed, urgent phone call to the school's legal counsel), and he was taken to Children's Hospital for evaluation, where it was determined that Webber's blood alcohol level was a whopping .10, that he would have to stay overnight for observation, but that there would be no lasting ill effects.

At first Webber's parents, equal parts concerned and irate, threatened to sue the school district, Principal Coffey, and, of course, Josie Abrams, the Rhodes Avenue Middle School teacher who had brought a cocktail to school and stashed it in the staff refrigerator. On further discussion and acknowledgment of the school's long history of lenience involving the activities of their son, and because they were not the litigious types, the Gales agreed not to bring legal action against the school or the parties involved, after having been assured, completely and definitively, that Josie would lose her job, which, after a brief disciplinary hearing, along with some ancillary input from select colleagues, she, of course, and without argument, did.

Charges were brought against Josie, though. Once Children's Hospital reported the incident, it was legally required that an investigation be initiated.

The Andes spoke out against Josie during the disciplinary hearing. They stalked like panthers into Principal Coffey's office—I was there, too—and they took turns railing against her.

They had an aura about them, the golden glow of the righteously indignant. *I know for a fact that she once told a student that almost all Republicans are assholes. She once made a boy stay after school because he misbehaved and then she took him out for ice cream. What sort of example does that set? What sort of example?*

"Thank you, Ms. Brauer," Principal Coffey finally said, interrupting them, convinced by their litany or just finally exhausted by it, "but we are handling the situation. The situation is being handled."

. . .

"Josie," I said to her that very first night at her house, "this is not great. There's no getting around that. It's pretty bad. But it will be okay." I made my voice a low murmur, as if I were trying to calm a small, trapped animal. "You'll be okay." I didn't even believe it myself. But what else could I say?

Mark wasn't really talking to her, but he had made her some soup, which sat in a blue mug growing cold on the coffee table. Josie was on the couch, her legs tucked under her, wrapped in a heavy gray blanket.

"Mark is so mad," she whispered to me, as if that were the problem. After he set the soup in front of her, he had disappeared upstairs. We could hear the *thump* of his footsteps above us, muffled music, a rush in the pipes of running water: routine domestic sounds, but somehow hostile now.

A great gaping hole had opened up next to Josie, a cavern. Deep inside it was the possibility of comfort, relief. Forgiveness, it seemed, was already just an echo in the blackness.

"This is not the end of the world," I said. "I promise."

Josie nodded. Four months later, on an ice-slick overpass, she slammed her speeding car into the guardrail.

Fifteen

For her twelfth birthday, Hannah requested only one gift, and so we were obliged to give it to her. She wanted to go out to dinner with Chris and me.

"Sweetie," I said to her when she announced her desire a few days ago. "How about a camera instead? Or a new bike? Or one of them new-fangled camera-bikes!" She shook her head, and I saw the stubborn two-year-old who used to go limp when she didn't want to leave the playground—baby Gandhi, we called her; the three-year-old who ate only plain bagels and strawberry yogurt for a year; the four-year-old who wore her shoes on the wrong foot every day for six months just . . . because. "How about a pet monkey!" I said.

"Dinner," she said, fiddling with a long twist of her blond hair. "You and me and Daddy."

And so here we are, Chris and I, sitting across from each other at La Tagliatella Insolita. I'm halfway through a glass of white wine. The soft lighting has changed Chris's face into a reproduction of its past self, and I am filled with affection, a full-body memory knocking against other, more recent ones. I have a funny inkling about being here, about Hannah's intentions.

It's a windy, warmish night: April 1, the birthday nobody

wants. When Hannah was seven, she came home crying on her birthday. "No one believes me!" she sobbed. "Eight other kids said today is their birthday, too!" From the day she was born, people have not been easily convinced.

"Should you go check on her?" Chris asks. Hannah slipped off to the bathroom five minutes ago and hasn't emerged. He takes a sip of his wine and looks at me.

I shake my head. "Let's give her a few more minutes," I say. "Actually, I think she might be parent-trapping us."

"Hmm. Hayley Mills or Lindsay Lohan?" he says.

"Oh, that's impressive."

"We watched both a few weeks ago. Movie marathon." Chris sets his glass down, and then, without warning, everything is awkward, and we are unable to hold each other's gaze. We both turn to look out at the dining room, transfixed by it, as if a bear in a tutu has suddenly danced into the room.

La Tagliatella Insolita is our local restaurant, the place where they don't exactly know us but they definitely sort of recognize us, a little Italian café with better-than-average mushroom ravioli and pretty good eggplant Parmesan. It's nothing special, except that we've been here a hundred times, for birthdays, minor celebrations *(congrats on coming in third!)*, even just nights when, at the last minute, we realized that nobody had the energy to cook. And so it's ours, in that way, or it used to be: full of our mundane history and food that might not be surprisingly delightful but that never surprises us, which is its own kind of delight.

I'm watching a waitress walk through the dining room with four plates on her forearms. It's a marvel that we're here together, Chris and Hannah and I. Maybe there is a future for us that doesn't involve pain, an inching, quotidian life we can build together. I feel a surprising breath of hope. It turns out to be an actual breeze blowing through the front door as a family walks into the restaurant. Still, it's something. I turn to Chris and smile.

"I'm sorry if this is strange," he says quietly. "Being here together."

Hannah reappears from the bathroom before I can answer and slides into the booth next to him. "Hi, Mommy."

"Yo, birthday girl," I say, and she rolls her eyes, but she's still smiling. Her hair is brushed and shiny, and as she takes off her light jacket, I see that she's wearing a shirt I don't recognize, deep blue and long-sleeved, with a little splash of white daisies on one arm. Has Chris taken her shopping? There are these moments— every day, really; they pile up on top of each other—when I think my heart will stop from too much love and grief. But it never does, or at least it hasn't so far.

Chris slings his arm casually over Hannah's shoulders, and she leans into him. "Remember when you would only order spaghetti here?" he says to her.

"I'm ordering it tonight!"

I pretend to read the menu for a minute. Chris murmurs something to Hannah, and she readjusts herself in her seat, looks at her own menu, takes a sip of her water. "Mommy?" she says.

I smile, nod.

"Hannah wants to run something by you," Chris says. Maybe she does want that bike after all. Well, why not?

"Mommy," Hannah says again. Her voice sounds high and hesitant.

I feel a little hitch in my own breath, which is not enough of a warning for my slow brain. "What's up?"

"You know how I haven't been sleeping very well."

I reach across the table and pat her hand. "We will figure that out, sweetie. I was thinking about calling Dr. Gehr, you know, because you can't be the first kid—"

"—and so the thing is, it turns out I actually got, like, a really good night's sleep at Daddy's. Last week." She stops, puts her hands up to her face for a second.

"A good night's sleep," I say, terrified, suddenly. "That's great."

She takes her hands from her face and drops them to her sides. "And so I was wondering." She looks up at Chris, who nods gently. "Could I maybe stay with Daddy for a while?"

"Just for a while," Chris says quickly.

"Yeah, just a month or so, so I can get some sleep."

"She thinks it might help," Chris says. "And I don't know, maybe it will. Clean slate? Anyway, she'd see you during the day, so I don't see the harm."

They are so beautiful, my ex-husband and my daughter, my two loves. Their light hair gleams in the candlelight, their pale, matching faces full of worry. I'm gazing at them from the wrong end of a telescope. I would do anything to ease those identical lines of concern across their foreheads, their troubled eyes. "I'm really glad you got a good night's sleep," I say.

Hannah nods. And am I imagining it, the flash of a challenge in her eyes? The desperate tug of a dare? "So, it's okay with you?"

This is the truth: You lose some things because you didn't see the darkness rushing toward you. Some things disappear because it all snuck up on you so quickly and quietly, and you weren't paying attention. Okay. But once in a while a loss is preventable. You can stop it. And if you don't, you are to blame. The trick is knowing which is which.

Hannah and Chris are waiting.

"Oh, well, no." I shake my head. "No. Not at all." I lay the palm of my hand on the table next to the bread plate, stare at it for a second, lift it, then bang it down so hard that all of the dishes rattle, the wine sloshes, Hannah's water glass wobbles and almost tips. The family that came in a few minutes ago is sitting a few tables away. Like a mutant, three-headed animal, they turn and stare. "NO," I say again. Hannah looks at me, shocked, open-mouthed. Chris has an identical expression on his face that I would like to slap off. *No harm.* No harm? I feel a low growl in the back of my throat, fierce and primal.

"Iz," Chris says, "come on."

I ignore him, turn a laser focus to Hannah. "I'll stay up with you. We'll sit on the couch and watch TV shows about . . . boils. Cockroach invasions. I will stay up with you all night if you can't sleep. But you." I take a breath. When she was two days old, we brought her home from the hospital. I stared and stared at her, this brand-new, blinking person, and I wasn't sure if I loved her. I knew I would protect her, that I would do anything to keep her safe and alive, but I didn't know if I loved her. It took me a few more days to understand my heart. "You," I say again, "are staying with me."

My whole face twitches a little. Nobody says anything. The staring family turns back to their bread basket.

Chris clears his throat. "Well, then."

"Mom." Hannah says. She sighs. And there is relief in that tiny exhalation. I know it's there, even if she doesn't. *"God. Okay, fine."*

The waitress who had balanced plates on her arms has come to our table, is standing above us, pad and pencil in hand. "Are you ready to order?"

And I am so hungry. I'm starving.

. . .

I've gotten used to being at school without Josie. Some days it feels like a grown-up, darker version of the year Hannah's best friend Rooney moved away, and Hannah trudged off to school every day with a tragic expression and a stomachache. Except instead of moving to Seattle because both of her parents got jobs as software development engineers at Microsoft and pinkie-swearing to Skype every day and visit over spring break, Josie died.

There are other teachers at Rhodes Avenue with whom I feel a camaraderie—Bea Marcus, who tacks photocopies of her students' most hilarious mistakes onto the bulletin board in the teachers' lounge ("Slavery was an enema to the abolitionists"); Will Carrick, who pokes holes in his eighth graders' terminal self-consciousness by giving them random, nonsensical nicknames: iTunes, Gluten-Free, Our Lady of Paper Clips. But since Josie died, that kinship is vaporous to me, exposed for the superficial coping mechanism it always has been. These people are not my friends. It runs through my head as I sit at my desk grading papers or perch on the edge of a chair quickly eating my lunch: *Not my friends. They are not my friends.*

But sometimes, for a minute or two, I find myself giggling with Bea over the latest of her students' entertaining flubs, or brainstorming new nicknames with Will, or gossiping about the not-very-well-kept secret that Arthur Greene, the eighth-grade English teacher, and Violet Nowicki, the part-time librarian, both in their sixties and both divorced, are finally, after twenty years of flirting, hooking up. And maybe the world cracks open in those moments and a little bit of light comes in, and just for a few seconds I can not only imagine being happy in a world without Josie, but I'm actually living in that world.

And then the crack seals up and I'm back on familiar ground, and I remember to miss my friend, and I am relieved.

Sixteen

———◆———

For months, the phantom smell of latkes clung to the sweater I wore the night of Mark's party, even though I had washed it three times. When I held it close to my face, the whole evening came rushing back to me in a sensory, canola-oil-drenched flood of images, all culminating in Mark turning and walking away, fed up with me, done. Our meeting at the dedication of Josie's headstone on that dreary day, our brief embrace, resolved nothing. I thought that my punishment for losing Josie was losing Mark, too—although "losing Mark" didn't really describe it. My greasy fingertips all over Andi's silk shawl were a map of my intentions.

One night in April, I couldn't sleep. The air in my bedroom was stuffy and stale, like the inside of a broken refrigerator. I got up and opened the window, kicked off the covers, then pulled them back over me, then kicked them off again. *Maybe this is hell,* I thought: alone in my house in the middle of the night, stuck in an endless loop of thermal discomfort.

In the year since Josie had died, I had never once said the word "suicide," not out loud. But it played on the edges of my psyche, always there, raspy and ugly, and that night, in bed, I couldn't get rid of it. In fact, no one ever spoke of Josie's death as a suicide. We all pretended that her death was the result of a tragic accident—preventable, yes; it wouldn't have happened if she hadn't been driving too fast—but not deliberate. By our unspoken agreement, Josie had not killed herself.

At 4:40 a.m., in the silent darkness of my room, I sat up in my bed and I said it out loud. "Josie killed herself."

It didn't sound right, but it didn't sound wrong, either.

I got out of bed and made my way to the end of the hallway, my footsteps graceless and loud in the empty house. The noise didn't matter. Hannah was at Chris's. I poked my head into her messy room; I imagined her face, her pursed lips, the way she sometimes flung her arms over her head in her sleep exactly as she'd done when she was a baby. *Be asleep,* I thought. I would have taken her insomnia. I would have sacrificed all of my sleep for Hannah, forever. My chest was tight with love for my blameless baby. I loved her so much when she was at Chris's!

I felt my way down the stairs. The house was dark, but not sinister. I liked it this way. It reminded me of the darkrooms I'd spent time in in college, the comforting blanket of velvety blackness holding the promise of what was to come, that slow reveal. I felt my way into the kitchen. The digital clock on the oven glowed green: 4:43. I turned on the light and the coffeemaker, took the milk out of the refrigerator. I was thick with tiredness. A smudged coat of exhaustion lay over every bit of me.

This life: scattered papers and leftover lasagna, a silver barrette on the countertop and books and coffee and a scribbled note taped to the refrigerator, *Mommy, can it be true? We are out of ice cream!* What on earth could turn a person away from it, what seething despair or failure of attachment? I had spent thirteen months not asking this question, terrified of the toxic sludge that would surely spew out of me if I did. But I was asking it now.

And I found, to my surprise, in my messy kitchen in the dark early morning, that I wasn't angry with Josie.

I poured myself a cup of coffee, made it milky and sweet, and sat down at the kitchen table. There was a lacy fringe of frost on the window, and the crescent moon was still high in the black sky, crisp and sharp, like a little cookie. I blew on my coffee.

I wasn't angry with Josie, and I didn't blame her, but I couldn't explain her death, either. Even after all these months, it was an unanswered question, a vast expanse of pain.

At seven fifteen, I called in sick. In truth, my eyes were burning from lack of sleep, and my head ached, so it was easy to commit to the part. I made my voice extra husky on the phone, and Carol Wall, the school secretary, tsked with sympathy and told me to drink tea with honey.

I splashed some water from the kitchen tap on my face and downed the last few gulps of lukewarm coffee. I had not spoken to Mark, really spoken to him, in months. Mark! My loyal confidant, friend of my youth. I felt the urge to see him, to say to him: *It's okay now, it's not our fault,* mixed up with something else, a feeling somewhat less benign, but still inchoate. I got dressed quickly. Ten minutes later, I was on my way to his apartment.

. . .

Did I think he'd be there, at seven forty-five on a Friday morning? Did I think that my desire to see him could conjure him? I knocked, softly at first, then with more urgency. No one answered. He must have had an early class at one of the community colleges he worked at. Andi—I hadn't even thought about Andi, about what I'd do if she were home; I'll admit I wasn't operating at maximum capacity. But Andi was at school, of course. I stood in the hallway outside his apartment and turned in a circle, as if the freshly painted tan walls could tell me what to do, as if the

thick green carpeting under my feet would offer up a solution.
I wanted to talk to Mark. At the very least, I would leave him a
note. I banged on the door one more time and wondered if my
exhaustion combined with this vague sense of psychic lawless-
ness, this emotional unhinging, was a little echo of how Josie
had felt—the desperate need for solace coupled with the jangly,
hopped-up, insistent impulse to do something. Anything. The
worst thing.

Well. I'll take most of the responsibility for what happened
next, except for this: Mark had continued their questionable
habit of leaving the key under the mat. I used to tell Josie, over
and over: If a burglar wants to break into your house, where's
the first place he would look? And Josie would laugh dismissively and say, "He? Why do you presume the burglar is male?"
which was of course not the point and was also more pre-
scient, I guess, than either of us thought, because here I was.
Once when I went over to their house, Josie had run to the store
and had actually left me a note taped to the screen door: "Iz, the
key is under the mat." It wasn't a good idea back then, and it
wasn't now.

I let myself in. I was just going to find some paper and a pen
and leave a note on the kitchen table, something like *Mark, I'm
sorry we haven't been in touch lately* or *Mark, I'm sorry I ruined your
holiday party, I'm sorry I hated you for moving on with your life, I'm
sorry, I'm sorry, I'm sorry.* Something like that. And then I was
going to leave.

Their apartment bore an untidy resemblance to how it had
looked the last time I'd been here, on the night of their party.
There were books and papers on the coffee table now, a pair of
pink running shoes next to the couch. It was a "before" picture,
cluttered and homey and lived in. The surreal impossibility of
our small existence struck me with shuddering force—the idea,

probable but unproven, that life continues without us, in classrooms and living rooms and queen-sized beds. It surprised me, as it always did: the asteroid shock of it. Life goes on, for the living. Whose stupid idea was that?

In the kitchen, an open box of cornflakes and a bowl with the soupy remains of milk and soggy cereal sat on the table. The coffeemaker was on. I walked over and flicked it off, glanced around for a pen and paper. In the doorway, in a green robe, sleepily rubbing his eyes, was Mark.

"What are you doing back, honey?" he said, and then, blinking at me, utterly baffled, "Iz?"

"Hi."

"What the hell?" He reached out and touched his palm to the door frame. "What the hell?"

"I came over to talk to you." I smiled weakly, raised my palms, a gesture of supplication. My heart was pounding, and I suddenly saw this whole thing for what it was: a very, very bad idea.

"But . . . I . . . How did you?"

"The key," I said. "Under the mat."

Mark shook his head, to clear it or possibly to convince himself that I wasn't a dream. "I need some coffee," he said. "Do you want some? Why is the coffeemaker not on? Andi always leaves it on for me." He walked over and carefully touched the pot with the back of his hand.

"I turned it off," I said.

"Of course you did."

"I'm sorry I let myself in," I said. "I was just going to leave you a note."

Mark nodded, groggy. He looked vulnerable in his green robe, his skinny legs poking out, tender as a frog. Maybe this would be the best time to talk to him, after all, before he could rebuild his defenses for the day.

He took a sip of his black coffee. He walked into the living room as if I weren't there; I followed. "You've been avoiding me for a really long time," he said, "and now all of a sudden you need to talk to me so badly you break into my apartment?"

"Let myself in," I muttered. I couldn't tell if he was angry or bemused, but I had a hunch he was angry, because instead of sitting down, instead of asking me to sit, he just stood there, with his coffee, in the middle of the room. He took another sip and grimaced. "I'm sorry I turned off your coffeemaker," I said. "I thought nobody was home."

"Yes," he said. "That's what you should be apologizing for." But then he smiled a little.

I took a deep breath and tried to shove my hands into my pockets, but the pants I was wearing didn't have any pockets, so I just ran my hands down and up my thighs weirdly. "I came to tell you that I realized that it's not our fault," I said. "Josie's death was not our fault."

Mark stopped, midsip. "Iz," he said, taking a half step back. "What?"

I looked around the living room again and blinked hard against the pressure building behind my eyes. "Josie killed herself, right? She killed herself, but we can't . . . it wasn't . . . and so we can't blame ourselves."

Mark finally set his coffee mug on the table and sat down on the couch. "Jesus," he said. "Jesus Christ."

"She did reach out," I said, "and I wasn't always paying attention. But that doesn't mean it was my fault."

Mark nodded, a slow bobbing of his head. His face was dark with a day's growth of beard. He was like a Chia Pet.

"And it wasn't yours, either, no matter what was going on between you." There. I had said what I had come to say. We could get on with things now, I thought. I had freed us. I waited generously for Mark's gratitude. I hoped he wouldn't cry, but it was all right if he did.

Mark swiped his hand over his stubbly face, and then looked up to meet my gaze. "What the hell are you talking about, Isabel?" His voice came out in a low rumble, like he was trying to contain it. "What the hell are you saying?"

One of Josie's paintings was propped up against the wall in the far corner of the room, facing out. I had never seen it before. It was a send-up of a Degas, three ballerinas balanced at the barre and gazing dreamily into the distance, except the dancers were burly construction workers. Instead of tutus they were wearing tool belts, and instead of being lithe and poised, they were bulky, with huge guts. They struck graceless, lumbering poses. One had a droopy mustache, and the one on the end was reaching behind himself; you just knew by looking at it that he was about to scratch his ass. It was brilliant, in the way most of Josie's paintings and sculptures were brilliant: that is, it was also awful.

"You truly don't know what you're talking about," Mark said. "She didn't kill herself. She skidded into a guardrail. It was an accident. She didn't *kill herself.*" He practically spat those last two words. "Goddammit, Iz! She did not kill herself!"

He was wrong. He was so, so wrong. How could he tell himself this story, so clearly false? How could he live with the wrongness of it? I heard myself breathe in, a gaspy wheeze of oxygen, and then, there in the middle of Mark and Andi's living room, I disappeared—all of the molecules that collided to form me, Isabel Moore, the DNA of my thin fingers and my unruly hair and my wide hips and my high arches, dissipated in Mark's living room, became formless and chaotic, diffuse.

We could never know how Josie had died; we would just go on, living close to the emptiness. That was the best I had. It was, to my surprise, not nothing. Faster than a blink, those jagged fragments of me flew back together, so that only I knew it happened; only I would ever know.

"She's still dead, though," I said softly, "which is . . . fucking bullshit shit fuck."

"It is," Mark agreed.

I plopped myself next to him on the couch. "What's with that painting?" I asked.

"What do you mean?"

"Why is it not hanging up on your wall?"

"Guess why." He stretched his legs out and propped them on the coffee table.

"Andi hates it?" I asked.

"Andi hates it."

We sat for a while, next to each other, in silence. "Can I have it?" I asked.

"Yeah," he said. "That would actually solve a lot of problems."

I didn't want it. I didn't want to look at that painting every day and think, *I will never get her back,* but I got up anyway and I lifted the rough wooden frame and I lugged that terrible thing across the room and out the door and down the stairs, and I wedged it into the backseat of my car and I headed home, and I had no more knowledge or clarity than I had when I'd come.

But I had Mark back, maybe. With delicate, impermanent stitches, it seemed possible that something torn had been mended.

Seventeen

The day before Mother's Day, another forty-degree Saturday, I decide to take myself to a movie. Hannah is at Chris's now and will be spending the day with her friends Caitlin and Katelyn. Helene is at a wedding brunch for Nancy Teegarten and Ilene Solomon, the two members of her old group of girlfriends, the gay divorcées, who, it turned out, to everyone's surprise and most of all their own, really are.

It's been a chilly spring so far, wet and drizzly. I've taken to drinking my coffee outside early in the mornings, before Hannah is up. Barefoot, I gaze out into our small backyard, and the world looks primeval, green and misty and empty. I get the feeling humans do not quite belong here: there should only be dinosaurs, cold-blooded and hungry, chomping through the ferns. And then the caffeine kicks in, and I'm myself again.

One benefit of the weather is that our students' spring fever has been kept at bay. Normally, in May, an electrical current runs through them, every one of them, first slow, then fast, one to the next to the next, deep through their central nervous systems, and its single message is: *Bust out!* They begin a communal snuffling and snorting, like wild horses or pigs. One day they're in small groups, scanning an e. e. cummings poem, and the next they're laughing hysterically at a broken pencil, a sudden rain shower, a creaking chair that sounds like a fart. The younger ones forget rules they've known since September, push each other in the cafeteria, hurl themselves, en masse, through doorways. The older ones, the eighth graders, are occasionally caught hugging in the supply closet or a bathroom stall. They stage fake fights on the playground that sometimes become real ones without warning. They veer from joyous to cruel, and sometimes you can't tell the difference, and you can never keep up. The last weeks of school are bearable, but only just.

But this year the students are mellow and polite, February students, because although their brains know that the school year is careening to a close, their bodies are clueless, slowed and dulled by the wind and the rain. I miss the warmth, but I appreciate the calm.

Chris has been in his apartment for three months now—long enough to feel as if we are teetering on the razor-sharp edge of something permanent.

I called him this morning. I told myself that it was because I couldn't remember who was supposed to pick Hannah up from Katelyn's this afternoon, but it was written on my calendar and circled in black: PICK UP H, 6:00.

The phone rang and rang. I felt twitchy and embarrassed, like I was an eighth grader calling a boy I had a crush on. *What's the math homework?*

"Hey," I said when he finally answered, "I'm wondering who picks up Hannah today."

"It's you," he said. His voice was low and sleepy.

"Of course it's me! Who else would call you on a Saturday morning and ask whose turn it is to pick up Hannah?"

Chris yawned. "I mean," he said, "it's you. You pick her up

at six, and she's with you until Tuesday. Don't you remember? She'll have all her stuff with her. I hope."

"Did I wake you?" I asked.

"A little."

We'd woken up together on hundreds of Saturday mornings: thrilled, when we first started dating; late and luxurious, early in our marriage; ungodly early, when Hannah was tiny. And now, by ourselves, in separate houses. "I'm sorry."

"Hannah and I were up late watching that show you hate. *Skin Diseases of the World.*"

"Nice."

"It was fun. We had chips and guacamole."

"Ew," I said.

"I know." He yawned again, and we were both silent for a while.

"Okay. . . . Six o'clock."

"Right. Hey, do you still want me to come take a look at the dishwasher?"

"Well," I said, "it's still not working. I mean, I haven't gotten it fixed. I was hoping it would fix itself, actually. But I don't want to put you out."

"No," Chris said. "It's fine. I'll come by later this afternoon. Does that work?"

I wondered if this meant we were going to sleep together. I wondered if "fixing the dishwasher" would become our code, and then, later, something we would laugh about, a phrase we would remember almost fondly, with nostalgia, when we were safely back together and had no need for secret codes and liaisons. My skin felt tingly—*Skin Diseases of the World!* A little termite of hope gnawed its way into my chest cavity. "That works," I said.

There were kitchen noises in the background, *clink*s and

clanks. "Uh-oh, sounds like Hannah's making breakfast," Chris said. "I better go."

"Get the day started," I said, and swallowed hard.

"Bye, sweetie," he said, and then, quickly: "Bye, Iz."

. . .

I clean the kitchen, grade some papers, pass the morning alone, then finally, a little adrift, decide to drive myself to the movie theater early. It's in Gooseburg, a little village thirty minutes from the city, far enough away that I can comfortably sink into anonymity. Chris and I used to go to movies here, back when it was an unrenovated theater with a crowded and slightly dingy concessions counter, two screens, and purple carpeting that smelled funny. Now it's a multiscreen movie house/café where waitresses wander up and down the dark aisles whispering, "Can I get you another basket of fried eggplant?"

I park in front of the theater and realize that I have forty-five minutes to kill, so I walk over to Praise Cheeses, my favorite vegetarian sandwich shop, run by Seventh-day Adventists with a sense of humor.

I wouldn't say I'm starting to feel good. I wouldn't say that. I would say that I'm starting to realize that I can take a breath and look around, survey my surroundings, and find a flicker of happiness in the things I recognize: my mother, pulling out a plastic grocery bag from her purse and securing it onto her head to protect her hair from the rain. Chris, answering the phone with his warm unguarded morning voice. Hannah, humming to herself in the kitchen. I will admit that it's useful to note certain not-unpleasant moments. All the sad things that have happened are different in scope, in quality, *in fact,* from all the sad things that haven't happened yet. There is comfort in pausing.

I'm standing in line behind a very petite woman wearing a

high ponytail and a purple polka-dot sweater that can only have come from the children's department. I remember Josie calling my attention to a similarly child-sized woman once and whispering to me, "Look, it's Polly Pocket!"

I'm smiling at this memory and considering the grilled tempeh with Lettuce Pray and Let There Be Light mayo. I'm thinking about Chris coming over later, to fix the dishwasher. I'm thinking about how hungry I am and how good it will be to sit alone at a small, solid table and not even pretend I'm waiting for someone, just to eat my sandwich and watch people go by.

And that's when I see them.

They're sitting at a cozy table near the window, warm light flooding their faces like a religious painting, full, fizzy drinks in front of them in jewel tones of emerald green and garnet red: a man who closely resembles my husband and his companion, a very small, pointy, foxlike woman who looks unpleasantly familiar.

At first it's like seeing something so weird and impossible your mind immediately rejects it: *It's snowing in August?* Your brain spirals, trying to invent a plausible explanation, anything, anything at all—*It's January, and I've been in a coma for five months. Oh, I forgot I moved to Australia!* But then, depending on your constitution, you rearrange your thoughts, and quickly or slowly—but eventually—accept the impossible. Chris and Dr. Gwendolyn Grieco, our couple's therapist, are having a romantic vegetarian lunch together.

I press my shaking hands against my thighs, turn around, and take stock of the line that is rapidly growing longer behind me. I have two escape options: head back outside against the crowded restaurant's traffic or slowly ease my way through the line to the front and pass by Chris's table.

I glance over at the two of them. Dr. Grieco is saying something, gesturing with her hands. Chris is leaning on his elbows, gazing at her, enthralled. He stops one of her hands midgesture and grabs it, turns it over, examines it. She quits talking, looks at him.

He read my palm, too, on our first date, on that Fourth of July picnic fifteen years ago. "Whoa, check out that head line!" he said to me. "I wouldn't want to get into an argument with you, Madam Brainiac! Mmm, and your love line.... It starts late," he said softly, "but it's deep."

"Oh, please," I said, flushed. "You don't believe in this nonsense!" I let my hand stay in his, resting there.

He looked up at me and smiled such a private, sizzling smile, full of heat and promise, all my bones melted. "Maybe I do."

Dr. Gwendolyn Grieco throws back her head and laughs. The sandwich shop is packed, a Saturday lunchtime rush, but her laughter is as loud as a bell; I think I can hear it ringing over all the noise, jangling, clinking, clanging in my skull. Or maybe I'm just imagining it.

But suddenly I'm like one of those mothers who can lift a truck off of her child by herself, powered by pure adrenaline and fire. I can practically feel Josie's hands on my back, pushing me forward. *No way, Izzy. No fucking way.* "Excuse me," I say, bumping into Polly Pocket, tearing through the crowd, making my ill-considered beeline to their table. "Excuse me, excuse me." And then I'm standing above them, a mute waitress. Today's special is rage!

I have one fleeting moment of perverse pleasure on seeing their faces, their thunderstruck faces, Gwendolyn Grieco's lovely olive skin draining of color and turning a seasick shade of greenish gray, Chris's mouth dropping open and then closing like a big stupid tuna's.

But then that pleasure is gone, and in its place is shame: a full-body transfusion of it.

"You are . . . ," I squeak, not knowing what will come next. My heart is cracked, shattered; an avalanche of shards cascades down, down to the floor. I fix my gaze on Gwendolyn Grieco. "You are . . . a really bad therapist!"

Dr. Grieco, well trained, places her hands flat on the table in front of her. Her nails are short and neat and shiny; she's the kind of woman who probably indulges in a weekly mani-pedi but doesn't want it to look like she does. "Well, I'm not your therapist anymore," she says quietly. "Which you know, of course." She glances at Chris, who doesn't meet her gaze but instead looks down at the table—at least, I think, ashamed.

There's a little girl at the next table who has been staring at me the entire time. She's gnawing on a slice of green apple, and she can't take her eyes off of me. Her hair is a fuzzy tangle of brown curls, and she looks like she's about two. I feel a piercing stab of love for her, for this tiny stranger, unsculpted, all beating heart and hunger. Nobody knows that a running clock in my brain still calculates the ages my babies would be, my own private doomsday clock, counting forward from my personal apocalypses. And, yes, there would be a two-year-old, but never mind about that.

Dr. Gwendolyn Grieco is still talking. She's midsentence, *and so it seemed to me,* when I stop listening. I smile and wave bye-bye to that staring baby and then it's shockingly easy: I just turn and leave.

· · ·

I'm halfway down the block from the café, shivering in the joyless spring chill, when Chris catches up with me.

"Isabel." He's jogging toward me, a little out of breath. I pick up my pace. "Isabel!"

"I'm actually going to a movie right now," I say. "I'm meeting someone. I'm late." An older couple holding hands walks past us; the man nods. Ahead, two teenage girls in identical short plaid skirts are all exaggerated gestures and hysterical laughter. If Hannah were here, she'd be studying them like a scientist. One of them does a cartwheel in the middle of the sidewalk. "You are *completely insane!*" the other one shrieks.

"Iz." Chris reaches out to touch my shoulder, then thinks twice, pulls his hand back.

"Did you get new glasses?" He's wearing small, black, rectangular frames. They used to be a little rounder, slightly larger.

He pauses for a second, smiles, barely, lifts his hand to the edge of the frames. "I broke mine last weekend playing basketball. . . . Good job noticing."

That's what I used to say to Hannah when she was little and she made an observation about something, anything—a new box of Kleenex in the bathroom, an ant on the sidewalk. *Good job noticing!* Chris thought it was the most ridiculous thing to say to a child, the most absurd example of overpraising. *Good job swallowing that water,* he would say to her. *Good job having toes.*

And Hannah, clever child, not more than three or four, would giggle like crazy and give it back to Chris: *Good job sneezing, Daddy. Good job walking to the refrigerator. Good job having a face!*

"Yes, I'm an excellent observer," I say now, aiming for soul-piercing sarcasm but sounding, even to my own ears, pathetic.

Here's what I expect Chris to say: *It's not what you think. It's not like that. There's nothing between us. It's not what it looked like. Ha-ha-ha, this is all just a crazy misunderstanding!*

Here's what he says: "Iz, oh, God. This is hard. I don't know what I'm doing. I don't know. Honestly, I don't. I'm sorry. I promise I would tell you if anything ever . . . if I ever, if things got . . . whatever. Of course I would tell you."

He wrings his hands and stares hard at the ground. He looks like a little boy, trying to talk his way out of a jam. *I swear I didn't copy my answers!*

"She is our couple's therapist," I say, my teeth chattering with cold and ache.

"Was. She was our therapist. She's not anymore." Chris's light hair is a little shaggier than I remember; it fluffs out like feathers in the wind. "She made sure, you know, that we were done with counseling. She was insistent about that."

"How professional of her." I look away from Chris, scanning our surroundings. We're standing near a crosswalk, this busy avenue intersecting a leafy neighborhood. A scrap of paper flutters close to my feet. In front of a nearby house, a dog barks. "She's a gem," I say.

"I . . . I . . . I," he says, still wringing his hands.

"Great," I say. "That's good to know."

"Iz."

I shrug. "It's fine. It's kind of sketchy, to be honest. A little bit in the moral *gray area,* I think. But whatever! Whatevs!" And then I walk away again, getting more practice at leaving than I ever wanted.

. . .

I make my way to my car, as panicky and wound up as an overstimulated baby. I can't process the information I've been given. I get into my car and barely make it home before I power down into a three-hour nap.

When the doorbell rings, hours later, I'm still on the couch, but I'm awake. Through the living room window, I catch a glimpse of Chris on the porch and sink down as low as I can into the cushions.

"Iz!" Chris calls, and knocks. "Izzy, come on!" He rings the doorbell again and then knocks again, loudly.

I introduced Chris to my mother fifteen years ago, at a Greek restaurant. Over stuffed grape leaves and spanakopita, he told her colorful anecdotes of internecine strife at the state DNR office, and she told him a gossipy story about the local celebrity who recently threw a fit in the waiting room of the dermatology clinic where she worked. (*It was Carolyn Stafford, the weekend anchor on channel six, but I'll deny it in a court of law!*)

I could tell she liked Chris, and I was giddy with relief: I knew I was going to marry him. Afterward, when he went to get the car, she said, "Isabel, he's wonderful."

I nodded and grabbed her arm and whispered, "He would definitely hide us in an attic!"

Helene tilted her head at me and paused for a long moment, and then she said, "Well, let's hope it won't come to that."

"Isabel," he calls through the door. "Please let me come in!"

In an hour, I'll get up. I'll brush my hair and my teeth, and I'll check to make sure there's not a splotch of toothpaste or a large coffee stain on the front of my shirt that would make Hannah cringe and say, *Mom, are you even aware that there are mirrors in our house?* I'll get in the car and I'll drive to Katelyn's, where her cheerful mother will greet me at the door. *The girls were terrific,* she'll say. *Delightful!*

I'm so glad, I'll say. *Thank you. Thank you so much,* and Hannah will see me from the other room and smile, recognizing me as her mother.

That will be later. For now I hunch low on the old, forgiving couch. Chris knows I'm here. He might even be able to see the top of my head. He knows this trick.

He still has his key, of course, but it seems that, as a small concession, he's not going to use it.

I reach up behind me and feel blindly for the cord of the window shade and, as carefully as I can, I pull it down. Unfortunately there are three more windows in this room, all of which look out onto the porch, and none is as easily accessible to me at the moment.

"I see you," Chris says. He's come around to the window. His voice is disconcertingly close, a little tinny and distorted through the glass. "I want to talk to you. I'm sorry, Iz. I don't know what to say. I really am!"

. . .

Years ago, when Hannah was about four years old and we were happy, the three of us went for a little hike on a Saturday morning. It was late September, and the world pulled us into it—the explosion of colors in the trees; the sweet, melancholy whiff of autumn. We drove to the Audubon Nature Center and took an easy path through the woods, crunching on the fallen leaves, Hannah skipping ahead, shouting, "AY-kern! AY-kern!" every time she saw one. She was collecting them in her mitten, naming each one as she dropped it in—Mindy, Greg, Kansas City, Sneaky Pete. She still has that acorn collection, twenty or thirty of them lovingly stored in a cookie tin.

Chris held my hand as we walked, and together we gazed upon our daughter with an almost-shameful pride, the thing you secretly harbor but can admit only to the bearer of the other half of your child's DNA: *We made her. Can you believe we made her?* She sang to her acorns, and Chris warmed my hand with his, and I was suddenly overwhelmed with the knowledge that this was a moment to pay attention to: this day, this air, these two people. I felt the perfection of the moment and, inside of it, I felt its demise. I was almost dizzy with it.

"Britney," Hannah said tenderly, dropping another acorn into the mitten. "You will be delighted to meet your friends."

"Weird kid," Chris whispered to me.

We emerged from the wooded area into a clearing, and an expanse of prairie opened up ahead of us, the thick grass mostly faded to a dull brown, a few hearty purple flowers still in bloom. In the distance was a bird tower. We meandered toward it. A wooden staircase wrapped around the inside of the structure. It was a little rickety looking, but Hannah had raced over to it and was already halfway up the first set of stairs. Chris jogged to catch up with her, but I took my time. It was warmer out in the open; the sky was a deep, cloudless blue. By the time I got to the bird tower, Chris and Hannah were already at the top.

"Come up, Mommy!" Hannah called. She waved to me from the narrow observation ledge. Her blond hair blew in her face, and her red jacket reflected the sunlight. "There are *telescopes!*"

"It's gorgeous up here," Chris called, his hands on Hannah's shoulders. "You can see for miles!"

I shook my head. The steps made me nervous, and I was never a big fan of high places. "I'll stay down here," I yelled to them.

I didn't want to see for miles. I didn't want to peer into a telescope and spot the highway in the distance, the farms on the periphery, the birds in formation. I wanted to stand at the base of the bird tower and crane my neck toward Chris and Hannah, bathed in sunlight, golden. Love was foolish and inevitable. We were just waiting to be shattered by it. The days were finite, full of awe.

. . .

"Iz!" Chris shouts again from the front porch. He taps on the glass. "I'm not leaving until you let me in."

I sigh and get up stiffly, walk to the front door, unlock it. Chris steps inside and then gazes past me, and a look of surprise passes over his features, as if he doesn't recognize what was once his. He takes off his glasses and cleans them with his T-shirt, puts them back on. His body sags a little.

We stand together in the doorway, and neither of us has a clue. "I have to go pick up Hannah," I say, even though we both know it's two hours too early. The soft, late-afternoon light casts a homey, orange glow in the living room, a little cosmic taunt.

"I'm sorry," Chris says, an echo of all the dumb "sorry"s of our marriage: *I forgot the eggs, I used the last of the shampoo, we're out of coffee.*

I shrug. "It's okay." My voice comes out croaky, scratchy from my long nap.

"It's not," he says.

And it's really not, but maybe eventually it will be.

Eighteen

And so I find myself here again, at another meeting of the Relationships in Transition support group.

And has it been two months since I last laid eyes on Cal Abbott's kind face?

"We'll see each other again soon!" I'd said through the half-open car window in my driveway on that spring day: hopeful, confused, disoriented as a blind puppy. And did he say, in response, "Perhaps we will," followed by the car's whirring shift into reverse, the automatic thunk of the doors locking?

And did I, very briefly, cyberstalk his ex-wife?

And have I somehow, finally, just barely gotten used to my new living arrangement, the house-sounds in the night I alone must investigate, the broken appliances that I have to fix by myself or (more likely) replace, insane asylum days with Hannah followed by solitary-confinement ones without her? Yes, yes, yes, and no: not really.

I'm a refugee from happiness with nowhere else to go. And also, oh, I want to see him again. I do—even though every time I imagine sitting down beside him on an uncomfortable chair, or standing near him as I load up a paper plate with an embarrassment of tiny brownies, my left eyelid starts to twitch.

"You go without me this time, darling," my mother said this

morning. Her voice sounded gravelly, weary. "It should be your thing, not mine."

"*Come on,* man," I said. "This is your fault. You were my dealer. You got me hooked! Hooked on the wacky weed!"

She sighed. "Sweetheart. Are we talking about the same thing?"

. . .

"All righty," Jillian says. She makes a little looping motion with her index finger, like she's letting us know she thinks we're all crazy. But it's an instruction, of course, and so fourteen of us in the basement of the East Side Community Center obediently drag our folding chairs into a perfect circle.

It smells musty and sweet down here, as if ripe late-spring mud were trying to reclaim the building, beginning a slow seep through the walls. Jillian sits down primly and folds her hands on her lap. "Hello again to you all, and a warm welcome back to . . ." The room is silent. I look around at the vaguely familiar faces, the broad strokes of vulnerability and not-quite-dead optimism brushed across their features, all of our features. What effort it takes some days just to get into your car and drive somewhere. Park. Walk downstairs and find the right room. Not run screaming out the door. "Welcome back to . . ." Jillian says again, nodding in my direction.

"Oh! You mean me!" They've been coming here every week, I guess, coalescing into a tightly knit group of sufferers, a company of misery. "Isabel Moore." Sometimes when I say it out loud it doesn't even sound like my name, just its component parts. *Is a bell more what?*

"Why don't we go ahead and introduce ourselves, because I think there are a few new faces since you were here last, Isabel!"

Cal, five seats away from me, whispers to a pretty brown-haired fortyish woman in business casual. He smiled politely at me when we walked in, said hello, but that was all; now he's twinkly eyed and chuckling with Liz Claiborne. I'm jealous, although of course I have no right to be. I imagine the two of them, locking eyes empathetically over somebody's tragic tale of marital betrayal, then making out in his blue Prius in the parking lot, his hands caressing her shoulders, fingertips running down her spine. I can practically hear her, humming with pleasure, quiet as the car's engine. In my mind they suddenly, confusingly, become one, Cal's new lady love and his car: compact, attractive, energy efficient. My stomach squeezes like a sponge.

"Say your name and a little bit about yourself," Jillian says. "Maybe something interesting or important happened since the last time we saw each other? Something challenging, or something that has helped you grow?"

Across from me, Harrison the great big bald man smiles shyly at Lee Ann, the young divorcée, his pinkening face betraying him. Lee Ann fiddles with a clip in her hair and stares at her lap, half smiling, too.

How did I not see until now that this support group is a lonely hearts club? Of course it is! This is why everyone here has changed out of Cheetos-stained T-shirts, why the women are wearing just enough makeup, the men in pants of the nonsweat variety. It's why we put up with Jillian's textbook exhortations, her desperate, hopeful group trust games. It's why we're here. The Relationships in Transition support group is a meat market! Our tenderized hearts are on display for the taking.

"Well, I'm Neil," the man next to me is saying. "Something interesting in my life is, uh, Rainy, my 'girlfriend'"—Neil made air quotes here, his fingers groping in front of him like lobster pincers—"she dumped me for a dude who works at the co-op, I swear to God I think his name might be Kale, and they're going on a friggin' cross-country bike trip. Which is what she and I had been planning. So, yeah." He laughs bitterly. "That's something interesting."

Jillian pauses, her eyes darting. She's still so new at this, so green. She shakes her head a little, recalibrating. "All right, Neil. Thank you for sharing."

"And," he continues, as if Jillian hadn't interrupted, "I've been thinking, you know . . . wow. I pretty much sacrificed my whole family for Rainy. My wife and kids, and for what? I . . ." He presses his fingertips against his eyebrows for a moment and takes a gasping, broken breath. The room is silent. "I'm on my own now," Neil says. "I really, really fucked . . . excuse me, *screwed* up."

Barb, whose husband left her for polyamory and who seemed, at the last meeting, to be percolating a rich and hearty loathing for Neil, tsks sympathetically. Cal gives Neil a consoling nod, then touches his lady friend's arm—just for the briefest second, but I see it. Neil looks around the room and scratches his beard absently, *scritch-scritch,* like it's infested.

"Thank you, Neil," Jillian says after a pause and nods at me. "Isabel?"

I'm going to waive my turn again. I suppose there is something comforting about being here, but I'm not about to share my deepest secrets with Cal and Ann Taylor and the rest of these sorry strangers, to watch their faces and calculate their judgments or endure their pity. Grief beats its leathery wings under my skin. My friend is gone. That's enough. That's everything! Pass! I pass!

"I . . . um . . ." *My best friend died in a car accident just over a year ago. Her husband is in love with a woman with perfect hair who is partly responsible for her death. My mother had a stroke and she's get-*

ting old and kind of grouchy and will one day die, and nobody has ever loved me like she does. My daughter, on the other hand, hates me. And my husband is dating our couple's therapist. Former couple's therapist! I flutter my hand around in front of my face like I'm swatting away an imaginary mosquito. Everything about me is cracked, busted, beyond repair. What part of my life isn't a relationship in transition? "My dishwasher is broken!" I say, quite loudly as heat rises to my face. I inhale and swat away a tear.

The room is silent now, the air swollen with my humiliation. Cal gazes at me as if he's examining a frog under a microscope. Eileen Fisher looks at her feet. Next to me, Neil, who until moments ago held the record for most embarrassing outburst, breathes in and out through his nose with little whistles.

Jillian, poor Jillian. She's just staring into the middle of the circle, her mouth open slightly. If there were a caption underneath her, it would say DUMBFOUNDED.

Cal clears his throat. "My toaster has been acting up lately."

. . .

It's raining hard when the meeting finishes, one of those late-spring midwestern thunderstorms that whips up out of nowhere. The sliver of sky visible out of the basement window has gone black, and lightning sparks through the darkness.

Jillian taps the schedule that's posted near the door. "Don't Let Your Diabetes Beat You has this room in ten minutes," she announces, "so we need to clear off the dessert table quickly."

"It's the end of Relationships in Transition," Neil whispers to me, leaning too close and scratching his beard again. "Time for us to *break up!*" He chuckles at his own joke in time with a sudden loud boom of thunder.

The last time I was here, Neil had ditched his family for a

twenty-four-year-old hippie chick, and now he's miserable but clear eyed, surveying the wasteland he created. Barb, who practically vibrated with fury two months ago, seems different now, too, maybe sadder but less coiled, as if those vibrations finally shook something loose inside of her. And Harrison and Lee Ann—there's something between them, unlikely but undeniable. It occurs to me that everyone here is changed, whether by time or by friendship: everyone but me.

Another flash of lightning, another low rumble of thunder. Hannah used to climb into bed between us during thunderstorms, trembling. Even after they'd rolled away and all was calm, she'd beg to stay with us. *I'm still scared!* And although our bed was too small for three and she clung to me like a barnacle and Chris wanted her to go back to her own bed, I always agreed, because I knew: just because the skies were clear didn't mean you should let your guard down. Fear is tenacious, ungovernable.

I get up and gather my things, my sweater and purse, then hurry to the back of the room and grab my untouched package of store-bought chocolate-chip cookies from the table and stuff it into my bag. I need to get out of here fast, before I bump into Cal and his girlfriend in the hallway, probably hand in hand, gazing into each other's eyes, murmuring about how lucky they are to have found each other here, amid love's ashes. *I'll pull the car to the door so you don't get wet, sweetie. Don't be silly, Calvin. We can make a run for it together. I'm not made of sugar. I won't melt!*

I'm rushing up to the first-floor exit when the fluorescent lights in the stairwell flicker off and then, a long few seconds later, back on. Barb, a couple of stairs behind me, lets out a startled little yelp. "Oh, my!" Her voice echoes as if we're in a cave.

Rattled, I push through the heavy door at the top of the stairs and into the entryway. Harrison and Lee Ann are already huddled together in the doorway, giggling, his bare, meaty arm slung protectively over her thin shoulders.

The lightning is spectacular, wild, dangerous. Lately I've been trying to vault over my skeptical heart and find traces of Josie in the natural world. Why should the devout be the only ones who get to talk to their dead? So I've been looking. Is her spirit alive anywhere? In the red-tailed hawk who occasionally comes to perch in the low branches of the elm tree in our backyard? In the unexpected rainbow that arced over the green garbage bins in the alley behind Rhodes Avenue a few weeks ago? Of course, the only thing I feel when I silently ask a tulip if it's Josie is ridiculous. The only place I've ever felt even a fleeting glimpse of my dead, dead, dead friend is in the black sky of a thunderstorm, the angry hard pellets of cold rain, the flashes of electricity that could kill you. I know Josie's not actually there, in a storm, but that's what it feels like to miss her, mad and irrational and altered.

I want to be home, right now, in my bed, huddled under the covers. I dig around in my bag for my keys, feel for their reassuring edges.

And that's when I remember that I walked here. "Crap on a cracker."

"Still worked up about that dishwasher?" Cal is standing behind me. Next to him, Anne Klein adjusts her skirt and gazes out the wide window.

"I just remembered that I . . . don't have my car." Two hours ago, it seemed like a good idea to take a nice, mile-long stroll on a warmish night.

"Oh, that's too bad," Cal says. "Well, see ya around!" His girl-friend looks at him, her eyebrows raised. "Kidding!" he says. "I'm kidding. Isabel, please allow us to drive you home." *Us.*

"Oh, but I don't . . . this isn't that bad!" I'm trying to quickly gauge the depth and truth of the connection between Cal and this woman, trying to decide if I could tolerate being the mortified reject in the backseat, witness to their giddy rain-drenched affection. I'm thinking that risking my life walking through tree-lined streets in a thunderstorm might just be preferable, when another flash of lightning fizzes through the sky, followed by another, and then another, and then a triple-strength crack of thunder as loud as a bomb.

"You're right!" Cal says. "It's not that bad."

His ladylove extends her hand to me with a little sigh. "We haven't been formally introduced," she says mildly, "although Cal has told me about you. I'm Joy Peterson."

Joy. I've never met a happy Joy. She's wearing a breezy, light green cotton shirt and a black skirt. There's a delicate gold chain around her neck with a tiny oval pendant that rests in the dip of her clavicle, like a little cat's tongue. She's sexy in a precise, fine-boned way that makes me feel like an elephant.

She squeezes my hand. Joy Peterson has a surprisingly solid grip and a quick release. She didn't speak during the meeting, but I imagine her as the recently divorced mother of a pair of rowdy eight-year-old twin boys, and that her handshake is a reflection of her parenting style: firm, no-nonsense, a little bit heroic. *Mason, Trevor, you boys go to your rooms right now! Do I sound like I'm kidding?*

We wait a few awkward moments until it's clear that we've reached the scientific limit of our comfort level with each other here in the entryway, and then we make a dash for the car. We are, of course, soaking wet by the time we scramble in, and very quickly the chemical-floral-doggish scent of wet hair fills Cal's little Prius. Joy, in the front seat, pats her head, and then turns around to me and gives me the tightest smile in the history of smiles, a very slight stretching of her lips across her teeth.

"Thank you for this," I say to her, trying for a sisterly bond: *Thank you for the ride, but you and I both know what I really mean; thank you for letting me interrupt your date; Cal and I have a little history, sure, but don't worry, I'll step out of your way; he's yours now, this hunky older fella.*

But Joy just smooths her hair again and turns back toward the front of the car. "Don't thank me," she mutters.

It's loud in the car, but I'm pretty sure I hear Cal chuckle to himself, unable to mask his delight with the situation—two women in his car, younger than he is by decades, and are we vying for his affection? Clearly we are. It strikes me for the first time since I met him, and with the mighty force of the previously ignored obvious, that Cal is a player. My hair drips in my eyes, and my shirt is damp against my body. And something else: a nervous quickening; desire, for once without scrutiny. That long-dormant dragon suddenly twitching its spiny tail.

The rain hammers the Prius, and the thunder is an almost-constant drumbeat. The streets are dark and mostly deserted. We hydroplane through an enormous puddle, and Joy lets out a high chirp of fear. Cal is driving west, away from my house. I'm quiet in the backseat, waiting.

"Oh," Joy says, after a few minutes. "Oh, you're dropping me off first?" The disappointment in her voice is like a missed note in a familiar song. She recovers quickly, like a professional. "Yes, that's fine. Good idea. Thank you, Cal. I do need to get home." From behind, I see her raise her hands to her throat. She's adjusting the clasp of her necklace, recentering the pendant.

After ten more minutes he pulls into the steep driveway of a small blue house on a busy street, across from a shopping area: an empty video store with a FOR LEASE sign in the window; Lucky Shrimp, a Chinese takeout place; and Fashion 4ward, a down-market women's clothing store. Joy has her hand on the door handle before the car has even stopped moving.

"Hang on," Cal says. "Wait." He gets out quickly and jogs around to the passenger side with an umbrella that he seems to have procured from thin air. He opens it, and Joy steps out of the car and under the umbrella with an economy of moves, bal-letically. She tilts away from him as they walk to her front door, arranging as much physical space between them as she can. The sky is brightening behind her little blue house. The rain still thrums on the car's roof, but it sounds less menacing now, not an artillery, just a cloudburst.

I watch as they pause at her front door. Cal is getting wet, holding the umbrella above Joy's head as she searches in her bag. I'm thirty feet away in the cheap seats, but I can see the drama play out between them: Cal says something; Joy shrugs. Cal says something else, gestures with his free hand. Joy nods, slings her bag over her shoulder and turns away, stabs her key into the door, turns halfway back to Cal.

And then she's inside her house, and after that who knows: maybe her grubby twin boys rush to her for hugs, or the babysit-ter greets her with apologies for the mess, or her little sister, who is visiting from Indianapolis, says hello from the couch where she has just started watching *The Notebook,* and how about she starts it over so they can watch the whole thing together? Or nobody is home, because nobody else lives there, and Joy slips off her wet shoes and turns on the light and breathes in the lonely quiet and feels a tiny pinprick of grief over this one small lost possibility.

Or maybe none of those things. It's impossible to guess.

. . .

Cal is quiet as we pull out of Joy's driveway and head back toward my neighborhood, and I'm still in the backseat, which suddenly and again feels unbearably awkward, so I say, "Are we there yet? I'm bored! Are we there yet?"

"Don't make me turn this car around," Cal says sternly, and here we are, pretending that this man who is almost old enough to be my father is my father. Cal turns onto a quiet side street and pulls over. "Would you please sit in front with me?" he says.

"Joy seems nice," I say, next to him now. "Is she a Turk?"

"Worse," Cal says. "Much worse. I believe she's a Swede."

"Oh, boy," I say. "I knew a Swede once. *Knew*, if you know what I'm saying." Now that we're alone in the car, it's more true that we haven't seen each other in two months.

"She is a lovely person," Cal says. We're stopped at a red light, five minutes from my house. The rain is down to a drizzle, the sky smudgy and pinkish, as if it's embarrassed by its recent display. "I told her that, at her door. I said, 'You are a lovely person,' and then she just went inside."

"Yeah, that makes sense."

"Isabel," he says. "Do you remember at the first support group meeting when Jillian suggested we keep a pen and a notebook by our beds, and every morning, before the day starts, write down one thing we're looking forward to that day, and one thing we're apprehensive about?"

"Uh, no. But I haven't been paying the best attention at these meetings."

"Well, I've found it to be a useful exercise," he says. "Therapeutic, really. And every Thursday morning for the past two months I've written, 'Seeing Isabel.'" He's looking straight ahead. I can't tell what this admission has cost him, if it's cost him anything.

"Wait, is that under the 'looking forward to' column, or the 'apprehensive about'?"

"'Looking forward to,'" he says, "definitely. At least for the past few weeks."

We're almost at my house. Cal glances at me quickly: his face kind, his green eyes familiar now.

I feel the loss of Chris all over my body. It announces itself in the strangest ways: a weight in my knees, a twinge in my right cheek, an ache in the night. I feel it now, liquid, changeable. Is this the secret of human existence, the biology of loneliness?

We're in my driveway, we're inside the house, in the dim living room, kissing frantically.

He runs a hand through my still-damp hair, rests his palm on the back of my neck, whispers something in my ear that I can't quite make out.

I take his hand and lead him upstairs.

I lead Cal to the bedroom that Chris and I shared, and in this way it becomes mine, transformed.

It's a shock of nerves, embarrassed thrill, and it is also the saddest story I've ever heard. It sounds like this: goodbye, goodbye, goodbye.

Acknowledgments

My deepest gratitude to Jennifer Jackson and Julie Barer for brilliant feedback, endless patience, and calm waters. I am so lucky to have you two. Sincere appreciation to my wise and insightful friends and colleagues: Carolyn Crooke, Elizabeth Larsen, Jill Hekman, Korinthia Klein, Annie Rajurkar, Liam Callanan, Jon Olson, and Christi Clancy. A big thank you to Emma Gillette for Charm School. Thanks to Sue Betz for eagle-eyed copyediting. I am indebted to my parents, Ann and Jordan Fox, for a lifetime of confidence, encouragement, and leaps of faith. And my whole heart is full of gratitude to Andrew Kincaid for two decades of love and support. Thank you doesn't even begin to cover it.

ALSO BY

Lauren Fox

STILL LIFE WITH HUSBAND

Meet Emily Ross, thirty years old, married to her college sweetheart, and personal advocate for cake at breakfast time. Meet Emily's husband, Kevin, a sweet technical writer with a passion for small appliances and a teary weakness for *Little Women*. Enter David, a sexy young reporter with longish, floppy hair and the kind of face Emily feels the weird impulse to lick. In this captivating novel of marriage and friendship, Lauren Fox explores the baffling human heart and the dangers of getting what you wish for.

Fiction

FRIENDS LIKE US

For Willa Jacobs, looking at her best friend, Jane, is like looking in a mirror on a really good day. Strangers assume they are sisters, and they share everything: an apartment, clothing, groceries, and the challenge of making rent on part-time jobs. Together they are a fortress of private jokes and shared opinions, with a friendship so close there's hardly room for anyone else. But when Ben, Willa's oldest friend, reappears and falls in love with Jane, Willa wonders: Can she let her two closest friends find happiness with each other, even if it means they leave her behind?

Fiction

VINTAGE CONTEMPORARIES
Available wherever books are sold.
www.vintagebooks.com